The Hour of Lost Words

*Is an hour enough to say what
was left unsaid?*

NATASZA SOCHA

Contents

For all those who miss someone…

Acknowledgement

Thank you to everyone who shared with me the stories about their loved ones who have passed away — their feelings, emotions, thoughts, and the silent conversations they still have with them.

The Hour of Words

*What can someone abandoned by words
possibly say?*

Anna Kamieńska

"If you had to quickly name one thing, you're with me for, what would it be? "

"Mayonnaise".

He stared at her in astonishment.

"Seriously? That's the first thing that came to your mind?"

She nodded.

"You like mayonnaise as much as I do. That's important".

***

A good morning doesn't always promise a good day. Sometimes the world can turn upside down in just a few hours. You talk about mayonnaise early in the morning. You're pleasantly relaxed, your body enjoys the slowness, your mind is in a controlled state of lethargy, and you're observing every minute of your life. It's one of those Tuesdays when everything is in its place, just as it should be. No misunderstandings, no unpleasant chills running down your spine causing tension. Sometimes one day of the week gives strength for the rest - rainy Thursdays, dull Saturdays, and ordinary Mondays.

And that's why it should be perfect. From morning till evening. Except our whims and desires don't always match those that were planned for us.

"Stop. You can't place a comma where there's a period".

That sounded somewhat unpleasant but unfortunately, true. Catherine liked her husband's apt comparisons, the metaphors he skilfully juggled daily. No wonder, he was a writer after all.

But the last thing she needed now was flowery language. She just wanted someone to explain it all to her, maybe promise that the course of events could be reversed, that there are exceptional circumstances and that thanks to a time loop the reality could change. There are situations where the right words become the most important thing. They then organize the perception of the world, straighten things out, and gently soothe the pain.

"Your mum is gone. You need to be strong".

Catherine suddenly felt a dislike for her husband, as if a wall had grown between them. It had grown here, in the hospital corridor, from the words that should never have been spoken. She looked at her husband coldly, then turned her gaze away. In fact, he could leave now, along with everything he had to say. Sometimes someone's absence is better than poorly chosen words.

She saw her mother and talked to her just yesterday. Why can't we predict that someone will disappear from our life in a moment? It's unfair. Besides, they hadn't finished an important conversation, the first one that was different from others in a long time. Usually, it had been about cleaning, the impact of dust on human life, something standing or hanging crooked, and about the cat that peed in the house too often.

"But it's a house cat, mom".

"He could learn to go outside".

"And then punch in the door code to come back"?

But yesterday was different. Her mother even gave up polishing plates ("don't leave them wet, they'll have white spots"), sat at the kitchen table, and started stirring the sugar bowl with a spoon. Three turns to the right, one to the left. Catherine initially ignored this spectacle, but curiosity won.

"Why do you stir more times to the right than to the left"?

Her mother shrugged.

"Are you happy"? – she asked suddenly.

It was as surprising as if she had announced she had adopted a lion in Kenya and was moving there.

"But..."

"Just answer me. Now".

"Yes..." – Catherine hesitated for a while.

"Good for you. Although... I don't quite believe you".

"Mom..."

"I have to go. But we'll talk about it tomorrow because you can't keep everything silent. I warn you, it might be a shock for you".

Catherine was completely taken aback, unable to speak at that moment. She opened her mouth, then closed it, and then opened it again. And it went on like that.

"You remind me of a fish out of water" – her mother noted.

"Mom, should I know about something?"

"Yes... Just as I should hear something from you. But you're silent. I'm leaving now, I have a movie date".

"With dad?"

Her mother suddenly laughed so loudly that the cat fled the kitchen with a scream and disappeared under the wardrobe.

The cat's name was Maurice.

***

Death is selfish. It doesn't prepare anyone; it doesn't explain its actions. It comes, takes, leaves, and no one can file a complaint. It's minimalistic in its endeavours. It extinguishes breath. It closes the eyes. It cuts conversations in mid-sentence. Calculating like an actress who will do anything to get a role. Or like Maurice, who would even sit next to a dog for a liver treat.

When Catherine was twelve, she had a strange dream, but only now could she interpret it. Everything in it was slowed down, like in nature documentaries, and after a while, it froze in stillness. She saw bees hanging in the air. She saw wind tangled in the treetop but also motionless. Just like the birds on the branches and the smoke from the chimney. Like the woman in front of the house and the child on the bicycle. Catherine walked through this paralyzed landscape, looked around, and searched for any signs of life. She wanted to touch the bee frozen in the air but feared it would disappear. And with it the whole landscape.

It wasn't a good dream, she has never forgotten it.

And now it has become reality.

She stood in the middle of the hospital corridor and realized the world had just paused, even though there had been so much movement in it just a moment ago. Maybe for a fraction of a second, maybe for a little bit longer, she felt time stood still. And only she continued to breathe and hear her own heartbeat. Everything else was in lethargy synonymous with death. Just a breath ago, the world was spinning, only to freeze now, no one knows for how long.

"I would like to be alone" – Catherine said, turning her back to her husband.

Suddenly, everything returned to normal. The clock in the corridor was moving its hands, people started walking, respirators and other devices were humming and beeping, and in the distance, the elevator doors could be heard opening. Someone was just delivering lunch, and the smell of tomato soup reached Catherine's nose. Tomato soup tastes best with rice, although some prefer it with noodles - this absurd and somewhat out-of-place thought popped into her head. And also that tomatoes for the soup should be roasted in the oven beforehand to bring out their flavour.

Her husband couldn't comfort her, which further threw her off balance. In a difficult situation, touched by sadness and helplessness, he wasn't able to say anything wise. This word juggler, a master of perfect sentences, had apparently lost half the phonemes, and with those left, he was not capable of creating anything special. Maybe he was a graphomaniac, as some critics occasionally wrote about him? Maybe he could neither write beautifully nor speak well? Maybe it was just a pretty package? People often succumb to illusions. A handsome author who knew he looked good in blue shirts and medium-length hair (his trademarks) couldn't possibly write poorly. And when he added a smile, the melancholic-intriguing kind, the world used to buy everything from him.

"Crap in a wrapper" – she muttered now, even though she knew she was being unfair. And that she was venting her own anger and despair on her husband mainly because he stood nearest.

Now he said he would wait outside the hospital, then added something about the fragility of life, but she didn't want to listen anymore. It was clichéd and banal; a writer shouldn't use such comparisons.   The   worst   thing   about graphomania is that the words turn out to be empty. They become puffballs, leaving only dust when stepped on.

"Mom..." – Catherine said aloud, then squatted, hiding her head between her knees. "This can't end like this; you wanted to talk to me. And not necessarily about scrubbing pots with citric acid. You know so well that conversations, books, and movies shouldn't end this way. Well, unless there's a sequel... "

"Will there be one?"

****

The mother-daughter tandem is like an effervescent tablet dropped into sparkling water. It fizzes, foams, and overflows the vessel. Once, in school, Catherine conducted an experiment with baking soda, vinegar, and water. She placed a cup on a plate and covered it with aluminium foil. She cut a hole in the foil, poured in two tablespoons of water, added baking soda, and waited for it to dissolve. Finally, she added two tablespoons of vinegar. And then, the 'lava' erupted - frothy bubbles filled with carbon dioxide. It was quite beautiful, though dangerous.

Catherine and Marianne functioned just like that. Like a volcano. They were a culmination of opposites, divergent opinions, and conflicting views. Sometimes they argued for the sake of arguing, just to stand one's ground. As if it were a competition for the last word. The one who would lose her arguments paradoxically gained strength for the next quarrel. She had to win at all costs. To balance the score. To start all over again.

"I don't like pumpkin. Don't buy it, I hate the taste" – Catherine said.

"First of all, pumpkin is healthy, packed with vitamins, low in calories, and fat-free. It promotes metabolism and prevents obesity."

"But Mom, I'm not obese. Besides, you're talking to me as if you're in a pumpkin quiz. I just don't like pumpkin. You don't need to worry about my metabolism. It's fine. My doctor agrees."

"Secondly, pumpkin is also known and widely used in cosmetology. For dry skin, you can apply a mask made of pumpkin pulp, cooked and blended with a tablespoon of olive oil" – her mother continued, apparently uninterested in her daughter's opinion.

Catherine took a deep breath and looked at Maurice, seeking support but finding none. Cats rarely care about human problems.

After a second, she announced, enunciating each word:

"Mom, I have masks with vitamin C, and probably some with other vitamins too, and they work perfectly. They moisturize, firm, cleanse, and even rejuvenate. They might even heal the psyche. I won't buy a pumpkin to cook it, blend it, and apply it to my skin. Never. And your pumpkin pushiness only reinforces my conviction that it's not for me. Blah, blah, end of discussion."

"Thirdly, pumpkin tastes wonderful. You just need to know how to prepare it."

"Blah, blah... but I can cook!" – Catherine shouted.

"Stuffed pumpkin, baked with rice, sweet or spicy... Pumpkin pie, cream soup, salad..."

'Fuck!' – Catherine heard a scream in her head. She could almost taste the bland flavour and smell the insipid scent of the vegetable. She felt nauseous, although she wasn't sure if it was because of the pumpkin or the conversation about it. The more it was discussed, the more she hated it. Despite its richness in vitamins and minerals. Despite its global popularity, especially in November. And despite all that Halloween PR.

Most of their conversations were like this. Always nervous, confrontational, spoken in slightly raised voices. Each wanted to prove the other wrong, forcibly pushing their own opinion. They never really listened to each other. Neither had the patience to hear the other out and give themselves a chance to understand, accept, or even just consider what the other had to say. You don't always have to agree on everything. But you shouldn't disagree just out of spite.

Before Catherine's wedding, she and her mother went to Masuria together. They were supposed to spend a week, just the two of them, to bid farewell to their old lives and prepare for what was to come. Catherine rented a room in an old cottage, spacious, with two beds, a beautiful old wardrobe painted with flowers, and a large round table. The bathroom, in shades of cornflower blue, had a light blue bathtub.

"I would have preferred a hotel" - her mother said.

"I thought it would be nicer here. We can cook for ourselves, no one will impose meal times on us, it's peaceful and quiet, and we even have a whole apple tree to ourselves" - Catherine praised the place.

"I would have preferred a hotel" - her mother repeated, then unpacked her suitcase, carefully arranging everything on the shelves of the old wardrobe, sat in a chair, and picked up a book.

"Maybe we could go for a walk?"

"Maybe later."

"Or maybe I'll just set up the deck chairs in the garden?"

"If you must..."

"Or maybe I'll just kick myself for all my mistakes and sins?"

Her mother only raised her eyebrows theatrically at the sound of the profanity and bit into an apple from the tree she had previously scorned. The cornflower bathroom did not impress her either.

The entire week passed on imagined comparisons between what they had and what they could have had if Catherine had chosen another place. It wasn't a vacation, but a duel of arguments. They returned tired, angry, and somewhat resentful. But then came the wedding, and mutual grudges melted away in the candlelight, dissolving completely over a four-layer cake, three layers of which her mother relished. Only the pistachio one made her grimace.

"I'm glad you're happy" - Marianne said. And it sounded sincere.

For a moment, Catherine breathed a sigh of relief and entered married life a bit more calmly.

Over time, however, it got worse. The more often they met, the more distant they were becoming. Their conversations begun to boil down to exchanges of unnecessary words that irritated Catherine and made her skin itch, as if someone was constantly teasing her with an allergen. When too many redundant words suddenly appear, they start to cling to the entire body, attacking from all sides and making it hard to breathe. Like a boa constrictor encircling its prey.

"Cooking doesn't seem to be your passion" - her mother would say, and Catherine would only grimace.

"Should it be?"

"For a wife and future mother, cooking should be fundamental. Food is the foundation."

"But I don't like cooking."

"You can't hide it. But you can always try harder. Your cucumber soup has no flavour."

"Strange, there are cucumbers in it."

"But no dill, and you add too little cream."

"Am I allowed to dislike dill?"

Marianne ignored such questions, but whenever Catherine served soup, she always found dill in it. She would then set her bowl aside and ostentatiously eat a sandwich.

Who won?

***

Catherine returned to her apartment late in the evening. She couldn't walk around the city forever, especially in December, on a frosty day without snow, which she eagerly anticipated every year. Not this time. A power failure would be useful, something that would switch off those damn lights, wipe the smiles off the faces of plastic Santas, and cover up the silvery wings of artificial angels. One of them was coated from head to toe with silvery glitter, which sparkled in the glow of LED lights. Its face shone eerily, and its slightly parted lips revealed silver teeth. It didn't look like an angel at all, or at least not the kind associated with Christmas. But why do we assume angels must be beautiful? They could just as easily have noses like cauliflowers, crooked teeth, greasy hair, bitten nails, and pimples on their chins. An angel doesn't have to be perfect. What matters is that it fulfils its role.

Catherine looked at the angel's face once more. It reminded her of someone. Or perhaps it was just an epitome of sadness? An allegory of all the bad thoughts that had been haunting her recently. Of everything that has just happened. It was hard to believe that only a few days ago, she was simply happy. The brutality of reality can be compared to life on the savanna. One day, an antelope and a lioness bask in the sun next to each other, and the next, the lioness feels hunger and pounces on the antelope, which, in a split second, is drenched in blood. The idyll disappears. Cut. The end of the film.

It's not good to face death in December. Maybe January would be better? No, the beginning of the year is a promise of something new. A time for resolutions that evaporate within two weeks. Lists of pledges end up in the trash, and everything returns to normal. How about February? Yes, February is a nondescript month. A transition between winter and spring, perhaps shortened for that reason. February lacks character. Still cold, but annoyingly so, because no one wants to wear woolen hats and thick coats anymore. No one wants to blow on frozen hands or drink litres of tea just to stay warm. People are tired of scraping ice off car windows and shuffling their feet at bus stops. They've had enough of the cold and the gloomy sky. Somewhere in the distance, March looms, full of crocuses, hyacinths, and tulips, full of that indefinable smell of slowly awakening life. It's March that people long for, impatiently counting down the days of February. People are always waiting for something. They cross off days on the calendar and foolishly rejoice that another Tuesday is gone, that Wednesday and Sunday have passed. What are they rushing for? Their own funeral? Do they want to send out the last invitations to a party that nobody enjoys?

Yes, death should come in February. In that ugly, useless month. With some strange Valentine's Day in the middle, which she has never liked.

Catherine stopped in front of a shoe store. From every boot, shoe, slipper, and even a wellie, a colourful bauble peeked out and sparkled coquettishly. It was unattractive and didn't capture the spirit of holidays. Clearly, someone had no idea how to decorate, so they just added a festive touch to what was already on display. Red, yellow, and silver balls. Probably plastic as there were fewer and fewer glass ornaments in stores.

These shoes were ugly too. Some were even dusty, as if they hadn't managed to shake off autumn. Catherine heard her mother's voice in her head: "You don't need to be reminded that every pair of shoes needs care and maintenance, do you?"

It had always annoyed her when her mother would nod significantly and repeat that sentence, looking at Catherine's muddy boots. And she would raise her finger, which seemed absurdly long, accusingly pointing it straight at another sin committed by Catherine.

"I'll wipe them with a cloth in a minute; they won't suffer for a few seconds" - she would answer dismissively. She didn't like cleaning shoes; it seemed completely pointless, especially since they looked exactly the same the next day as they did before cleaning.

"Sure, you know better. But remember, mud is best removed with water, and then the shoes must be thoroughly dried."

"Mom, give it a rest. I wear these boots every day. I'm not going to spend half the day maintaining them when I'll be wearing them again soon."

"So they can get ruined, right?" - Marianne would just shrug, sigh, and leave for another room, and Catherine would immediately feel she should apologize, though she didn't quite understand for what.

Only Maurice didn't care about any of it. Cats can't be bothered with nonsense.

Catherine touched the display window. She looked again at the rather dusty black patent leather high heels. Clearly, no one liked them, or they weren't in fashion at the moment. But as a child, she had dreamed of such shoes. They didn't need heels, but they had to shine and have a small bow in front. The foot looked entirely different in them. As if it belonged to a princess, adding prestige to the rest of the body. Plus, glittery tights, and one immediately felt like they were in a fairy tale. Not even a splatter of spinach on the plate could spoil that feeling.

"Patent leather should not be waterproofed; it should be cared for with a special cream for polished leather and then polished with a soft, preferably flannel, cloth" - she whispered to herself now and wiped the tears welling up in her eyes with the back of her hand.

She didn't want to cry, as it happened too often, lately. She wanted to somehow stop the sadness attacking her from all sides, but after a while she gave up. She would let the tears flow; no one was watching her, after all. People have recently stopped looking at each other. They passed by thoughtlessly, not paying attention to anyone else. She even liked this urban anonymity; sometimes it was better than someone's excessive interest. Now she could walk through the December city and cry as much as she wanted, even sniffle. She could indeed sob loudly. Who cared? Most people looked at their feet as if focusing only on their own steps to avoid tripping over a curb. Others slid their eyes over the faces of passing pedestrians, not registering them at all. Sometimes they stopped to look at a display, especially when something was moving, dancing, or spitting out artificial snowflakes. Kitsch in December was something acceptable, even expected. It heralded what most people were waiting for. Not always with great joy and solemnity, but they were waiting nonetheless. Christmas was a kind of magical boundary between what had already happened and what was to come. A transition from old to new, much more meaningful than New Year's Eve. Perhaps because the latter was simply too loud. With its disco music, concerts in big cities, with songs that sounded identical and bad.

"I don't like this kind of music" - her mother would say. – "They scream chaotically, and the melody escapes them somehow."

Catherine didn't like it either, but her mother's categorical tone annoyed her even more.

"The days of Paul Anka and The Beatles are over, Mom. People enjoy this now" - she would reply.

"Because no one taught them to listen to good music."

"But everyone is entitled to their own opinion."

"So I understand you have no problem with this howling?"

"I just don't like such categorizations."

"But one can't to listen to this!"

"YOU can't. That's different."

Marianne would usually at this point ask Robert to turn on something else in the bedroom, so she could go there, put on headphones, and not be bothered by anyone. She would adopt a martyr-like expression, which instantly triggered aggression in Catherine, though she tried to keep her nerves in check.

You can't really yell at your mother, especially not on New Year's Eve. Nor can you start stomping, screaming, and, God forbid, swearing. So in those situations, she would close her eyes, try to calm herself, and even use a special *ujjayi* breath. She had read somewhere that it restores a sense of peace and balance. It didn't for her, but at least she didn't kill anyone.

She looked at her phone.

It was twenty past eight. She had seven missed calls, all from Robert, of course. And one message: a small heart from Martin. No comment, no unnecessary questions. She texted Robert saying that she was on her way back, replied to the heart with a black one, and leaned her forehead against the cold window for a moment longer.

"Is everything alright?"

Someone had noticed her after all.

An elderly man with a dog was walking past the shoe store and was clearly puzzled by the sight of a lone woman, now sobbing quite loudly. The dog also looked at her curiously. He even came a bit closer and sniffed her leg.

She looked at them, dazed.

"Nubuck and suede leather should be brushed with a rubber or wire brush. All stains should be removed with a soft cloth or sponge soaked in a light soap solution. If the shoe is heavily soiled, clean it with a soft sponge soaked in water with salt" - she said, looking the man straight in the eye. Then she wiped her nose with her glove, turned around, and walked towards her apartment.

The dog barked three times. And you could really hear the astonishment in it.

***

"How did this even happen? What went wrong? People don't just die suddenly! Just like that… without reason!" - Catherine stared at the doctor, completely unable to understand what he was saying. She interrupted him, not even trying to give herself a chance to hear his voice. She felt as if everything around her was spinning, the walls leaning towards her, and the floor spreading out in different directions. She felt as if people were getting closer and then moving away, and the fluorescent lights were glaring into her eyes. And that the IV stands near the hospital beds had suddenly grouped together and were looking at her expectantly, as if participating in some hysterical spectacle. She even wanted to walk over to them and scream that they shouldn't stare like that. And to buzz off.

Finally, the doctor grabbed her by the shoulders and shook her.

"There was a reason; I'm trying to explain it to you. Anaphylaxis. A severe allergic reaction that sometimes, unfortunately, leads to death. When an allergen enters the body, it can trigger the release of strong chemical mediators that primarily affect the vascular system and smooth muscles."

Catherine giggled suddenly.

Chemical mediators?

Smooth muscles?

Why do doctors use such words? Why do they bombard you with terms that ordinary people don't understand? Maybe it's deliberate, to distract you? So the patient focuses on these strange words and doesn't break down.

Chemical mediators. It's absurd to talk to people like this. He might as well have been speaking Chinese, with a bit of Shanghainese mixed in.

"What happened to my mother? Why did she die?" - she finally whispered, as if she was a little girl who had just got lost at a huge, colourful fair.

"Was your mother allergic to anything?"

"I don't know, I don't think so…" - she stammered. "Are you talking about food?"

He nodded.

It's assumed that almost any protein found in food can trigger an anaphylactic reaction, especially in someone who is allergic. But the most common allergens are nuts, fish, shellfish, sesame seeds…

"Sesame. Yes, it's possible she was allergic to sesame. Something rings a bell, but I'm not sure."

"For some reason, she experienced an anaphylactic shock, swelling of the laryngeal mucosa, and blockage of the airways. We administered adrenaline, but unfortunately" - he spread his hands helplessly – "it was already too late."

Catherine didn't take her eyes off him. The doctor cleared his throat uncertainly and nervously rubbed his forehead with his hand. Apparently, he wasn't good at informing his patients about the death of their loved ones. He didn't know which words to use or whether to show compassion or just convey the message in a dry and concise manner. Underneath his unbuttoned white coat, she could see a checked shirt. Black and green. For a second, Catherine even focused on counting the buttons, and then she began to study the doctor's shoes in detail. Sporty, white and blue, with a strange, somewhat inflated sole. They matched his light jeans with slightly saggy knees.

"I'm really sorry, truly" - he added and walked away without looking back.

Catherine stood in the corridor for a moment, staring at the doctor's receding back, his white and blue shoes, and his white coat. Then she sat down on the floor and couldn't understand why people suddenly gathered around her, why Robert was pleading with her to stand up and drink some water, and why everything suddenly hurt so much.

Apparently, the first symptoms of anaphylaxis appear within a few minutes or several minutes after contact with the allergen. You can then feel intense anxiety, sometimes anxiety states, pressure, and headaches. Then comes ringing in the ears, paleness, a drop in blood pressure, increased heart rate, weak pulse, as well as severe shortness of breath, vomiting, abdominal pain, and diarrhea. Catherine felt as if she was experiencing exactly such a shock. Right here and right now. And that she would die any moment, and it would be a very fitting summary of what had just happened.

Because if she and her mother had different opinions on almost every topic, then only death could reconcile them in some way.

It is interesting whether they would be able to talk normally and calmly on the other side. Whether the awareness that they no longer had to try, that no rules, norms, or standards applied, would change anything. After death, you don't wear shoes, so there would be no problem cleaning them. You probably don't feel hunger, so no need to buy pumpkins and benefit from their blessings. Dirty hands and uncombed hair wouldn't matter either. Just as unwashed windows and cake frosting that is not sweet enough.

Would they still argue after death?

Would they still try to have their way?

If death equalizes everything, then surely the reasons for quarrels, bickering, and conflicts disappear automatically.

Catherine walked into the hospital bathroom and turned on the cold water tap. Then she looked in the mirror and realized that there would be no more arguments. Because it was only her mother on her own who had crossed to the other side, and even if she wanted to say something, Catherine wouldn't be able to hear her anymore.

***

The apartment was eerily quiet. Her father merely waved a hand at his daughter in greeting and went to his room, or rather, sat wearing his headphones in front of the TV and immersed himself in a movie. It was *Die Hard*, but Catherine couldn't remember which part it was; after all, they all seemed alike. Bruce Willis's bloodied face appeared on the screen, and her father muttered something under his breath. It was evident that he was completely engrossed in the action, so she retreated to the hallway.

Two weeks had passed since Marianne's death. And four hours.

Catherine stood for a few minutes with her eyes closed, as if waiting for her mother to come out of the kitchen and tell her to hang up her coat and put her hat on the radiator because it was probably damp ("It's a good trick, tried and tested many times").

"I'll count to ten" - she whispered under her breath and squeezed her eyelids even tighter. Then she added another ten. She promised herself that if she heard the sound of church bells, Marianne would indeed appear. It wasn't entirely fair, since it was close to six o'clock and Catherine knew perfectly well that she would soon hear six chimes.

One, two, three, four, five, six...

But her mother still didn't appear, so she didn't grimace at the sight of the muddy boots. Nor did she tell Catherine to wash her hands, because it's on them that the worst germs and bacteria are.

Catherine waited a little longer, sighed, opened her eyes, took off her shoes, hung up her coat, put her hat on the radiator, and went to the bathroom. She turned on the light and leaned her back against the green tiles. Not much had changed here in thirty years. A small, uncomfortable bathtub, in which it was barely possible to stretch out one's legs. The washing machine, and above it a shelf with laundry detergent and fabric softener. In the mirrored cabinet, her mother's cosmetics were still there. Nourishing night cream with calendula. And moisturizing day cream. Catherine unscrewed the jar and sniffed the contents. The cream smelled pleasant - fresh, floral, a bit milky. There was also a lipstick in a pale pink shade, aloe tonic, and nail polish remover. Cotton pads in a transparent container and a green pumice stone for feet. Body lotion, half empty, and two nail files. All the items looked as if someone was about to use them, as if they were just waiting for their turn.

Lipstick.

Catherine remembered how a few months ago she watched her mother bustling around the kitchen. She observed her in silence then. She couldn't recall the last time Marianne had spontaneously smiled. Even her wrinkles had softened, ironed out by the lack of smiles. She had dry, somewhat parchment-like skin, irises the colour of pale sky, and narrow, pursed lips. Sometimes they almost completely disappeared, so Catherine quickly asked some question to make the lips reappear. And so her mother could keep talking. She hadn't worn lipstick for a long time, nor had she worn mascara. She used to love lipsticks in all shades of pink, she had quite a collection, but that must have been a long time ago. There was only this one left, pale pink, almost untouched. Though she had the feeling that her mother's face had seemed a bit more alive recently... Or maybe it was just an illusion.

Catherine carefully put the cream jar, the lipstick in its golden case, and the tonic bottle back in place. She adjusted the pumice stone and nail files, touched the bottle of body lotion. She didn't know whether she should throw all this away, store it, or perhaps leave it as it was. She feared that getting rid of these cosmetics would mark some finality, although the worst had already happened. She closed the cabinet and put her hand on the mirror. Her mother would have been angry. She didn't like it when someone left fingerprints on it; and what annoyed her most were toothpaste marks.

"Catie, please come here immediately and clean the mirror. Also, tighten the toothpaste tube and wipe the toothbrush dry" - these were the sentences she heard when she was seven, nine, and even sixteen years old. For half her life, she had to polish the mirror, although she always tried not to splash toothpaste while brushing her teeth.

"Mix vinegar with water in a half-and-half ratio".

She hated the smell of vinegar, but once a week she thoroughly cleaned not only the bathroom mirror with it, but also the one in the hallway and the wardrobe in her mother's room.

No streaks. Streaks were unacceptable.

This time, however, she left a handprint on the mirror and went to the kitchen. Marianne was still there too. Her scent, her way of arranging containers of rice, flour, and sugar, her green tea with prickly pear and jasmine, instant coffee, the shortbread cookies with jam she bought at the nearby bakery, and on the stool, an apron with cherries folded neatly. Under the sink in a tin container were potatoes, already smelling slightly of soil, and two slightly rotten onions. Catherine threw them into the trash, and soon after later added the potatoes.

And then quickly took them back out. She grabbed a small knife with a wooden handle and peeled the potatoes. She threw them into a pot, salted them, and half an hour later put them on her plate, watching them steam.

The last potatoes that Marianne had bought. Probably "Hinga," a late, starchy variety, oval tubers, quite small, yellow skin, light yellow flesh, red-purple flowers. Or "Bryza," tasty, mealy, but difficult to store. Maybe that's why they had a bit of an earthy taste.

Catherine finished eating and touched the edge of the empty plate with her hand. It was white, with a border of roses and a gold rim. Her mother only used this set on great occasions, but when those were finished, she moved the plates from the attic to the kitchen cabinets, where they took up permanent residence.

"Everything becomes ordinary somehow" - she said then. "Even plates have lost their specialness. But at least they're not sleeping in a box."

Catherine used to like them very much, but over time they seemed just kitschy to her. Now she washed this one, dried it, and wrapped it in a newspaper. Then she took rice, flour, sugar, oatmeal, salt, and a bag of buckwheat from the cupboards. She decided she would do the shopping for her father tomorrow and restock. But these things she wanted to take with her. Probably no one took buckwheat as a memento of the deceased, but it was all the same to her.

"Dad, I'm leaving now. I'll come by tomorrow, bring you some food, and clean the fridge"- she said to her father, but he looked at her rather dazedly.

"Okay, very well" - he adjusted the headphones on his ears.

Did he even care about Mom's death? Or was it just his way of coping with the truth?

Bruce Willis fighting the whole world, car chases, and fast-paced action that's hard to tear away from? A parallel world he retreated into, to avoid thinking about the real one?

Catherine looked at her father for a moment longer, but he didn't seem to notice her. She put on her boots and took her hat off the radiator.

She smiled. It was nice to put it on. To feel the warmth.

Putting hats and gloves on the radiator was really a good idea. From now on, she would always do that.

***

December twenty-third. Christmas Eve, a day perhaps even more soaked with hopes than Christmas Eve itself. Catherine woke up at five-thirty and, although it was still dark outside, she got up and went to the kitchen. She always wondered what someone's life looked like after the death of a loved one. How could you be a daughter on Monday and a half-orphan on Tuesday? A wife on Wednesday and a widow on Thursday? It was brutally categorical.

She sat down at the white wooden table and placed an empty mug in front of her. She would have liked to have some coffee, but she didn't have the strength to get up and turn on the machine. She might have eaten a piece of poppy seed cake that Robert had brought from his mother, but the cake was in the fridge.

"Too far" - Catherine thought. So she just imagined cutting a slice, placing it on a white plate with a border of roses and a gold rim, and then drinking warm coffee. The clock ticked quietly, but when she started listening to it, it became difficult to escape the sound after a while.

Tick-tock. Tick-tock.

Louder. More brutal.

Finally, Catherine stood up and took the clock off the wall. She removed the two batteries from inside and placed them on the table. The clock stopped, a bit surprised at what had happened, and she sat back in her chair. Silence filled her completely, just as it should. It allowed her to view reality not so much from the head level, but rather from the heart. Or maybe the soul, if one did not doubt its existence. Her head was swirling with thoughts, unorganized, chaotic. They tried to turn into a scream. Sometimes, when they succeeded, Catherine would wake up calling out to someone in the middle of the night. She had no control over her own fear. Fortunately, for that particular scream some pills were found.

Now she needed silence. Silence freed her from the weight of bad thoughts, from unpleasant emotions, and from the pain that came back in waves. From the internal noise. Thinking was a trap; silence was the antidote. Now she wanted to be alone with herself, giving up everything, even the illusion that time could be turned back and that her mother wouldn't eat those damn sesame cookies. For the first time in a long time, she didn't need any words. Not neutral ones, nor comforting ones. She finally found the strength to find herself in the silence.

Catherine hadn't bought a Christmas tree this year and forbade Robert from celebrating the holidays in any way. Of course, he didn't listen to her.

"Christmas Eve is an evening of memories, a kind of poetic-reflective collage. It might actually help you. There's no point in pretending that Christmas won't come this year, that it will bypass us widely, and Christmas Eve will be suspended. Imprint your mother's memories on it. At least try."

She didn't want to listen to him anymore.

"Death is part of life" - he added, because he liked to have the last word.

Maybe in other circumstances, she would have even found it quite an accurate observation, but not this time. Death is death, an independent element, not connected with anything, least of all with life. It appears out of nowhere and cuts off the oxygen supply. The pulse stops, and the eyes that so eagerly look around suddenly become empty. Catherine felt a surge of anger rising to her throat. How can you just decide for someone? Without asking, without warning.

When she was twelve, her mother sent her to a summer camp. When Catherine came back, she no longer found her old room. It was renovated and rearranged. The old wardrobe and bed were gone, replaced by new furniture. Her old dolls, teddy bears, and the big plush elephant her father had brought her from Hungary were also gone. Catherine didn't know how to react. She wanted to cry. Someone had cleaned her room, taken her favourite things, and imposed a new order.

Now it was the same.

People love stability, even if it only concerns dolls in a child's room. Habits. Routines. Templates. Maybe it's boring and not very progressive, but it's their own. You can't clean for someone else.

"Not sleeping?" - Robert entered the kitchen but didn't even look at her.

She didn't answer. Lately, she preferred to stay silent more often, having evidently concluded that words wouldn't change anything. Robert couldn't comfort her or reach her, and it was clear he was already tired of the whole mourning process. He had no idea that Catherine's silence was a form of self-therapy for her. He just sulked and ostentatiously did his own laundry. His relationship with Marianne had been correct, bordering on slight impatience. He didn't like her frequent visits, which he often emphasized in conversations with Catherine. She, too, had had enough of her mother, who had been dropping by almost every day without warning in recent years, as if it was her duty. As if on her to-do list, it said, "Check in on Catherine and Robert."

"I'm sleeping" - she finally said provocatively. "I'm sleeping, so try not to wake me."

Robert shrugged. He opened the top cupboard and took out a mug. He turned on the coffee machine and stood for a moment with his back to Catherine, waiting for the water to heat up.

She closed her eyes. Robert had barged in with all his noise - hitting the mug against the table, pouring water, clearing his throat, and yawning loudly. Even his bathrobe made unpleasant sounds. It was unbelievable how someone's presence could be so intrusive, pushing into the hard-earned comfort zone where Catherine was trying to find herself. Even

Maurice felt contaminated by the noise and started flicking his tail nervously. Catherine knew what that meant. A cat tantrum.

She would have liked to leave the house now.

She raised her head.

Why not? She was allowed to leave whenever she wanted; she didn't have to explain herself to anyone. Robert had come into the kitchen, and she was leaving it. Action, reaction. If someone had been watching from the outside, they would have seen only people walking around the apartment. It wasn't worth looking for any hidden meanings in it. Robert appeared in the hallway as she was putting on her shoes.

"Are you crazy? Where are you going?"

"It's quite a nice feeling to surprise him like this," she thought.

"I'm going for a walk."

"At this hour?"

"Are there specific times for walking in December?" - she asked calmly, although she really felt like screaming again.

It was his fault.

She didn't wait for an answer, just pulled her hat over her ears and left without looking back. Sooner or later, she would have to end it.

"When will you be back?" - she heard him calling out.

"When pigs fly," she muttered under her breath.

*

There is a certain bench. Metal, with peeling black paint. It stands in a small park, close to a pond that is frozen over today. It's not a well-known spot, hidden behind a large witch hazel bush, whose sweet scent is particularly alluring in winter. Catherine found it without trouble, as if guided by a GPS. As if something led her to this exact place, even though she had never been there before. Along the way, she noticed a café that was already open, so she stepped inside and bought a hot vanilla drink.

"Do you open this early?" - she asked.

"In December, always. Hard to believe, but quite a few people come in before seven" -

the bartender replied. – "Almost as if they can't sleep."

She smiled faintly.

"Would you like some cinnamon in your coffee?" - he asked, and then he threw in a cinnamon cookie, too. "On the house."

Cinnamon, of course. It's almost Christmas.

"What's your name?" - she suddenly asked, surprising even herself. She wasn't the kind to start talking to strangers. But the bartender has a sad, forlorn look, though he was putting on a brave face. And he had given her a cookie.

"Alex."

"You look like something's bothering you?"

"More like devouring me. But…"

"Okay, I get it. I don't like talking about my problems either. You know why? Because to strangers, those problems usually don't seem so bad. If I told you my mother died, you'd think,

'Old people die, it's the way things are.' And in a way, you'd be right."

Alex didn't even attempt to smile. It was clear he was in a dark place.

"I'll be going. Have a good day, despite everything" - she said as she was leving.

The drink was disgustingly sweet, but it didn't bother her. Each sip sent a pleasant warmth through her body, momentarily soothing the hopeless melancholy that had gripped her for nearly a month.

She entered the lamp-lit park, passed the pond, circled a large chestnut tree, and headed towards the blooming witch hazel. It's amazing that there are shrubs that choose this exact time of year to showcase their best. Then again, they have no competition, so they can be the most beautiful. She parted the branches and saw the bench.

"Has it always been here?" - she asked herself.

She sat on the edge of the bench and closed her eyes. She held the cup in both hands, occasionally sniffing, as the vanilla scent was better than the taste.

December twenty-third. Seven nineteen. It was still dark outside, and the first snow of the year began to fall. A bit shy, delicate. Catherine finally smiled. In a shy and delicate way, too, as if afraid to allow herself more.

Snow has something magical about it. Especially the first snowfall, with tiny flakes just beginning their winter adventure. Catherine reached out and caught a few snowflakes.

"I would like to ask you so many things. And tell you so much more" - she said aloud. "But for some strange reason, I have always put it off for later, probably because there's always a tomorrow."

It's hard to believe that sometimes tomorrow just disappears.

Catherine closed her eyes.

Marianne was sitting at the other end of the bench. She was wearing a green dress made of a slightly transparent, soft fabric that Catherine remembered from her childhood. She had once secretly worn it before going to school, wrapping the excess fabric around a belt so the dress wouldn't drag on the ground. Her mother noticed that, and Catherine was punished by not being allowed to go to a friend's birthday party.

"Mom, I just wanted to look like you" - she had tried to explain, but Marianne was unwavering.

Catherine still had her eyes closed, yet she saw her mother. The psychologist, whom she was referred to while still in the hospital, told her in one of their sessions that sadness is never one-dimensional. It consists of many layers that sometimes overlap and can even create a state similar to a half-dream. One is then so deeply immersed in their melancholy that they can't be sure if what's happening to them is real or just a figment of their imagination. Sadness is longing. And longing is a desire.

"How much time do I have?" - Catherine asked quietly.

"An hour" - Marianne replied.

"Can I ask you anything?"

"Ask."

"Am I dreaming?"

"I don't know if that matters", Marianne replied calmly. "Ask something else. Ask about us."

"Tell me, why did we fight?"

Marianne initially remained silent, but after a while she began to speak. Calmly, thoughtfully, choosing her words carefully.

"I was hurt by your attempts at separation. The fact that you began to oppose me while I sought identification. Though identification is also a cause for competition. Not about which of us is better, but about who will dominate the rival."

"The rival?"

Marianne nodded.

"I know, it's silly. I admit, I often found myself being less mature than you. I felt that in some ways, you surpassed me."

"That's impossible."

"And yet. I mean maturity, and maturity isn't about age. It's about life skills and how we respond to reality. To the surprises we receive, both the good ones and the crappy ones.

Somewhere along the way, I think I got stuck. I didn't want to acknowledge that I was losing my position as the leader. That independence is a natural cause of events. The problem was that your independence exposed my weaknesses. It sidelined me."

Catherine grabbed Marianne's hand. And then she slowly lifted her eyelids.

Marianne turned her face towards her. At first, she was thirty-one and had just given birth to Catherine. Tears of joy streamed down her cheeks, and her eyes were smiling. Then she was thirty-five, sitting with little Catherine in a sandbox. And finally, she was forty, forty-eight, fifty-two, sixty-three. Beyond that, there was nothing, although there should have been, and Catherine wanted to scream at her now. That you don't eat cookies with sesame seeds, knowing they can cause an allergy. That you don't die so young.

"I didn't know they had sesame. I bought them by weight at a small bakery near my apartment. I didn't pay attention the ingredients, and I didn't taste the sesame. Besides, I never imagined it could be deadly for me. They were just cookies. It's even a bit embarrassing to die because of cookies. I'd prefer not to boast about that publicly."

Catherine buried her face in her hands.

"I still can't believe it". She whispered, then asked after a pause: "What did you want to tell me that Monday? You know, the last time we saw each other."

Marianne wrinkled her nose playfully.

"I'm a bit embarrassed. Maybe we can talk more about mother-daughter relationships some more, and then what I'm unsure how to express might naturally come out?"

Catherine raised her eyebrows.

"You messed up? You of all people are perfect."

"I did get carried away a bit, that's true. But I don't regret it."

"Mom…"

"I'm just piquing your curiosity. Let me enjoy this for a moment."

Catherine shook her head, then started drilling a hole in the slightly frozen ground with her boot.

"Do you know why I left the house so early today? I couldn't stand Robert and his noisy bathrobe that rustled so terribly."

Marianne chuckled.

"I know the feeling. Your father used to drive me crazy with his loud apple crunching. He'd keep his mouth closed, but I could hear everything. That crunching was like a locust invasion. It drilled into my head so much that after a while, all I could think about was his teeth attacking the flesh of the apple. And let me tell you, it was even worse with carrots."

Catherine couldn't help but laugh.

"Do you know what's truly important?" - Marianne asked.

"Are you talking about apples and crunching?"

"No, now I'm switching to a much more serious topic. After all, I am your mother."

Catherine glanced at her expectantly.

"To be a good enough parent. Not perfect, or ideal, but the kind of parent a child turns to you when they have a problem. You stopped confiding in me. And now I know why. I meddled too much with you. I tried to change you to make you more like me. And I didn't want to be dethroned. I refused to accept that this was how it was supposed to be. That I needed to step aside and sometimes just observe what you were doing without necessarily commenting on it."

Catherine clenched her fists.

"Now I see that I didn't make anything easier for you. Often I even provoked arguments just to convince myself how different we were. I wanted to prove to myself that we had nothing in common and that everything separated us. Your life was coloured by the past, mine by the present, therefore we had no right to understand each other. That's how I explained it to myself."

Marianne smiled gently.

"It was foolish. Insecure, but still foolish."

Catherine felt warmth on her cheek. She swallowed.

"Mom, that pumpkin pie... Remember? You mentioned it to me once but I don't think you ever shared the recipe."

"Because you didn't want it. Besides, you don't like pumpkin."

"I didn't like its strong presence during that conversation. But that pie somehow haunts me."

"I always made it with whole meal flour. But you can also use regular flour mixed with bran."

"I'll buy whole meal" - Catherine said, smiling. She then pulled an old receipt and a pen from her coat pocket, carefully noting down all the ingredients to ensure she could bake the same cake as her mother.

"Now for the filling" - Marianne said.

It suddenly dawned on Catherine that she could listen to her forever. Even if she had to hear the word "pumpkin" three hundred times and be convinced that it was all she should eat from now on. Words in this missing hour took on new meaning. Each one was ripe, juicy, like the best apple straight from the tree.

"That sounds delicious"- Catherine whispered. "Really."

"Will you tell me who he is? And why are you seeing him?" - Marianne asked unexpectedly.

Catherine lowered her head. That question had never been asked before. There had been reproaches, accusations, even warnings that she would come to regret it. There had been stories Marianne had heard from others, stories that never ended well. And yet, not once had the essential question been asked. Now it had to be answered at once - no beating around the bush, no preamble, no explanations. No justifications either.

"He... he likes mayonnaise."

Marianne's eyes widened.

"I take it Robert prefers ketchup?"

"It's just that I have never met a man who loves mayonnaise as much as I do."

"I see" - Marianne said nodding solemnly. "A mayonnaise-man, well, that's actually quite an argument."

Catherine burst out laughing.

"I know how it sounds, but that's exactly why I fell in love. He actually sees me. When he looks at me, it's only me he sees. He dies not look to the side, not somewhere over my head. There's no impatience in his gaze, just calmness, and tenderness."

"And Robert?"

"Robert does enjoy the sound of his own voice. Every other voice feels like a disturbance, an uninvited note in a melody Robert knows by heart and has no desire to alter."

"Do you want to get a divorce?"

Catherine slowly began to nod.

"I do, Mom."

For the first time, she said it out loud. At last she articulated something that had until now filled her with fear. It's not easy to leave someone without a compelling reason. What would she say in court? That her husband doesn't look at her the way she wished he would? That he uses too many metaphors hiding the real issue behind them? That sometimes he cannot tell a fictional character with the person he lives with and forgets that it's her who needs more of his attention? That his words, no matter how often or eagerly spoken, mean very little? And that he never bought her mayonnaise, even though he knows she loves it?

Those aren't real arguments.

It was a hysterical vision of her life with Robert. Exaggerated, saturated with longings she couldn't quite put into words. And the court expects specifics. Clear and simple statements about differences in character or incompatible expectations.

He wanted sex, she didn't. Or the other way round.

He lost money in a casino, she was unfaithful.

Those were blunt, powerful words, something you could build a divorce petition on. And how would her argument sound?

There was no tenderness in his touch.

There was no interest in his gaze.

There was no substance in his words.

There was no trace of her in him.

Could the court possibly measure the level of tenderness? List the parameters of interest? Weigh the meaning of words?

She hadn't talked about it with anyone because she wasn't entirely sure what she was actually accusing Robert of. Only after she met Martin did she realize what she had been missing.

"Who is he?" - Marianne asked.

Martin was an IT specialist. A precise, analytical mind. Logical, methodical. Numbers, order, linear thinking, step by step, planning, operating with figures, literalness, attention to detail. There was in fact nothing about him that should have fascinated Catherine. No spontaneity, creativity, imagination, dreams. And she had always thought that was what she was looking for. Colours. Images. But it wasn't true, and Catherine told her mother that now. And finally, she added:

"I'm simply looking for my own reflection in someone else's eyes."

***

Love is an essential part of life. Not the grand, pompous kind overflowing with exaltation, but the kind made up of the missing pieces of the other person. In truth, no one is complete. A human being is full of holes, ambiguities, and unfinished fragments that can only be filled by the right person. They, too, have their own missing bits and are searching for someone to fill them. When these two people finally meet, the puzzle is complete at last.

Catherine wondered why it was so hard for her to decide to have a child. She was thirty-two, lecturing English literature, she had a husband, and a three-room apartment. These were solid foundations – such as people usually strive for before taking the next step.

A child.

Everything pointed to adding another layer to these stable foundations and enjoying the next milestone on her life's to-do list. And yet, Catherine couldn't. Or maybe she didn't want to. Or perhaps… a bit of both?

She met Martin in a rather ordinary way, during the international conference "All That

Gothic," organized with the Department of American Literature and Culture. She gave a lecture; he was also handling the technical side of the conference. Their eyes caught, and then they started talking, debating. They even managed to find time for a coffee. Gradually, the pieces began to fit together more and more, and Catherine felt like she was becoming complete, smiled more often, opened her eyes wider. She even began to walk differently, more boldly, more steadily. And she no longer kept her eyes fixed on the ground.

Marianne noticed this change too.

"Don't do this" - she said one day.

Catherine immediately understood what she meant. She looked at her mother and pressed her lips together.

"Don't do this," Marianne repeated, then began scrubbing the pots with determination.

They didn't return to the topic for a while, although Catherine felt her mother watching her, saw how she noticed all the gradual changes, even if no one else did. Yet, from that moment on, things between them began to unravel even more. Every conversations ended with a spark of conflict.

"We don't measure out detergent by eye."

"Mom, give it a rest. I've always done it this way."

"The required amount of detergent is indicated on every package" - her mother wouldn't back down.

"Stop it."

"If you followed the rules, starting with something as simple as laundry, maybe following the bigger ones would come easier to you too."

At such moments, Catherine would immediately retreat. First, she would stop listening and mentally disconnect, and then she would simply run out of the house and walk aimlessly, breathing deeply. She met Martin once a week. Magical Tuesdays. She had the day off at the university, and she turned that freedom into a few wonderful hours with a man she could, without hesitation, imagine having a child with. He fulfilled those needs in her that she had long buried deep inside.

"I know what you mean" - Marianne said now. "Passion is a hunger. And hunger must be satisfied. For a heartbeat, everything disappears. Family, obligations, work, commitments. The entire world becomes that other person with whom you want to share every second."

That was exactly how it was with Catherine. She knew that passion is like an adventure - enticing and tempting. That it is a risk, a surprise, a surge of emotions, and a thousand question marks. And that's what thrilled her the most. Because passion allows you to lose yourself in desire, to deceive, to lie, to create your own reality. But sometimes, it also opens your eyes.

"You have no idea how much I understand you" - Marianne lowered her gaze.

"Will you tell me now?"

"Not yet. Ask me about something else" – those things that tormented you the most.

Catherine didn't want to look at the clock. Her mind was tangled with sentences never spoken and thousands of questions left unasked. Why is it always hardest to talk with your mother? Is it shame? Genetic embarrassment? Fear of exposing your own weaknesses? This time, there was no room for fear. Because there's simply no time for it.

"Why didn't you ever hug me?"

Marianne lowered her head.

"I wanted you to keep your feet on the ground. To know how to handle different situations. Touch makes you soft."

"That's not true" – Catherine objected. "Touch gives you strength. Martin taught me that."

"And Robert?"

"Robert only knows how to charm with words. He enchanted me, that's true. Enchanted me for over ten years, and I can't say it was all bad. But now I know - it wasn't enough. And his words were just empty."

"It's worse when there are no words at all" - Marianne said. "When they appear less and less until one day, they're gone."

"What do you mean?"

"Your father taught me to how to be silent. We never really talked – not truly. He didn't like it. Each year, it got worse. I could count on the fingers of one hand the words he spoke to me in a month. If I were Robert, maybe I'd know how to arrange them into something beautiful, maybe even a compliment, but unfortunately, I never had that talent. I only heard scattered words. Emotionless, impersonal. Commands, sometimes instructions. I even learned to distinguish between the types of grunts and half-syllables. And the degrees of intensity when he crunched apples."

"Is that why you stated coming over more and more often?"

Marianne nodded.

"I came to talk. About shoes, about laundry detergent. About what cleaning agents to use and how to pack a suitcase for a vacation. About how delicious and healthy broccoli is and how to transplant cacti. I didn't speak to to teach you anything – I spoke to let out all the words your father had locked in my throat. Do you know what he once told me? That he didn't like the sound of my voice. And that silence is perfect. So, I sank into that silence, because I had no other choice. There was a time I wanted to spit out all the words he had taken from me, but he looked at me so dismissively that it left me speechless. So, I just kicked the chair he was sitting on."

Catherine looked at her in astonishment. Her father was indeed silent, but she had never suspected it could hurt her mother so much. Robert, on the other hand, used words often and eagerly. Catherine lived surrounded by words. Just as sounds make up a musical piece, and colourful dots on a canvas create a painting, words evoke emotions, carrying specific value and meaning. You can't live without them. Sure, sometimes they miss the mark, sometimes they are just empty shells, but they still fill everyday life. They give it some meaning and in their own way are simply indispensable. Can one live without words?

"I didn't know" - Catherine whispered.

"Because I never told you. The problem between mothers and daughters often lies in keeping silent about things that should be discussed. It leaves room for discussions about nothing. Such rambling that it straightens the folds in your brain."

"Like when you tried to convince me that cheese should be stored on the top shelf of the fridge?"

"Exactly. Or when I tried to convince you to add lemon balm to boiled potatoes."

"That was awful" - Catherine laughed. "You brought it every day and stubbornly threw it into my pot."

Marianne helplessly spread her hands.

"I wanted to convince both you and myself that my words meant something, that they mattered, even if your father thought otherwise. I wanted someone to listen to me and for my words to have some effect. I hoped that eventually, you would start adding lemon balm to potatoes yourself and putting cheese on the top shelf. That would have been confirmation for me that my words weren't falling into a void. I must honestly admit, though, that potatoes with lemon balm are disgusting."

They fell silent for a moment. Catherine wanted to move a little closer and maybe even hug her mother, but she was afraid that any sudden movement would ruin everything. She feared the bench would disappear; the missing hour would shatter into thousands of seconds, which would then scatter through the park along with the chance for more questions.

"Do you remember when you were the happiest?"

"On the day you were born. When I nestled my face into your warm neck and then, when you instinctively squeezed my finger. I thought then that I never wanted you to let it go."

"But you know I had to do it?"

Marianne nodded.

"You can't prepare for that. Separation is more painful than childbirth itself. But instead of understanding and accepting it, I started to struggle to regain control. Now I see that."

"Do you remember the summer by the sea? I was nine then, and my hair was impossible to comb. It was stiff, salty, and messy. But it was mine."

Marianne bit her lower lip.

***

What's left of us in adulthood is a sum of how many times we were broken in childhood. How many times our hair was cut without our consent, a toy thrown away without asking, how many times we were sent to camp despite our paralyzing fear of separation. The number of all these little things, seemingly insignificant, grows with each passing year until it finally starts to claim small victories. Fear of making one's own decisions. Acceptance of manipulation. Freezing one's own needs.

"We're going to the hairdresser's" - Marianne said back then, and although Catherine tried to protest with tears, her mother was unyielding. "Look at yourself. Your hair is tangled, damaged, and completely dried-out. Besides, I don't really like braids."

"But I like them" - Catherine said softly.

Her hair was cut the very same day.

Life is made up of images. A memory may be long, stretched out, yet it always ends with a shot that sums it up. Had Marianne embraced her daughter then and promised that her hair would grow back, perhaps the image Catherine constantly saw wouldn't have been so terribly sad.

"One should lose parental rights for such things" - Marianne admitted now.

"Well, perhaps it's not about the rights, but some sort of punishment would be appropriate. Like a ride on a rollercoaster, which you despise even more than the remnants of toothpaste on the mirror."

***

When Catherine met Robert, she quickly succumbed to his words.

"You're so melancholically flirtatious" - he whispered in her ear, and Catherine found herself even more enchanted.

It took her some time to realise that Robert wouldn't actually listen to her. And that he disliked blunt, genuine words that exposed his narcissistic personality.

"Writers don't like criticism" - she learned that quite quickly. "Especially from their loved ones, and even more so from those who don't know a thing about writing."

"I teach literature. I think I have some understanding" - she tried to argue with him, but Robert only gritted his teeth and looked away.

"Reading and writing are two different things."

"As a reader, I know what I like and what I don't."

"But your opinion isn't objective. It's not even a composite of several tastes, but just your feeling. And that means you could be mistaken."

Catherine shrugged.

"I believe I'm objective. I like your books, so theoretically, I should enjoy everything. But that's not the case. Not with your latest novel."

Robert was furious. She saw the vein pulsing on his forehead and could't help but notice his hostile gaze.

"You don't know a thing" – he snapped.

"Possibly" - she tried to defuse the tension. "It's just that the main character doesn't convince me."

"Fortunately, he'll convince others" - Robert cut the conversation short, and then spent the next three days in a masculine version of a sulk. He wouldn't speak, cooked for himself, and locked himself in his room.

This bothered her; she always tried to placate him, but a narcissist can be unyielding. She sympathised with her mother even more now. How to live in a world without words?

Robert's book didn't sell well, the critics weren't gentle either. They pointed out exactly what his wife had mentioned earlier. Catherine felt no satisfaction from this; she simply wanted her husband to admit she was right, apologize, and acknowledge her insight. And that sometimes it's worth swallowing criticism, even from the closest person. But he seemed to remain convinced that the opinion of an English literature lecturer just coincidentally aligned with the critics' views. And that it still didn't mean anything. He didn't let her read his next manuscript, so she stopped asking.

"They say actions speak louder than words" - she said now. "Perhaps it's true?"

Marianne shook her head.

"That's nonsense. A word is a signal that someone cares. That you matter to someone. I didn't need orations, speeches, or long stories. I just wanted to feel what someone once called love, interest, and tenderness. Words allow us to live because they touch our emotions. When someone doesn't want to talk to you, you start listening only to yourself. Words let us share our dreams and secrets. And sometimes they can save us. If your father had talked to me, if he had wanted to converse, I probably wouldn't have overwhelmed you with my presence, I wouldn't have flooded you with a torrent of unnecessary words, chosen on the spot, just to say something."

Catherine smiled at her memories.

"What did you just think about?" - Marianne asked.

"I remembered the time Robert had swollen eyelids. He spent all night in front of the computer, and he really did look rough in the morning. You gave us a whole lecture on cucumbers that day. We couldn't interrupt you. And then you went on about massages and herbal infusions. It was terrible; I thought you were in some kind of a trance and talking just for the sake of talking, and those massages, herbs, and cucumber were just an excuse to drown us out, to silence us."

Marianne smoothed the folds of her green dress.

"I'm sorry" - she said, but Catherine quickly shook her head.

"No, no, I understand now. I finally understand."

Marianne lifted her head and looked up at the sky.

"I like snow," she smiled at the swirling snowflakes. "Did you know that each snowflake contains dozens of ice crystals? And they need about fifteen minutes to fall to the ground. Sometimes it felt like I was just such a snowflake.

And that when I touched the ground, I would finally disappear."

Catherine sniffled.

"You touched it too soon."

"I don't know. Maybe everyone has their own tempo. Some are carried by the wind, like those snowflakes, so they swirl in the air a little longer; others rush toward the ground at breakneck speed."

"Like us back then on the sled" - Catherine suddenly remembered.

Childhood memories were clearer now and came back to her more and more often. Good and bad. Until recently, Catherine had seen only fragments, some blurry images or bits and pieces of what once was. A plate with unfinished cucumber soup, she never liked, a sandwich spread with mayonnaise, which she loved, an open wardrobe in her mother's room and scarves scattered on the floor, her father sitting in an armchair, or maybe just his back. Everything oddly torn out of context, sometimes funny, sometimes frightening. Memories often got mixed up, transformed, so Catherine wasn't sure if what came back to her had really happened or was just a fragment of her subconsciousness.

But the sled ride looked like a complete picture now, full of vivid details, both dynamic and emotional. As if it all happened just yesterday.

January. Icy, frosty, yet so fascinatingly white that people forget all the other colours. Mom picked Catherine up from kindergarten earlier than usual, and when the little girl went outside, Marianne proudly showed her the wooden sled.

"These are for you. An older man was selling sleds at the market. He made them himself, a few pieces, and they sold out immediately. I thought you've never ridden a sled, so maybe... now?" - She winked at her.

Catherine had rosy cheeks, a red nose, and warm ears under a green woolen hat. She had a warm heart and warm hands hidden in her mittens. She laughed loudly, and so did her mom. They sledded down fast, without braking, screamed at the top of their lungs, and laughed at every fall into the fluffy snow.

"It's strange that people so rarely remember the good times" - Catherine observed. "Did you know that in English, there are about a thousand words to describe positive emotions and over two thousand for negative ones? Why do I remember the day you had the hairdresser cut my hair, the day you cleaned my room and threw away my dolls, but I only remembered the sledding just now? Surely it all balanced out somehow."

Marianne looked at her with a smile.

"Do you remember the ring from the fair?"

The ring was gold-coloured with a red stone. It shone brighter than the stars in the sky, at least that's what Catherine thought. It was also much easier to obtain. Although Marianne initially resisted, she eventually gave in and bought it for Catherine. Fifteen minutes later, the colourful balloons and wooden birds, the cotton candy, and the glazed gingerbread had disappeared. Because Catherine lost the ring in the crowd and now stood before her mother, crying. The world stopped existing for her because the loss was too great.

"Did you take it off your finger?" - Marianne asked.

"I don't know" - Catherine sobbed. "Maybe for a moment, because I wanted to see if it sparkled in the sun, but I thought I put it back on."

"It must have fallen out."

Catherine hung her head.

And then Marianne hugged her, took her by the hand, led her to the stall, and bought the same gold ring with a red stone.

Two women closest to each other don't always have to agree on everything, and it's okay for them to argue. They can make mistakes and do foolish things. A mother and daughter are a strong tandem of two independent individuals, a tandem powered by love. Catherine finally understood this.

"Will you tell me now?"

"I fell in love."

"No!!! You too? With whom? Do I know him?"

"Her."

Catherine froze and resembled a fish taken out of water.

***

Three days after her mother's death, Catherine called Martin. She did that when she could finally speak normally. When her voice returned and her words began to form somewhat coherently.

"Are you angry at her?" - he asked.

At first, she wanted to deny it, but suddenly she realized that this question perfectly reflected her emotions. Yes, she was angry. She was furious at her mother for suddenly going silent. For stopping her visits, her meddling, her advice, her talks about cucumbers, dust, the best times for vacations, and whether a dog is smarter than a cat. For asking why Maurice meowed so strangely. Someone who constantly flooded them with tens of thousands of words had suddenly stopped and gave her the silence she didn't want.

"Yes" - she finally admitted. "I'm furious, bitter; I'd love to scream in her face what I think about all this. I feel like, in a way, she had her way again. She did something without consulting me, and she did it out of spite."

She almost cried into the phone.

"I lost my sister at the beginning of this year. We weren't close; I don't even know why. She moved abroad, and we lost contact. Probably because we used to misunderstand each other completely. We argued about everything, and the difference in our opinions was so great that we both concluded it was better to stop speaking to one another. Sometimes it seemed impossible that someone like her could be my sister."

"I don't know what to say. I'm terribly sorry… How did you lose her?" - Catherine asked.

"A train accident. Eight people died, and Joanne was among them. And you know what? When it all finally hit me, when I realized I'd never see her again, I felt anger. I was furious that she never called, even though I sent her holiday cards. That she broke off contact even more than

I would have wished. And that, in a way, she left me alone. Even though she lived in Denmark, she was still my older sister, my family. And suddenly, she was just gone. And now…" - he paused for a second.

"And now what?"

"I'll tell you later. Right now, you have to go through your anger. And then denial, sadness, and slow acceptance. Until you come to me smiling again. But it will take time, and I'll be waiting."

Martin said exactly what she needed to hear. His words hit the mark, even if they weren't as beautiful as Robert's. It's a pity she never told her mother about Martin. Although that wasn't the most important thing right now…

***

"What? HER?" - Catherine asked. "Mom, that sounds more surreal than your presence here. And the fact that we're even talking."

"I met her in the library about two months ago. I don't know if she prefers women or men, at least in a sexual sense. We didn't get to that stage, although I can say with certainty that I fell in love with her."

Catherine covered her mouth with her hand.

"But how?"

"You see, in our case, the conversation worked just like your mayonnaise. Cristine spoke to me, listened to what I had to say, and then began to speak again. And from that moment, our conversations became the driving force for everything. We called each other, wrote, met, and talked endlessly. Only nights interrupted us, but we had to regenerate sometime, after all, we were of a certain age."

"Mom…"

"Wait, let me finish. Cristine is seven years younger than me and she is a widow. She loves books and loves discussions. And - allow me to steal your comparison - she looks at me and sees me. And I see myself in her eyes. That's how it was, right? And that was enough for me."

Catherine shook her head in disbelief. Indeed, in the last weeks before her death, her mother had visited less often than usual. It only struck her now. She had forgotten to come on Saturday. And on Sunday, she had only stayed for an hour. Even Maurice was puzzled.

"I felt he missed you in his cat way" - she said.

Marianne laughed.

"Maybe I was too much for him."

"Did you really fall in love with her?" - Catherine whispered.

"Yes. Perhaps platonically. There probably wasn't any eroticism into it, though I'm not sure. I just felt happy. And I had butterflies in my stomach, though I had been sure that expression only existed in cheesy novels. But those butterflies do exist. Your insides levitate, and you have no idea why, and you just feel light. I had such a deficit of closeness and conversation that the butterflies emerged almost immediately from their hidden cocoons. I even wondered if I should leave your father and move in with Cristine."

"Did she suggest that?"

"Imagine she did. She, too, had feelings for me. She confessed this while we were baking a strawberry roulade together."

"Mom, I think I'm shocked."

"I absolutely understand. And I'm mad at myself for not having introduced you to Cristine. For not daring. Even if it would have seemed an absurd conclusion to my old age."

"You're not old."

"Alright, my maturity of late cherries. Those in August. Staccato, if I remember correctly."

"Don't you regret that it didn't work out?"

"Very much. But here, the degree of regret is somewhat different. It's mainly about acceptance. Coming to terms. I don't know everything yet, I'm new here."

"I wanted you to meet Martin so much" - said Catherine quietly.

Marianne looked at her and smiled gently.

"And I wanted to meet him, too" - she replied.

"But you looked at me with reproach. As if you constantly threatened and reminded me that I was making a mistake."

"Because in a way, you were disrupting my stability" - Marianne admitted after a while.

"Yours?"

"Yes. I was used to you and Robert. To you as a married couple. To your apartment, to frequent visits. I even wanted to be a grandmother already and have another reason to visit. Your father had fallen completely silent in the last two years. He practically only made sounds that matched my questions. Whether he was hungry, whether he wanted pancakes, whether he had any laundry. Those sounds were everything he gave me. When I realized you were having an affair, I got scared. But this fear wasn't about you, but about what would happen to me" - she lowered her head. "I felt a kind of anger. I was hurt that you didn't come to me, didn't ask, didn't want any advice. The fact that you were cheating on Robert hurt me more because I took it very personally. And you were silent. You didn't want to admit it, though it was obvious you were somewhere else in your mind. Your face changed with each passing day. As if someone was painting the missing pieces of happiness on it."

Catherine looked at Marianne, intrigued.

"You think happiness is divided into elements?"

She thought for a while.

"Happiness is never complete; otherwise, it would be hard to enjoy. If you have everything, you lack nothing. So you can't feel happiness when you get something because you already have it."

"I think I'm a little lost."

Marianne pushed a stray lock of hair from her forehead and wrapped herself in a soft shawl that had been hanging on the back of the bench until now.

"That man clearly knows exactly where your pieces of happiness are. He knows how to find them and give them to you, like flowers from a bouquet. I know what I'm talking about. Though not for long."

"Do you think Robert noticed anything?"

Marianne shook her head.

"He couldn't. Robert is a narcissist. Only what he does is worth attention. And perfection doesn't consider rejection because it doesn't fit into its self-worth."

"Mom…"

"Yes?"

"You know you probably would never have become a grandmother?"

Marianne looked at her questioningly.

"What are you trying to tell me?"

"I found out a few weeks ago. Because, you see, for the first time in my life I felt that I wanted a child. That I was ready and I wanted to be a mom."

"With Martin?"

Catherine blushed.

"I know it's silly because I've only known him for a few months. But that certainty came suddenly. Without question marks, without fear and uncertainty."

"But?"

"Hyperprolactinemia."

Marianne looked at her daughter, not understanding much.

"Don't speak in riddles. What kind of devil is that?"

Catherine sighed.

"I went to the gynaecologist to ask about possible preparations for pregnancy. No, I didn't talk to Martin about it; I wanted to find out everything myself first."

"But what is this hyperprolactinemia?" - Marianne asked again.

"High prolactin levels. Its elevated levels may indicate pituitary gland tumours or thyroid diseases. Prolactin is responsible for producing and secreting milk in pregnant and breastfeeding women. Unfortunately, in non-pregnant women, high prolactin levels can inhibit ovulation."

"And that's how it is with you?"

Catherine nodded slowly.

"Why didn't you tell me?"

"You know why."

Marianne closed her eyes.

"And Martin?"

"He doesn't know either. Mom, I want to have a child with him so much. You know I even thought about adoption? Although the doctor told me that hyperprolactinemia can be treated and that I shouldn't give up. Often, pharmacological treatment is enough."

"You will have that child" - Marianne said suddenly. "You can trust me. I'm already on the other side and have access to certain information. Even as a novice."

Catherine pulled her knees under her chin. The snow was still falling, now even more heavily, but she didn't feel cold. The flakes swirled in the air; a few of them settled momentarily on her navy blue coat. Once, she saw a snowflake under a microscope. Apparently, those tiny six-pointed stars look best when the air temperature is zero degrees. In severe frost, they're no longer so charming; they lack that pure, flawless structure because the frost destroys it.

She looked at her mother.

"How do you know I'll have a child?"

Marianne smiled.

"I know, trust me."

Catherine bit her lip.

"And you know you can speak beautifully? Not just about dust and cucumber masks. You speak beautifully about life. And about me. About Cristine, too. I regret not coming to you earlier, not telling you about Martin, not asking your opinion, not hearing about the pieces of happiness. Sometimes one gets so wrapped up in their anger, stubborn to the end. It harms oneself the most, but you realize it only after some time. God, how stupid I was."

Marianne pondered.

"In our way, we're similar. Because I also didn't use the right words. And it's words that colour our lives, make them special. Poor vocabulary means a poor emotional life. Instead of choosing words with a positive message that would strengthen us both, I focused on the empty and irrelevant ones, so you didn't want to listen to me. And you were right. You can't talk about nothing just to make a sound. What we talk about is significant. It came to me too late." - She sighed.

Catherine sniffed.

"We both got tangled in the wrong words. We both chose them so they lost their meaning even before we said them. Why can't people talk? Sometimes Maurice is more convincing than me."

"Because talking about feelings, about what hurts us or makes us happy, is embarrassing. It exposes our weaknesses, removes the armour of toughness."

"But you're my mom. Why do we need armour?" - Catherine was astonished.

Marianne sighed.

"Perhaps because parents should be strong? Stronger than their children?"

They both fell silent and looked at each other. A mother and a daughter. Two people closest to each other who thought they were divided by everything.

"Mom, I can't imagine tomorrow's Christmas Eve without you" - Catherine whispered. "Besides, I haven't prepared anything. Father will come, and I don't even have a cheesecake. Robert brought some poppy seed cake from his mother and probably some dumplings, but I didn't make anything."

"You don't have to."

Catherine looked at her in surprise.

"And it is you who is telling me this?" - She laughed quietly.

Marianne shrugged.

"The compulsion to celebrate. Now I see that there were more baubles on the tree and polished cutlery than the holidays themselves required. But I have a good recipe for a no-bake cheesecake". - She winked at her. "You can make it even tomorrow morning. Or a strawberry roulade. It goes to the hips but also straight to the heart. Pure happiness in pink."

"I'll make a pumpkin pie. Maybe not very traditional, but it will have symbolic meaning for me. And Robert can eat his poppy seed cake."

"But I didn't finish the recipe, and we don't have much time left, about seven minutes. You need to take the dough out of the fridge, roll it out, line the tart pan with it, prick it with a fork in several places, and pre-bake it in a preheated oven at two hundred degrees for about ten minutes. Once pre-baked, pour the filling, sprinkle with chopped cheese and pumpkin seeds."

"And how long do I bake it?"

"Fifty minutes."

"Mom?"

"Yes?"

"I love you."

The Hour of the Blue Notebook

A family circle cannot be drawn with a compass.
Stanisław Jerzy Lec

The Storebæltsbroen Bridge spans the Great Belt, connecting two Danish islands - Funen and Zealand. The accident occurred around 7:35 AM. A passenger train, consisting of two IC4 diesel train sets, was traveling from Aarhus to Copenhagen. A total of one hundred and thirty-one people, along with three railway employees, were on board. Meanwhile, on the opposite track, a freight train carrying empty, tarpaulin-covered trailers belonging to the Carlsberg brewery was speeding by. A fierce gust of wind dislodged one of the trailers, which fell onto the track where the passenger train was approaching. Despite the train's emergency braking, the collision with the trailer was unavoidable.

The Storebæltsbroen, which connects the Danish cities of Nyborg and Korsør, remained closed for several hours. Rescue operations were underway. The authorities evacuated everyone to the mainland, though the strong winds made the operation challenging. A storm raged over the Baltic Sea.

When Martin first read these reports, he didn't yet know that there had been fatalities. A total of eight. Among them were his sister Joanne and his brother-in-law Ebbe. His mother broke the news to him, and then she simply hung up, leaving Martin to realize that he needed to go to see her immediately. Even if she pretended she could cope, even though she was a strong woman, he knew he couldn't leave her alone, at least for the next few days. A few weeks after their father's death, she'd had a heart attack, and the doctor said it was due to a severe stress reaction. If Joanne hadn't kept her wits about her and called an ambulance, they might have lost their mother too.

He jumped into his car right away, and during the drive, he tried to push thoughts of death, the accident, and the inevitable event he was so unprepared for out of his mind. He behaved as if he wanted to delay it all until later, focusing now on his mother, handling necessary formalities, and concentrating on the tasks at hand.

"A passenger train, traveling on the double track, collided with a piece of the damaged trailer. The steel beams tore into the front of the passenger train, causing severe damage to the lead carriage. It's likely that the fatalities were found here." Martin gritted his teeth and turned the radio off.

He continued the journey in silence.

Joanne. Five years older, though sometimes it felt like fifty. Always serious, always critical of any display of humour, especially the absurd kind. She took life seriously and didn't like to laugh. Sometimes Martin thought she was an alien, sent to them from a planet where laughter was forbidden. They rarely played together because, to Joanne, Martin was just silly and ruined everything. Like that time she organized a professional game of hospital. She was both nurse and doctor, while he was supposed to be the patient, injured in an accident, lying with a pained expression on the bed, wrapped in bandages coloured red with markers.

"But I don't want to just lie here without moving. Can I at least have a piece of chocolate?" - Martin asked, squirming on the bed, while Joanne was preparing for surgery.

"Stop it! You're ruining everything again! Have you ever seen a dying patient getting chocolate?"- she snapped at her brother.

"But I don't feel like I'm dying at all" - Martin protested, even trying to chuckle but immediately fell silent under his sister's stern gaze.

"Calm down and lie still. I'll have to examine your severe injuries closely, and who knows, maybe even amputate your leg."

Martin jumped up excitedly.

"What's 'amputate'? Will you draw something on it? Maybe a dragon? Or a knight? Or both, and I'll color it in later."

Joanne just snorted.

"No, silly. Amputate means to cut off."

"Yowwww!" Martin suddenly screamed and leaped off the hospital bed. "Cut off your own legs! I'm going to Mom's for pancakes. And I'll tell her you're crazy."

Of course, Joanne was furiously mad at him afterward and didn't want to play with him for several days, even though he promised that she could cut off both his ears, so he could pretend he couldn't hear, especially when Mom asked him to clean his room.

Over time, they played together less and less. Eventually, Martin came to the conclusion that he didn't really have a sister, just a teenage "something" that lived with them, had no sense of humour, locked itself in its room, wore black clothes, and was never invited to any birthday parties. A weirdo.

He parked in front of his mother's house and took a deep breath.

Was Joanne really always so serious? So sullen? Memories started playing in his mind like colourful slides they used to watch together. Some were chaotic, others frayed, and some simply unfinished. But there was laughter in them too, and a kind of tenderness he had long forgotten. And then, once again, he saw the closed door to her room and his sister's cold gaze.

"Jo, what on earth have you done?" - he muttered and entered the stairwell.

As usual, it smelled of wet leaves. Martin actually liked that smell. It reminded him of childhood.

At first, he couldn't believe it. It was a kind of denial that served its purpose. Martin convinced himself that Joanne had gone much farther than Denmark, and since she rarely contacted them anyway, not much had really changed. Besides, he hadn't even attended the funeral.

"What do you mean? We weren't invited?"

After what he heard from Joanne's lawyer, Martin instinctively glanced at his phone's display, as if to confirm whether he was speaking with a living person or had fallen victim to a malicious bot.

"I didn't know a funeral required an invitation. I suppose only the King of Denmark was given that honour?" - he retorted sarcastically, though the lawyer was merely conveying the information politely.

His mother listened to the conversation and looked at Martin questioningly. When he finished, he spread his hands helplessly.

"Apparently, they had long decided that if either of them died, they didn't want to turn the funeral into a spectacle."

"We're not allowed to go?"

"There's no point. The funeral has already taken place."

His mother took a deep breath and sat down on a chair.

"How is that possible? When?"

"The day before yesterday. Typical Jo. She always got her way. Never liked people, so she probably figured they would only annoy her at her own funeral."

"But we're family."

Martin bit his lip.

"Apparently, that doesn't grant us any privileges. Mom, calm down. We'll go there someday, visit the cemetery, and tell her exactly what we think of all this, okay?" He winked at his mother, trying to lighten the mood.

But still, he felt a pang of sadness.

A few months later, out of nowhere, a feeling of anger arose within him. Rage, even fury, that Joanne had just cut herself off from him like that. And that she never replied to the cards he sometimes sent for her birthday and Christmas. Maybe because they weren't serious enough? Because they didn't fit her vision of traditional greetings, which she found acceptable?

Once, for her birthday, he wrote that she was as old as Niagara but just as breathtaking. And for Christmas, he came up with a rhyme that he thought was particularly funny:

"Health, happiness, and good cheer! Don't choke on the carp's bones, dear."

It's possible, however, that Joanne considered it a classic display of idiotic humour and decided not to respond to such absurdities. So, eventually, he stopped trying too. She only wrote letters to their mother three times a year - the last one always arriving in December, in which she would rave about Danish Christmas. Martin tried not to yawn as their mother read the letter aloud, but when she almost dozed off on the second page, he took the letter from her hands and began to recite in a deep, serious voice:

"Salmon and herring prepared in various ways, shrimp, lobsters, crabs, sole fillets in sauce, fried sausages called *medisterpølse*, and frikadeller meatballs with red cabbage and beets. Good Lord, how many times can we read about this? Besides, who in their right mind eats meatballs on Christmas Eve, followed by pork tenderloin with mild onions, black pudding with syrup, liver pâté with bacon and mushrooms... Where are the dumplings, borscht, and poppy seed cake? Where's the humble cabbage with mushrooms?"

Their mother chuckled, wiping away a tear, while Martin pretended to be so stuffed that he could barely breathe, his belly swelling more and more.

"And to finish it all off, rice with cherry sauce. Hallelujah! Oh no, wait, wrong holiday.

So, let's sing 'Lullay, Baby Jesus,' stuffed like a Turkish pasha."

"Martin, stop it, or I'll have to scold you" - his mother laughed, wagging her finger at him. "And as punishment, you'll get meatballs on Christmas Eve."

Yet, one day, it pained him to think that Joanne would never send another letter like that, never again describe all those dishes, never bore them with Danish customs, and never call on Christmas Eve to wish them well. They would never hear anything from her again. He once managed to talk to her, though Joanne, as usual, wasn't very forthcoming.

"Are you as fat as a whale after all that food you've stuffed yourself with?"

"No, just normal."

Of course. It couldn't have been any other way. When was that? Two, three years ago?

Martin pressed his lips together.

"Don't you think it's cruel to just disappear like that? I understand that we had our childhood and teenage problems, that we didn't always get along, but this time you've really gone too far" - he said loudly, staring at their shared photo hanging in their mother's bedroom.

He was five then, she was ten. And they didn't look alike at all. Martin was grinning, showing gaps in his teeth and a face smeared with chocolate, while Joanne looked straight at the camera, serious and a bit angry, as if posing next to such a fool was exhausting. But there was something that connected them. The freckles, the nose, the mouth. The same eye colour, the shape of their faces. He was wrong. They were very much alike. That photograph reflected their characters and temperaments as well. That's probably why their mother had it framed and hung it on the right side of the bed. There were other photos there too, mostly of Martin, who apparently liked posing for pictures. And he often smiled.

"You really pissed me off, sis. I never even got to meet Ebbe, although he looked like a decent guy in the photos. Not to mention my niece... Everything has to be your way, as usual. And I can't even protest because you can't hear me. You have always been selfish, but this time you've gone a bit too far. I never thought it would end like this. Sure, things weren't great between us, but what you did really threw me off balance. No, not just a little. I'm seriously pissed off. You never gave a damn about everyone" - he added, though deep down, he knew it wasn't entirely true.

When their mother peeked into the bedroom, Martin quickly turned his head so she wouldn't notice his wet eyes. He couldn't even remember the last time he cried. Probably during Star Wars, when Leia died.

He sniffled.

"I found some of Joanne's mementos in the attic. Do you want to go through them?"

He nodded, though it surprised him that his sister had left anything behind. When she moved to Copenhagen, she meticulously cleaned out her room as if she didn't want to leave any traces of herself. He would even joke that she should disinfect everything with cleaning fluid. Whatever she didn't take, she threw away or gave to others. But there wasn't much, because Joanne was, in a sense, a minimalist. Mainly in expressing emotions, but also in the way she disliked surrounding herself with things. The Scandinavian lifestyle must have suited her well, with its philosophy of *hygge*, *new nordic*, and God knows what else.

"She forgot about a cardboard box in the wardrobe. It stayed in its place. Maybe she didn't notice it because there was a blanket on top of it" - the mother said. "I found it once and thought I'd keep it as a memento. I even thought about giving it to her someday, but there was never an opportunity. So it's been lying there for years, and maybe... maybe now's the time to take a look."

When Joanne had her daughter, their mother was convinced they would finally meet. She hadn't been invited to the wedding, nor had Martin. Joanne had only informed them that it was a small ceremony and they didn't want to make a fuss. Apparently, there hadn't even been the traditional cutting of the groom's socks or the bride's veil.

"Cutting socks?" - Martin had been baffled at the time.

"I don't know, that's what she wrote in the letter."

"Fascinating customs, maybe it's better we didn't have to take part in that."

When Else was seven months old, Joanne came to Warsaw for a symposium on the future of hospitality in Europe. That was the one and only time she decided to let her mother see her granddaughter. She came literally for a few hours, even though her mother had prepared a room for her, hoping they would stay longer.

"You're not staying the night?"

She was surprised when Joanne placed a small bag in the hallway, glanced at her watch, and announced that she didn't have much time.

"I have a hotel," she simply said, as if it were the most obvious thing in the world. "Besides, I'm leaving for Warsaw tomorrow morning. I already have a train ticket."

"But here's your home. And your own room."

Joanne smiled politely, remarked that the strawberry cake smelled exceptionally tempting, and that little Else looked very much like her

Danish grandmother. She spent almost the entire time sitting on the edge of her chair, as if afraid to settle in, as if sinking into the armchair or sofa would mean she intended to stay longer. Else slept the whole time, and their mother didn't know whether she was allowed to pick her up and hold her, even for a moment.

Joanne looked different somehow, even more distant than usual. Dressed in an elegant black dress, a grey blazer, shoes with a small heel, and her hair styled in a sleek bun. She wore tiny heart-shaped earrings and a pale peach-coloured lip gloss. She looked pretty, youthful, but a bit like a stranger who had accidentally walked into someone else's home. The conversation mostly revolved around how lovely life in Denmark was.

"Next year, we're planning to move out of the city and live in Helsingør. It's about fifty kilometres north of Copenhagen, on the northern coast of Zealand. Charming landscapes. There's going to be a new hotel there, and I'm going to be the manager" - Joanne emphasized the last word, as if to underline that she had made it, that she was someone important in her field.

But their mother only wanted to hold Else, to cuddle and kiss her, so the word "manager" didn't impress her much.

"Well, then" - Joanne said, getting up from the chair and looking around for her blazer.

"You're leaving already?" - their mother was surprised.

"I've stayed too long as it is" - Joanne replied, and she simply left with a sleeping Else in the stroller, claiming she would manage just fine, with a taxi already waiting downstairs.

"Maybe the little one should stay with me? You've got a conference, who's going to take care of her then?"

It was a strong argument, but Joanne was well-prepared.

"I've hired a nanny."

"But why? And a stranger on top of it."

"She's a qualified professional recommended by the hotel, just for such occasions."

"Martin will be back in a few days, maybe we can all meet?" Their mother tried everything.

"No" - Joanne replied quickly, and then after a second added. "I'm going back to Copenhagen the day after tomorrow."

When Martin heard about this visit, he felt that his sister had done it on purpose. She had brought Else for just a few moments to show her off and then simply left, even though she must have known it would hurt their mother.

In a way, it hurt him too.

***

The box was old, a shoe box originally. It smelled faintly of dust and a bit of laundry detergent, which their mother also kept in the attic. Martin sat down on the floor and placed the box on his lap. There was something magical about it - he was about to peek into the memories of his older sister, whom he would never see again.

He carefully lifted the lid and immediately smiled with nostalgia. A laser keychain? He remembered that gadget perfectly, a true marvel of 1990s technology. Joanne had a blue one, and he had a green one. They could play with them for hours, though Joanne always reminded him not to shine it directly into her eyes or blind the neighbourhood cats with the laser.

A floppy disk? He had almost forgotten what they looked like. Each one held about 1.44 MB, and sometimes it took a dozen of them to save a game. They played *SimCity* and *Mortal Kombat* endlessly back then. He probably went through five joysticks battling it out in the latter. Or *Worms*! It was a killing game, but so picturesque! A wonderful family of worms with an entire arsenal of fascinating weapons. The bombs were the wildest. He wondered what was on this floppy disk? Maybe *Pac-Man*, Joanne's favourite game?

"Oh, Christ, a Furby!" - Martin exclaimed, carefully pulling out the red, furry creature they constantly argued over. Furby was every child's dream, but unfortunately, they had only one to share. They had agreed that Joanne would play with it on even days, and Martin on the rest. He couldn't remember the last time he had it in his hands, but it was clear that his sister must have hidden it from him. Furby even had its own little bed in his room, something Martin would never have admitted, not even to Joanne. He had built it out of soap boxes, glued together and wrapped in silver foil, even making a sort of pillow. It would have been terribly embarrassing if anyone found out.

The box also contained figurines from surprise eggs, a few Pokémon Tazos, colourful beads for bicycle spokes, used phone cards, some postcards, receipts, stickers, and a notebook.

A blue notebook.

Martin took a deep breath. It felt like reading Joanne's diary would be a violation of some sacred boundary. She didn't write it for anyone else, after all; these were her private thoughts, poured onto paper. He probably shouldn't be reading them, even if Joanne would never find out.

The blue notebook was slightly faded. And very plain. There were no stickers, no doodles, nothing to give it any personalized touch. But that was exactly how Joanne was. She didn't like flowers, hearts, pink, or any of that girly, infantile stuff. A notebook was meant to be a notebook, not an artist's canvas.

Martin touched the cover, stroked the rough blue paper, and then opened the notebook at random.

If you have a more talented sibling, you might feel the understandable pressure to live up to them. To be interested in the same things, choose equally ambitious studies, help your parents. But is that really necessary? Remember, you are unique and don't have to be a copy of anyone else, even if that person is your sister or younger brother. Do they excel at something? You're better in other areas - for example, you're fluent in English, you have language skills. You read books quickly. You learn fast...

He swallowed hard.

A more talented sibling? This couldn't be about him, could it? Joanne had never taken him seriously. He was just the younger brother who annoyed her and had a silly sense of humour. It was really only their parents who were proud of how well he did in school, how he excelled in math and physics, won competitions, and received praise for the first computer programs he could create in elementary school. He had never heard from his sister that he was good at something, that it was nice to have a brother like him. A few months before the year 2000, the media had been talking about the apocalypse, predicting the shutdown of IT systems, power plants, and data loss. Twelve-year-old Martin knew perfectly well that nothing bad would happen and reassured his uncle, who was nervously backing up all the files he had stored on his computer.

"Uncle, relax, they'll figure it out. They'll add the right options to interpret the two-digit year, and it'll be fine" - Martin had said back then.

And, as it turned out later, he was right. Most applications and operating systems were indeed updated by New Year's Eve of 1999, and his uncle boasted to everyone that his nephew had known what to do all along. It was a pity their father hadn't lived to see it.

We are all born with different talents, needs, our own temperament. Use what you have and what you can do as best as you can. Don't let anyone make you believe that you're worse, that you're not doing well in life. Don't let yourself be constantly compared to someone else. You're very cool, and you should remember that. Very, very cool...

This couldn't have had anything to do with him. These notes were strange; on the one hand, they sounded like something Joanne would write, but on the other, he couldn't make sense of them at all. Nor could he fit them into his understanding of their relationship. Did Joanne feel inferior to him? Had someone said something to her, causing their relationship to become so strangely indifferent? Martin began to read aloud:

Psychologists say that so-called second children are often very independent, able to occupy themselves, not demanding too much attention, and are less selfish. They often try to live up to their older siblings but in a completely different field. This subconscious and involuntary competition allows them to develop new hobbies that might turn into lifelong passions.

He paused to think. Had he ever tried to compete with Joanne? When he was little, he had always admired her because she seemed so much smarter than him and intriguingly serious somehow. But over time, it started to bore him, especially since she never laughed at his ideas. She didn't share their parents' enthusiasm either; they loved his childish experiments and the first constructions he came up with on his own. Like the time he asked for a cardboard roll from a kitchen towel, aluminium foil, paper, and colourful beads.

"I won't give them to you because they're mine" - Joanne had said.

But then their dad came along, and he must have talked some sense into her, because she came to Martin's room without a word and handed him a box of beads and two sheets of paper - one blue and one black.

"I'll make something cool out of this and give it to you" - he promised her, but she just shrugged and left, muttering something under her breath.

Martin glued the silver foil to the black sheet, folded it, and wrapped it with tape, then hid it inside the paper roll. He attached a black circle with a cut-out centre to one end and a pre-prepared, cut-off piece of the roll with Joanne's beads to the other. Then he glued the two parts together and wrapped the whole thing in blue paper. He drew flowers, birds, and even two hearts on it, then happily took the object to his sister's room.

"I made you a kaleidoscope" - he announced, puffing out his chest with pride.

Joanne gave him a cool look, took the toy, but didn't even glance at it, just set it on the shelf.

"You're not even going to check if it works?" - Martin pouted.

"You could at least show some interest in what your brother made for you, right? Show some enthusiasm?" - his father had said, while their mother just shook her head.

Joanne had then stood up, put the kaleidoscope to her eye, and let out a series of exaggerated praises that Martin loved, but their parents didn't seem to appreciate much.

"Oh, wow, what a brilliant thing, you're an absolutely perfect child, I don't know what to say, oh, oh!"

That's pretty much how it sounded.

Being a younger sibling doesn't have to be a curse, though you've probably heard from your parents that since you're older, you should give in to your younger brother. Help him, give up your things. Good thing they don't want a kidney or a lung. You feel like you've been pushed to the sidelines, that your desires no longer matter to your parents. You feel resentment and the pressure of responsibility. You have to grow up on command and be almost like a second mom to your younger sibling. And yet you still want to be a child who can be spoiled! You want to be, at least sometimes, the pampered daughter. But remember that your parents haven't stopped loving you; they just love you a little differently now. They see you as an equal partner who should understand what it's like to raise young children. They expect your help...

Find the good in being an older sister...

What a load of crap.

They don't love you differently; they love you less. Love can definitely be divided into two unequal parts. It's a shame they don't write that in any of the guides. Everywhere it's just the same nonsense about how a new chapter in life doesn't mean a worse one.

They obviously weren't in my house...

Martin closed the blue notebook and took a deep breath.

But Joanne never complained! She never grumbled about having it worse, about having to take care of him, about feeling somehow exploited. Did he really poison her life? Did their parents favour him, and he just never noticed? Did they love him more? The very thought that one could receive less love than expected made him feel cold inside.

Joanne was gifted in languages, yet she didn't get into college. And she didn't even want to try her luck in other fields. She was indifferent to it. Yes, their mother was disappointed and said that their father would have been sad too if he had been alive. But their father had been gone for over fifteen years by then.

"Do you have any other plans? Any alternatives?" - their mother had asked, but Joanne just shrugged.

She eventually chose a post-secondary hotel management course, and after completing it, she went to Copenhagen for an internship.

And she stayed there.

Only children definitely have it the best. Their position isn't threatened, no brother or sister wants to dethrone them, and they aren't compared to anyone.

Joanne decided to have only one child.

When the anger subsided, Martin fell into a strange stupor. He couldn't focus on anything, and if it weren't for his business partner, he would have likely missed several deadlines. He was trapped in a lethargy, unable to break free, caught in some internal lock. On the one hand, he wanted to allow all these emotions, which came in waves, to wash over him; on the other hand, he instinctively pushed them away. He denied them, repressed them, and fled from his feelings.

He even came up with an absurd hobby - *gyotaku*, the art of painting a fish and then pressing its image onto paper. He remembered how much he enjoyed carving patterns into potatoes in elementary school, which were then painted and stamped onto paper like prints. When he found a *gyotaku* class, he signed up immediately, and from that point on, twice a week, he would paint fish with ink and press them onto rice paper. It was so absurd that he sometimes couldn't believe what he was doing, but he kept at it. Anything to stop thinking, stop reflecting, stop dissecting. So he painted and printed those fish, and sometimes crabs and octopuses, until he eventually concluded that he must have gone mad.

A moment came when he decided to confront his thoughts and feelings head-on. He herded them all into one place, sat across from them, and stared at them as if watching wild geese fly by or a line of cars on the highway. He observed his emotions - sadness, grief, anger, rage - and breathed them in, holding them inside until he began to accept their presence. After some time, he returned to the world of the living, though he still wasn't ready to fully say goodbye to Joanne. Sometimes, it felt like he had no skin, and even the smallest memory of her burned him to the core. He didn't understand these feelings. They hadn't been the perfect siblings, after all. He often thought that Joanne lived only halfway, while he was literally raving about everything.

"There's a shadow on the street. But I don't know whose" - he would say to her, for example, and wink.

"Stop it."

"Really. We need to check whether it passed through a transparent body or not. And did you know that a penumbra isn't actually fifty percent shadow?"

"Go away. You have your own room, so I don't understand why you keep coming into mine and acting all smug. I'm not interested in your shadow, penumbra, or any transparent bodies."

"So what are you interested in?"

"Silence. And there's no room for you in it. Only me."

"The absent, omnipresent silence of the universe" - he said in a serious tone.

"My own silence is enough for me. And only that."

"The stillness of matter's particles. But in nature, everything moves."

"Get out, you idiot."

Once, they went to a sports camp together. Martin was nine then, and Joanne fourteen. Two weeks in the woods, by a lake - canoeing, running, swimming, climbing in the rope park, and orienteering. One day, he ran to the tent where Joanne was staying with five other girls, but he quickly forgot why he had come.

"I have an older sister, but she's in college already" - one of the girls was saying.

"I have twin baby brothers. They're only a few months old, and it's impossible to tell them apart. I don't know how Mom does it" - said another.

"And I'm an only child" - Joanne said.

Martin froze just outside the tent entrance.

Only child? What about him? He wanted to correct her immediately and say she must be mistaken, but for some reason, he turned around and hid in his own tent instead. He didn't even feel like eating dinner.

The next day, he approached her while they were preparing for a kayaking trip and whispered:

"Why did you tell your friends you don't have any siblings?"

Joanne gave him a cold look.

"Were you eavesdropping?"

He shrugged.

"I heard it by accident. I came to see you yesterday because... because…" - he stammered a bit, and Joanne pursed her lips and started packing her backpack.

"Can't I at least be an only child during the holidays?"

"But why?" - Martin didn't understand.

"Because. And stop following me around."

At that camp, she was completely different from the way she was at home. She laughed, goofed around, volunteered for every possible activity, organized treasure hunts, and even helped in the kitchen, cooking a delicious pea soup twice - the best Martin had ever tasted. It was all so strange because as soon as they returned home, Joanne's energy vanished, and she became silent and withdrawn. Was it because she had a brother again?

"And now I really don't have a sister anymore" - he said aloud, feeling the deep pain of that realization.

In the afternoon, he went to his favourite sandwich bar. The bar was run by a small, slightly subdued woman, around fifty years old. She made the best sandwiches under the sun. When he discovered this place, he decided he would never make sandwiches himself again.

"You know, these sandwiches taste absolutely exceptional. It's a bit like those specialties we bring back from abroad. In France or Italy, all those cheeses and hams taste so divine that you almost become a connoisseur yourself, but when you're back home, it's just cheese and ham" - he said to her once.

The woman smiled at him, pleased with his compliment. Lately, however, she seemed sadder than usual. Maybe because he still hadn't managed to pull himself together. And sad people tend to attract others like them. Happiness attracts happiness, and melancholy is quick to notice another kindred, pained soul.

He didn't know if it was appropriate to ask her about it, so he just smiled awkwardly and ordered a sandwich with goat cheese and beets. He sat down at the blue table and placed the plate with the sandwich on it. He really liked this place. A small, cozy bar with seven tables, each in a different colour. He usually chose the blue one, though he also liked the purple one, the colour of ripe grapes. At the red table, two young girls were sitting, showing each other something on their phones and giggling contagiously. In any other situation, he might have smiled too, but now he didn't have the energy. The bar owner also seemed immune to the joy of others today. The yellow table was free, and at the green one, a woman in brown shoes and a dark dress kept glancing nervously at her watch.

"A date?" - Martin wondered, but the mystery was quickly solved when a young man walked into the bar and, after a few seconds, approached the green table. The woman stood up and began nervously smoothing her dress. She didn't know whether to shake the man's hand or kiss him on the cheek, so she just stood there, and he looked at her with a mix of curiosity, reproach, and maybe even a bit of anger before nodding and sitting down. Martin noticed that they hardly spoke to each other. Strange.

"Doesn't it taste good today?" - The bar owner approached him and gestured toward the untouched sandwich.

"I don't know, I haven't tried it yet" - he admitted honestly. "I'll take it home and eat it later" - he added, looking apologetic.

"Sure, I understand" - she replied, as if she knew exactly what state he was in. – "I'll pack it up."

As he was leaving the bar, the two young girls were no longer laughing but sharing music through earphones, while the older woman and the young man were still disturbingly silent.

Martin suddenly turned to the bar owner.

"What's your name?"

"Anna."

"Goodbye, Mrs. Anna. I'm sure I'll enjoy the sandwich" - he said, waving the sandwich wrapped in a blue bag before heading over to his mother's place.

He really didn't feel like going, but she had a package for him.

"A letter came for you" - she said before he could step inside, handing him a white envelope. "I think it's important" - she added, pointing to the address of a law firm.

***

"The guardian of a minor should primarily be the person designated by the father or mother, provided that this person has not been deprived of parental authority. Generally, parents, when appointing a guardian, have their child's best interests in mind. The designation can be made in a will, orally, or in writing."

"I don't quite understand" - Martin said, looking questioningly at the lawyer who had just read that sentence to him.

The meeting was taking place in a dark green office with large wooden windows that overlooked a park. In front of Martin stood an oak desk, and he sat in a soft, very comfortable chair upholstered in green velvet. The room was somewhat gloomy but also calming. There were no loud paintings or distracting gadgets to divert attention from what was important. Although the white horse head, presumably magnetized as it had paper clips attached to it, did catch his eye. Martin wanted to touch it, but that would probably look foolish.

"Your sister specified in her will that in the event of the death of both parents, the child should be cared for by her husband's mother, the child's grandmother. However, if, for any reason, she is unable to do so, custody of the child is to be granted to the deceased's brother - that is, to you" - the lawyer stated. "The family court in Copenhagen granted your sister's request and, after concluding the proceedings, placed the child in the care of her grandmother. Unfortunately, due to health reasons, the grandmother is no longer able to care for the child, so the process will be reinitiated, and if there are no objections, the child will be placed with you."

"But how can she be placed with me? I don't even know this child!" - Martin exclaimed in astonishment.

The lawyer looked at him with a serious expression. He was generally a rather grim and emotionless man, despite the fact that they weren't discussing apple varieties or the weather, but rather a little girl who was suddenly supposed to be placed in the care of an uncle she had never met.

"A guardian acquires the rights and duties associated with guardianship after taking an oath before the court. In this oath, the guardian assures that they will carry out their responsibilities with the utmost diligence" - the lawyer recited now, as if delivering a poem at a school assembly, fully aware that no one really understood him.

"I'm not even sure how old she is" - Martin said nervously, wiping his sweaty forehead with his right hand.

"Five."

"Five" - he repeated in disbelief. "A five-year-old girl who has never been to Poland. Oh, no, wait - she was once, but she was only a few months old and probably doesn't remember anything" - he added somewhat ironically. "And now she has to suddenly live in a foreign country with an uncle she's never seen before. I think we both have slim chances of success. Are you really saying my sister appointed me as the guardian of, uh…"

"Else" - the lawyer prompted.

"Yes, Else, I know. Did she really do that?"

"You have the right to decline, and the guardianship court can release you from the responsibility, provided there are valid reasons, such as unclear financial circumstances or poor health. However, please remember that if the parents designated a specific person, that choice should be given priority unless there are significant objections, such as being deprived of public rights or parental authority, or simply when there is a high probability that the person will not fulfil the duties of a guardian adequately."

Martin swallowed loudly. He didn't want to let Joanne down, but on the other hand, the entire situation seemed like some colossal absurdity. Was he supposed to become a father just like that, without ever even thinking about having a child before? He also didn't know how to break the news to Catherine, especially now when she had just lost her mother and was deep in mourning. How was he supposed to handle this, to reconcile it with his current life and everything he was used to?

"When would Else potentially start living with me?"

"Right after New Year's. She'll spend Christmas and New Year's Eve with her grandmother, who then has to undergo surgery to have an artificial hip implanted."

Well, yes. The elderly lady clearly couldn't take care of a five-year-old, even if she had the best intentions. And even if Joanne had chosen her as the primary guardian of Else.

He only knew the girl from the photos. Every now and then, his mother would receive a picture of her granddaughter from Joanne, which she would place in a box with a Danish flag sticker.

"Mom, don't you want to visit them? After all, Copenhagen isn't the end of the world" - Martin wondered.

Maybe she wanted to, but Joanne had never mentioned it.

Right.

She didn't even reply to his greeting cards. And then she decided that neither her brother nor her mother should attend the funeral. And now someone like that wanted him to take care of her child?

When he left the law firm, it was four in the afternoon. The October air smelled of autumn and everything associated with it. A bit of rain and mist, a bit of leaves, smoke, and simmering preserves, though that last scent came from a nearby bakery.

"Fresh plum buns available around the clock."

Nice. A constant aroma of simmering plums.

Martin took a deep breath, then got into his car and drove to the cemetery, to his father's grave. He preferred to visit in October, before the big November rush when the crowds ruined the intimacy of the place. The cemetery in October was only a few breaths away from All Saints' Day, yet wonderfully empty, peaceful, and still without all those plastic candles that stripped it of its mystery.

A ginkgo tree with yellow leaves grew by his father's grave. Some of the leaves had already fallen onto the stone slab. Martin never cleaned them up because they reminded him of a monochrome mosaic, though his mother was always annoyed afterward.

"Those leaves rot and leave stains on the granite" - she lectured him every time.

He crouched by his father's grave and touched the cold stone.

"Maybe it's for the best that you two aren't buried together" - he whispered. "Family tombs remind me of collecting stamps in one album. I know it's a silly comparison, but people don't necessarily have to lie next to each other after death, right? It's better if everyone has their own place because it doesn't change anything anyway. Some physicist once said that the soul is a collection of information stored at the quantum level and that when someone dies, the soul leaves the body, meaning it can move freely. So either your soul will fly to Denmark, or Joanne's soul will visit you. Maybe she'll be more sociable after death. I'd give anything to talk to her. You know she decided to make me a father? I'm supposed to take care of Else. Me, a guy who's never had a family of his own. What could I possibly teach her? How to press fish onto rice paper?"

Martin took a simple white candle from his jacket pocket, placed it by his father's grave to shield it from the wind, and lit the wick. He wanted to meet with Catherine today to talk about Else, but he still didn't know what to think of it all. He didn't want to scare her. They had only known each other for a few months, were still testing each other, cautiously touching their most sensitive strings as if to make sure they fit perfectly. Deep down, they both felt they were meant to be together. And that silly saying about two halves of an orange sometimes turned out to be true. But there was one problem. Catherine had a husband, and they had been married for quite a few years.

Once, when Martin was still a child, he couldn't finish a puzzle for over a week. It frustrated him, but he didn't want to give up. Eventually, Joanne came along and immediately found the wrongly placed piece.

"It almost fits, but you forced it in. Besides, these two brown pieces aren't identical. Look for yourself, they have different shades. You're supposed to be a genius, and you missed something like that."

She was right.

Years later, he thought it was just like Catherine and her husband. They almost fit perfectly, but he, Martin, was the right piece of

the puzzle, in the proper shade of brown. And
Catherine knew it too.

But should he tell her about Else now? He
couldn't take in the little girl; that would be
madness. Men have nine months to prepare for
fatherhood, and the lawyer had given him less
than three. It wasn't going to work.

***

Martin's apartment wasn't very big, but
he lived there alone. Two rooms: a bedroom and
an office, and something like a dining room
connected to the kitchen. The dining room had
been created somewhat artificially - Martin had
carved out two square meters from the bedroom
and one from the hallway, thus gaining a bit more
space.

There was no guest room because he
always found the term amusing. Besides, he
thought such a room didn't suit his lifestyle
because Martin didn't invite guests. He usually
met his friends in clubs or bars, and it never
occurred to him to host a gathering at home with
pretzels and chips. He didn't have a TV either;

when he wanted to watch something, he'd turn on his laptop.

And he liked spending time with Catherine in the kitchen. And, of course, in the bedroom. Although, when she first came over, the lack of a living room with a couch and TV really surprised her.

"You know, your apartment looks a bit like a person without an arm" - she laughed.

He stood in the middle of the dining room now and looked around. Could this apartment be adapted to the needs of a five-year-old child? Slim chances. He'd have to give her either the bedroom or the office. The office would be easier, as it would only require moving the books and binders to the bedroom, but that still wouldn't solve the problem. The room was simply too small. It wouldn't fit a bed, wardrobe, dollhouse, three hundred stuffed animals, dolls, strollers, and unicorns - everything a little girl absolutely needs. At least, that's what he thought.

He'd also have to paint it pink and buy heart-patterned bedding, read her bedtime stories, maybe even make up his own. He'd need to learn to cook healthy meals, braid hair, and somehow endure tea parties with dolls. It all seemed so unreal and disconnected from the reality he lived in that he just shook his head and decided he was definitely against it.

At least he was honest with himself.

Oh, right, the bathroom too.

There wasn't a bathtub, only a shower. Kids definitely prefer bathtubs. Foamy bubbles and suds. And a separate toilet would be helpful, so he wouldn't have to pee in front of the child. Every circumstance was against the idea.

Martin washed his hands and looked in the mirror. A young man with freckles, hair sticking up in various directions, and a slightly prominent lower jaw stared back at him. He had blue eyes and a mole near his left ear. His face suited a boy more than a man, someone who was running through life and wasn't planning on slowing down.

"Jesus, I'm floundering like a damn hamster in a cage" - he said to himself, then threw on his jacket and rushed down to his car.

He turned on the radio, set the navigation, bit into the sandwich he bought yesterday from Mrs. Anna, and started the engine.

"I don't know why I'm doing this" - he added, but since he had been gathering scattered memories of Joanne everywhere, he felt he had to go to the Drawsko-Wałeckie Lake District too.

Sometimes people make spontaneous and unconsidered decisions. And that's good. Planning everything is as boring as tomato soup.

"The most important elements in red wine are so-called bioflavonoids. They bring relief from allergies by stabilizing the action of cells that react to allergens. Bioflavonoids are also found in grapes, apples, and onions" - said a voice on the radio, and Martin couldn't disagree. He had always thought that wine should be drunk, even if you don't have an allergy. He would have gladly had some now, but he was driving.

The journey took him less than two hours. When he was a child and travelled here with Joanne for camp, it felt like it lasted an eternity. The centre was closed, but Martin simply climbed over the fence, made his way to the building that seemed to be the common room, and stood in front of a glass display case filled with brochures.

"When your child is bursting with energy - choose the multisport program. You'll find a bit of everything here: soccer, tennis, volleyball, basketball, dodgeball, floorball, badminton, skill games: ping-pong, foosball, boules, swimming, mini-olympics, fun competitions. And additionally, kayaking, swimming, water balloon fights, cannonball jumps, and water splash."

He was definitely the best at cannonball jumps. No one could hit the water with such force, causing it to spray everywhere and scare the fish.

Why did Joanne tell her friends she was an only child? That question returned to him with doubled intensity. If she didn't want a brother, why did it matter to her that he should take care of her daughter? Because they shared the same genes? That couldn't be the only reason. Martin looked around. A lot had changed; the tents had been replaced by small cabins, and the kitchen and dining room were now housed in a new, impressive pavilion opposite the common room.

He closed his eyes and tried to recall those two weeks.

They barely spoke to each other then. Joanne avoided him, and whenever he came running with a question, she immediately brushed him off. But he didn't care much because he had his friends and plenty of other attractions. Now, however, it all seemed strange. He kicked a pile of brown leaves, from which a dazed spider scurried out. The air smelled of smoke, just like it did when they sat around the campfire eating roasted potatoes. He even wanted to sit next to Joanne, but she shook her head and made a threatening face. But he still approached her for a while and said that as soon as they got home, he would tell their parents everything.

"I don't doubt it" - she said, fixing him with a cold stare. "I also don't doubt that you'll add something dramatic, so I get into more trouble. You little rat."

He shrugged and stuck out his tongue. After all, she started it. He didn't even remember if he ended up telling everything at home, but a few weeks later, it didn't matter because their father passed away soon after.

Due to stupid complications from the flu.

After that, they stopped noticing each other, although he sometimes tried to reach out to her. It was no use. His sister completely withdrew from both him and their mother. Everything seemed normal on the surface, but it was only an illusion. Joanne reminded him of a robot, carrying out all orders without any grimace, smile, or sign of anger or reluctance. She did what was expected of her, then shut herself in her room and sat in silence. She became illusory, lost her contours, and what filled her was nothing like the old Joanne. Martin couldn't understand this transformation, nor could he understand why their mother didn't notice and so rarely talked to Joanne.

It was getting late. The wind had begun its evening dance with the branches, the leaves swirling to the rhythm of an inaudible melody. Martin tried to locate the spot where Joanne's tent once stood, but the new cabins made it difficult to orient himself.

"I'm an only child" - he heard the words clearly again, so he clenched his jaw, climbed back over the fence, got into the car, and turned on the radio.

"Although there's still plenty of time until New Year's Eve, it's worth starting preparations now. Autumn is the perfect time for a comprehensive rejuvenation program. The earlier we begin, the better the results we'll achieve" - the announcer said.

"Alright" - Martin agreed. "Why not?"

"Planning to wear a dress that shows off your shoulders, back, and legs? Then you need to take care of your body. In autumn and winter, your skin is often dry and pale. The ideal solution to these problems is spray tanning."

"But I won't be wearing a dress. And definitely not one that reveals my shoulders, back, and legs" - Martin tapped his fingers on the steering wheel and turned off the radio.

***

November that year was quite unusual. As if it had forgotten it was the ugliest month of the year and was trying to show a better side. Warm, a bit windy, the trees still clung to their leaves, though most had already shed their yellow and red hues and were now dressed mainly in browns. They rustled enticingly and flirtatiously.

But Martin was immune to these flirtations. He had just come to the conclusion that sometimes isolation is nthe best solution. It helps to separate the thoughts that matter from those that create chaos. He couldn't stand it when someone had the upper hand over him, controlled him, tormented him, and wouldn't let go. And that's exactly what his mind had been doing for the past few months, releasing memories that Martin couldn't control.

"Filtration. It's impossible that I can't take control. After all, it's my own head" - he said to himself, and continued to practice the separation of thoughts with determination.

He decided not to tell anyone about Joanne's will. Neither his mother, nor Catherine.

He also decided that he wouldn't think about his sister or dwell on the past. And he resolved not to open the blue notebook again, to stop reading about siblings, rivalry, guilt, and regret. Negative thoughts disrupt harmony, and he wanted to find it again.

"Mom, I bought the horseradish you asked for, but I don't quite understand why you need so much."

"I'm making an elixir."

He nodded approvingly, though he had no idea why she needed a horseradish elixir.

"It's for strength, immunity, and generally for the autumn-winter blues" - his mother said.

And then she seemed about to mention Joanne, Martin noticed immediately, so he quickly interrupted her.

"Really, can you give me the recipe? Dictate it, I'll write it down."

"You need to peel the horseradish and grate it finely, then pour wine over it, let it sit in a dark place for three days, shaking it once a day. After that, strain the mixture through a linen cloth and sweeten it with honey. You should take it for three weeks, three times a day, about half an hour after meals."

This was how controlling your feelings worked. Martin focused on the horseradish and, in doing so, pushed thoughts of Joanne aside. And fortunately, his mother forgot what she had wanted to say earlier.

In some sense, his world returned to normal, though partly under the supervision of his strong willpower. Such an approach would sooner or later lead Martin into a dead end, but he didn't know that yet. His everyday life took on a superficial quality; all his actions were just lightly touched upon, as if he feared that any deeper reflection on what he was doing or saying would once again summon unwanted thoughts. And then he would have to descend lower, deeper, where the guilt began. When he saw children, he looked away, when Facebook showed him videos of fathers and children, he immediately turned them off, and when someone mentioned siblings in his presence, he stopped listening. With Catherine, he mostly talked about her, about what she liked, what she dreamed of, and why she so desperately wanted to visit Finland.

"To ride in a reindeer-drawn sleigh, just once in my life" - she replied, and for a moment, he weighed in his mind whether Finland was also part of Scandinavia. Like... Denmark.

"No" - Catherine said, smiling, and Martin realized he had asked the question out loud. "Scandinavian countries are only Sweden, Norway, and Denmark, but culturally and historically, Finland can also be considered part of them. And they are Nordic countries" - she added.

Martin quickly changed the subject.

Suppressing unwanted thoughts wasn't easy, but he was getting better at it. It involved constant self-control and anxiety about whether he was following his own guidelines. Over time, Martin became nervous because this self-discipline was exhausting. He became a prisoner of his own memories, which played cat and mouse with him. On one hand, he tried to push away thoughts of Joanne and her daughter; on the other, they kept coming back. And even if he reacted quickly and covered those unwanted memories with others, he still couldn't escape the original ones. Eventually, everything started to remind him of his sister.

Just like yesterday at the hairdresser's.

He was sitting in the chair, staring into the mirror, and saw himself at six years old. He had asked Joanne to cut his hair.

"Are you sure you want me to do it? I wouldn't want you to die of despair" - she replied sarcastically.

Then she took their father's clippers, draped a towel over Martin's shoulders, and got to work. She shaved him calmly, steadily, and precisely. Soft hair fell to the floor, and Martin watched in amazement as his new face appeared in the mirror. Suddenly, he felt older, almost grown-up, and that soon he would start dating girls.

He told Joanne.

"You're only six years old and more like a teddy bear than a man" - Joanne informed him immediately, then brushed the remaining hair onto the floor. "Do you like it?"

He nodded, but when their mother saw him, she threw up her hands in despair and complained that he looked like an unfeathered chick. He then pouted and pointed at Joanne.

"It was her. It was her idea" - he said in a tearful tone.

Now he felt a little foolish. He had indeed framed his older sister, and she wasn't to blame. She had just done what he had asked.

He grimaced.

"How are we cutting it?" - the hairdresser asked.

"With the clippers, on an eight" - he replied quickly.

"It'll be short, you know that?"

"I know".

In the afternoon, he stopped by the sandwich bar.

"Anything new?"

"Pear and blue cheese."

"Fresh pear?" - he asked, surprised.

"No, marinated in vinegar. My own recipe."

"How do you even find the time?" - he shook his head.

She shrugged.

"I've had a bit more time lately, so I fill it with what I like and do best."

He wanted to ask her about something else, but Anna looked at him as if she had cut the conversation short. Clearly, she wanted to avoid further questions that might lead to confessions. He understood her perfectly. People need time before they open up and pour out their sorrows. Before they let them go down the drain and finally start living normally.

So he ordered a sandwich and ate in silence, then clenched his teeth when he suddenly saw a girl on the street carrying ice skates. The memories returned again, even though he was doing everything to drive them away.

"Great" - he muttered under his breath. "Do whatever you want with me, I'm clearly too stupid to control you."

This time, they listened and immediately brought up the memory of Joanne spinning pirouettes while he tried to maintain his balance, taking his first steps on the ice.

"How do you do it so your legs don't slide out from under you?" - he whined, red with fear, effort, and excitement.

And she took his hand and they skated around the rink until he finally got the hang of skating and even dared to glide on his own afterward.

"I'm the king of the ice" - he declared after an hour, and Joanne tapped her forehead with her finger.

A tired and winter-weakened body needs support. For a while, set aside coffee, strong tea, and switch to herbal or fruit teas, like those with dried aronia or rosehips, which have calming effects and improve oxygenation of the heart muscle.

Martin turned off the radio and, out of sheer contrariness, brewed himself another espresso. He didn't care much about his heart muscle's oxygenation, nor did he seek any support from aronia fruits. In fact, lately, everything had become indifferent to him. Except for Catherine.

He fell into thought.

Love is often the meeting of two solitudes.

And it finds even those who have been in relationships for years. When he met Catherine, he realized just how lonely he was. He felt the absence of someone who was simply there, someone worth pulling out a second coffee mug for. He fell head over heels in love with her. It was something that had never happened to him before.

Even if he still had to wait a bit for her.

As the end of the year approached, Martin knew he would eventually have to make some decisions. He was already leaning toward refusal, yet something kept holding him back.

He pulled out his phone and dialled a number while standing in a large square filled with Christmas trees.

"Mom, do you need anything? I'm looking at some trees."

"Are you in the forest?" - his mother asked, surprised.

"No, I meant Christmas trees."

"But isn't it too early?"

"I don't know, maybe I'll buy one, and we can put it on the balcony? There's more choice now" - he babbled somewhat senselessly.

"Alright" - she agreed. "There should be an old brown suitcase in the basement. It has the Christmas decorations. You can decorate it right away."

"The baubles are in the boxes on the shelves; I know because I put them there myself."

"But I'm talking about those ornaments you and Jo made…"

Martin swallowed hard. His mother rarely hung those on the tree. She preferred her silver and gold pine cone-shaped baubles and silvery tinsel, along with the tiny warm white lights.

He didn't expect that anything had survived from the times when they made chains, wrapped candies in silver foil, and painted walnuts gold. Once, Martin even made a whole army of snowmen from ping-pong balls and several paper and matchstick hedgehogs. They weren't very pretty, but they took pride of place on the tree. Joanne had then covered a Styrofoam ball with a mass of tiny beads. It was very time-consuming, and Martin kept checking in on her to see how she was doing.

"Do you have to attach each bead individually?" - he asked, watching with awe.

She smiled.

"I've already made eight snowmen."

"Then go and make more. I'm creating something much bigger. But that takes talent and patience" - she explained.

Of course, he immediately complained to their parents that Joanne thought he had neither talent nor patience, but they quickly reassured him, explaining that it wasn't true, and soon after, the entire army of snowmen and hedgehogs took up residence in the tree's branches.

And what about Joanne's bauble?

Martin couldn't remember where it hung. Perhaps closer to the top, so everyone could see it right away? It was truly beautiful. Now it lay in the suitcase, wrapped in soft paper, but it still sparkled as it did over twenty years ago. The green, gold, silver, red, pink, blue, and orange beads shimmered, forming something like landscapes - a night with a moon on one side and a golden field with a large sun on the other. He didn't remember this at all. He touched the colourful bauble, and for the first time in a long while, he felt a pang of longing for his older sister. For her ironic remarks, her scepticism, even her anger when he barged into her room without knocking, sat on her bed, and demanded her attention.

"Go away" - she would say, but he just shook his head.

"Play with me."

"I don't want to."

"Did you know Tommy took my excavator?"

Joanne would sigh heavily.

"I don't care at all."

"He took it and said I stink."

"Maybe you do?"

Martin would then sniffle, and Joanne would escort him out of the room. But two days later, Tommy suddenly returned the excavator and even apologized. At the time, Martin thought his parents had handled it, but today he knew it was Joanne. Because she was the only one he had confided in.

It's a pity that only this bauble remained. After all, Joanne made beautiful chains and three-dimensional paper stars. She could even create an angel out of yarn, so it was all the more strange that none of those things survived. His snowmen and hedgehogs were still in the old suitcase, but most were damaged. He wondered if Else also made her own Christmas decorations and was curious if Joanne had shown her his picture, told her anything about her younger brother, and maybe even mentioned that he was quite nice?

His mother entered the room and glanced over Martin's shoulder.

"Should I make dried fruit compote for Christmas Eve?" - she asked. "Your snowmen are so cute, so funny. Look, some of them still have their eyes." - She smiled and picked up one of the snowmen.

Martin handed her Joanne's bauble.

"I don't remember where we got it. It's pretty. We can hang it this year" - his mother said and asked once more: "So, what about that compote?"

***

Martin left the house early in the morning. He wanted to call Catherine, but he held back. She was probably still sleeping.

Tomorrow is Christmas Eve. As always, he would spend it with his mother, though this time, it would be different. They would feel Joanne's absence more acutely than usual, even though the last time they had sat together at the Christmas Eve table was over a decade ago. They wouldn't read a letter from Joanne describing all those holiday dishes, pâtés, meats, and various sauces. Suddenly, it no longer seemed dull and stupid to him.

He would also have to think about Else. About how to talk to her. How to reach her. How to explain that, yes, they were family, but he had no idea how to raise a child. So he wouldn't take that risk. He still couldn't understand why Joanne had come up with such an idea. She had decided to entrust the care of her own child to a brother with whom she hadn't spoken for years and whom she often treated as a necessary evil? She had always been responsible, organized, and decisive. And he was her opposite. At least, that's how it always seemed to him.

Responsibility.

Was that the only reason he should take care of Else? Because he was an adult, so he automatically qualified as a guardian? Well, he would have to somehow explain in court that he wasn't capable of taking care of this child. He was alone (plus, he was having an affair with a married woman), had never planned on having children, led an irregular lifestyle, and often travelled. And the only connection between him and his sister was their shared blood. Maybe he could also mention that he liked painting fish and printing them on rice paper. They'd surely think he was a bit unbalanced, maybe even dangerous.

"Everything has gotten terribly complicated" - he said to himself. His gaze fell on the blue notebook lying on the table. He picked it up, then left the house, got into his car, and drove to a nearby lake.

He wanted to be away from people. Without people on the streets, without noise, without the sounds of the city.

He parked in a forest lot, pulled his hat down over his ears, shoved his hands into his trouser pockets, and walked toward the lake, to a small beach that, fortunately, was deserted at this time of year.

He noticed a bench. He had never seen it here before, or maybe he just hadn't paid attention to it. Black, metal, a bit scratched, with a strangely curved backrest. When he sat down on it, it seemed exceptionally comfortable and pleasantly warm. Almost as if it weren't made of metal. He stretched out his legs and stared at the still lake. It was quiet, still somewhat dark, although the sky was slowly shedding its nighttime navy blue shirt and discreetly donning a grey outfit, shaking off the first snowflakes.

One of them paused for a second on the edge of the bench.

Martin smiled.

Whether the crystals are flat, grow into stars, needles, or prisms depends on the temperature and humidity of the air and is related to the presence of weak hydrogen bonds - he remembered from his physics classes.

He closed his eyes.

When they were children, they used to came here often - he would jump off the pier straight into the water, while Joanne would cautiously submerge herself, slowly cooling her body. Just as she had been taught in her swimming lessons.

Their mother would pack sandwiches, meatballs, tomatoes, and apples in a basket, and their father would take his fishing rod, which was completely pointless because even if he managed to find some bushes to hide in with the rod, he had no chance of catching a single fish in all that noise. But perhaps that wasn't the point. He claimed that sunbathing tired him, while sitting with a fishing rod in the bushes calmed him down.

"But he never, ever caught a fish. At least I don't remember him ever doing so."

Martin shuddered, opened his eyes, and looked at the other end of the bench.

Joanne.

His sister, with her hair loose, reaching her shoulders, in a red sweater, grey woollen trousers, and single-fingered gloves, the kind they wore as children. Burgundy with white stars.

"We have an hour" - she said softly and looked at Martin.

They had blue eyes and similarly scattered freckles on their noses, which now, in winter, were almost invisible. They also had a similar shape of lips and a slightly protruding lower jaw. And a mole in the same spot, near the left ear. How could he ever have thought they had nothing in common?

Martin pulled out the blue notebook from under his jacket, and Joanne raised her eyebrows high.

"You found it" - she said simply.

"You know, you wrote about the Jacksons? How old were you then? Ten? Twelve?"

She shrugged.

"I don't know. I don't remember mentioning them."

"Then let me read it to you" - Martin said and opened the notebook. "The story of the Jackson family shows that a sister or brother can sometimes also be the greatest enemy. La Toya, even as a little girl, couldn't stand not being as famous as her brothers. She was jealous, frustrated, and often swore to herself that she would eventually outshine them. But there was no room for girls in Joseph Jackson's group."

Joanne laughed.

"Indeed, I had quite a knowledge of them."

"Jo, what really happened between us? I wasn't better than you at anything. I was just the younger brother who always got in your way. Did you feel inferior? Was it my fault?"

His sister looked him straight in the eyes.

"You'll probably deny it now, but our parents loved you more."

"No way…" - he shook his head but didn't finish because Joanne raised her hands.

"I knew you wouldn't agree. And I'll tell you, I also didn't accept that thought for a long time. But that's how it was. You were born premature, almost two months early. Mother nearly lost you, so when it turned out you'd survive, she took it as a sign from heaven, the most beautiful gift in the world. I was very happy back then, thinking I'd have a younger brother, someone who would be my real-life doll and, at the same time, someone who would be mine forever."

Martin closed his eyes.

"But it quickly stopped being all rosy, right?"

Joanne looked at him with a faint smile.

It didn't take her long to realize that Martin had taken everything from her, even if unintentionally. Their mother focused only on him, and their father constantly emphasized how gifted his child was. Child, not children. His brother's name was mentioned in all possible forms at family gatherings. And then they would add: "And there's also Jo". That's all. They had nothing more to say about her.

Martin bit his lower lip.

"Was I… was I mean?"

"You were" - Joanne confirmed. "When you realized you were winning the 'better child' competition, you started to exploit it. You tattled on me, complained, lied when I wouldn't do something for you."

Martin buried his face in his hands.

"I don't remember that" - he whispered.

"Do you remember the stress ball?"

The stress ball. A toy so simple, yet so genius. Just a regular balloon filled with flour, with a drawn face and yarn hair. You could stretch it and squeeze it in different ways. There was nothing extraordinary about this toy, yet every child wanted one. Joanne and Martin did too, but he was determined to find out what was inside, so he carefully snipped the stress ball with scissors. When flour started spilling out, he realized he might have just ruined it.

"Give me yours" - he said to Joanne, promising to clean her room as a reward.

"My room is always tidy" - she replied loftily and told him to tape up the hole.

"Will you help me?" - he asked, and when she started doing it, he ran to their parents, crying that Joanne had ruined his stress ball and was now trying to fix it so no one would find out. By the end of the day, he had his sister's toy and a new stress ball, while Joanne was punished by not being allowed to watch TV for a week.

"Yes, now I remember everything. I really did cut it with scissors and told our parents it was you." - Martin whispered.

"But as I recall, you got back at me by messing up my Tetris. I had that game on a handheld console, and I loved it more than anything."

"I didn't break it. I just took out the batteries, and you didn't even notice. But a few months later, you got a Transformer and didn't let me touch it for a moment."

Martin wrinkled his nose.

"Yeah, that happened."

He nervously rubbed his hands together and looked uncertainly at his sister.

"Joanne, I don't know Else" - he suddenly said.

"I know" - she agreed. "But I'm sure you'll manage. And that you'll take good care of her."

"Why didn't you come to Poland? Why did I never meet your daughter?"

Joanne took off her gloves and placed them on the bench. She had pretty, delicate hands.

"Do you really not know?" - She looked at him sadly.

"Just tell me."

Joanne lifted her head and looked up at the grey-blue sky, which was releasing more and more snowflakes. Some of them settled in Joanne's hair, forming something like a winter wreath.

Martin looked at her expectantly.

"I always remember what Mom said to me shortly after Dad died. From that moment, I knew that as soon as I could get away from here, I would run and never come back."

"Jo, what happened?"

"Dad died because of me."

Martin fell silent for a while. He had no idea how to react. What Joanne said was absurd.

"What? Dad died because of a sudden constriction of the trachea after being given antibiotics."

"Yes, I know" - Joanne said. "But on the day of his funeral, Mom yelled at me that it was my fault. Because he went out to look for me, got sick, and then caught that damned flu."

Martin was nine years old then, Joanne fourteen. And even though she was mature for her age, she still didn't know herself or the world well enough to understand what was happening around her. She was also burdened by the admiration and adoration for her younger brother. When Dad got sick and then died, she felt that she wanted to be like Ninny, the invisible girl from the Moomins. Ninny wore a bell around her neck so that everyone would know where she was. When she felt safe, her outlines would appear - a bow on her head, even a face - but when Moomin asked: "What's that?" the girl disappeared again, so offended was she. It was the same with Joanne.

Yes, she had left the house that day to visit a friend and had lost track of time because it was raining, and Martin had recently been explaining that the smell of rain was nothing more than a mixture of chemical substances, bacteria, and microorganisms, plant oils, and… pollution. He knew a lot for a nine-year-old, she had to admit. So she stood near her friend's house, trying to smell the rain, to understand what her brother meant, and completely lost track of time, even though she had promised to be back by seven.

Dad went out to look for her, and a few days later, he was lying in bed with a fever, chills, a debilitating cough, and excruciating pain all over his body. When he was close to losing consciousness, Mom took him to the hospital.

They gave him antibiotics, which only made things worse. He died a few hours later.

"You killed him" - Mom said to Joanne.

***

Catherine reminded Martin a little of Joanne, though at first, he didn't want to admit it even to himself. His sister had always seemed cold and unpleasant, but in reality, she was full of sensitivity and a subtlety that he had mistaken for passivity. It was a shame he realized it so late.

"What is she like, your Catherine?" - Joanne asked now.

"Calm. I like that just her being there is enough for me. When we're together, I feel safe. You know how? Like when we were alone at home, there was a storm, and you came into my room and read me stories. And then we built a fort out of chairs and blankets, and we hid from the lightning in there. How old was I then?"

"Three, maybe four" - Joanne replied.

"But also when that yellow dog from next door jumped out and tried to take my roll."

Joanne laughed.

As a child, Martin almost always had to be eating something. And when they went outside, he always took sandwiches, an apple, or a piece of cake with him. The neighbours' dog, yellow with a brown patch over one eye, also had to eat, and preferably the same things as people.

"He was yellow, wasn't he?" - Joanne recalled.

Not sandy, beige, or cream, but yellow, almost like dandelions in spring. They never met another dog like him. When Martin went outside, getting ready to eat his roll with pâté, the dog stood nearly nose-to-nose with him and opened its mouth wide. Martin froze in fear, but then Joanne walked up and whispered something into the dog's ear.

"What did you say to that dog?"

"That you were my little brother and he wasn't allowed to scare you. I also promised to bring him a similar roll in a moment."

"And he understood you?"

"Apparently, because he walked away, sat by the sandbox, and waited, remember?"

Martin nodded.

Joanne then went upstairs, spread pâté on a roll, and gave it to the dog, who from that time on was always the happiest to see her.

"You saved me."

"And then you told our parents that I was feeding the neighbors' dog with our pâté."

Martin shrank back on the bench.

"Did you get in trouble for that?"

"I received a lecture about how children in Ethiopia are starving, and here I am playing with food."

"I was a total idiot. Such an awful little brother, always tattling on you, even though you were saving me from trouble."

Joanne fell silent for a second.

"I admit, after a while, I didn't want to do it anymore" - she said after a pause. – "I wanted you to go away, to some genius boarding school. Maybe then they'd notice me again. Every bit of anger that could have emboldened me and allowed me to fight for myself again, I turned against myself. It hit me twice as hard and grew.

Over time, I think I even stopped liking you." - She looked at him uncertainly.

"I can't really blame you" - Martin said, rubbing his nose. "But I could have come to the funeral."

"Want me to tell you something? But don't tell Mom; she might not understand."

"I'm already scared."

"In Denmark, for several years now, the heat from crematory furnaces has been directed into the city's heating network and is used to warm homes. The idea is that the energy from cremation shouldn't go to waste but should be used for something beneficial. The Danes think it's very economical because it allows them to do away with expensive chimney installations."

"Jesus, Joanne, are you telling me that after death you warmed someone's apartment?"

"I think several."

"This is more grotesque than Mrożek's plays. I'm shaken. And you can be sure I'll never tell Mom about this."

Joanne giggled.

"Are you cold?" - she asked.

"I don't know. I don't feel it. I'm still thinking about you flowing through the city's heating pipes. Besides, I like winter and snow."

"So do I." - She looked up at the sky again. "You're going to tell me something interesting about snow now, aren't you?" - She winked at him.

He thought for a moment.

"Alright. The largest snowflake ever observed was thirty-eight centimetres wide and three centimetres thick. It fell in Montana in 1887."

Joanne snapped her fingers.

"Good one, but there's no evidence of it. There weren't any cameras back then."

"There weren't" - Martin agreed. "But it's still considered a world record snowflake."

"What else will you tell me?"

"That dry snow forms when flakes fall into a cold, dry atmosphere, which makes them small and powdery. And wet snow forms when they fall in temperatures just above freezing, causing the edges of the flakes to melt slightly and stick together, forming large, heavy snowflakes."

"That's physics" - Joanne remarked. "You were always a little genius."

Martin smiled.

"You used to sing beautifully" - he remembered.

"To the bathroom mirror."

"Who did you pretend to be?"

"Kylie Minogue, and sometimes Barbra Streisand." - She laughed.

"And… what's Else like?" - he suddenly asked.

Joanne brightened.

Else was exceptional. All parents say that about their children, but her daughter was truly a wonderful child. She loved to cuddle.

"She'd just come over and snuggle up, and that's exactly what I should have taught her. But I didn't know how. Else sensed it somehow, and she started gently touching me. Stroking me like a wild kitten who initially reacted to everything with some distrust."

"And Ebbe?"

"He hugged me too. And I think it was thanks to them that I survived the hardest times."

"How much time do we have left?"

"Half an hour" - Martin fell silent and lowered his head. Joanne looked at him seriously.

"Else is your niece."

"I know, Jo, but you can't just draw a family on a piece of paper. A mom, a dad, a little girl, a little boy, a dog, a cat, a hamster in a cage. A family needs to be felt, you have to want it. A child is something you plan for, not something you get as a gift."

"Sometimes there's no other choice. Do you want her to end up in a care centre, and then with strangers? Do you really think that's the best for her?"

Martin shook his head.

"Of course not. But..."

"Just try."

"But this isn't a game of Tetris that you can put on the shelf when you get bored."

"That's true" - Joanne agreed.

"Or Furby, which you secretly hid from me. I found him in that old shoebox. Did you ever tell me that the neighbour's cat stole him?" Martin suddenly remembered.

"Quite possible, but that wasn't true. Furby lived under my bed and only came out when you weren't home. It was my little revenge. I had my sweet secret, and Furby was all mine."

"Revenge?"

"For taking my room."

Martin closed his eyes. How old was he then? Ten? Eleven? Their father was definitely already gone. Joanne's room was much bigger, and Martin got the smaller one because he was younger. At first, it didn't matter to him, but after a while, he simply ran out of space. He kept bringing home old processors, floppy disks, broken computer parts, cans, lamps, cables, and wires. No wonder it was hard to even enter his room. Once, he dragged in a piece of tin fencing. It was bigger than his bed.

"Jo, let's switch. You only have a few books and two teddy bears" - he constantly whined.

Joanne's room was indeed quite minimalist. One day, she took all her toys outside and gave them away to the neighbourhood kids. She kept only one doll, two teddy bears, some puzzles, a few books, and Furby, who was partly Martin's. Even her wardrobe seemed empty. Unlike her friends, Joanne wasn't the type of girl who needed piles of clothes, bags, shoes, and scarves. She dressed simply and almost always in black and white.

One day, their mother decided they should switch rooms.

"Why?" - Joanne asked.

"Because you don't need as much space. And Martin is always building, constructing, and creating something. You can see for yourself that he barely fits with all his stuff."

"But this is my space" - Joanne tried to argue, even though she knew she had already lost. It wasn't a suggestion or a question. It was an order.

Two weeks later, Martin moved into her spacious room, and she ended up in his eight square meters. She didn't say a word, but she looked at him in a way that made him instantly regret the switch. From that time on, they talked even less.

"That was wrong" - he said now.

"It was. But the worst part for me was realizing that I had absolutely no one to complain to."

Martin was now struggling to hold back his tears.

"Why didn't I see this before?"

"Because every child is, in a way, selfish. They want to be happy in their own way, often not realizing that they're hurting others. It's probably normal. But do you know what's most beautiful about a child? Honesty. There's no guarantee that Else will immediately like you and want to live with you. Kids are brutally honest. You might find out that you can't make good pancakes, that you wear stretched-out T-shirts, and that you're boring."

"Me?" - Martin was surprised.

"If you don't participate in the doll tea parties, if you don't know the songs from *Frozen*, if you can't make a bike or an owl out of chopped vegetables, there's a good chance you'll be classified as boring."

"You're not making this sound appealing" - Martin admitted.

Joanne just smiled.

"Else is a picky eater."

"Great."

"You'll have to work hard to get her to eat anything other than a ketchup sandwich. But you only offer food when she's hungry. You don't push meals every five minutes and ask if she'll finally eat something. You give her time to get hungry. Unless it's rhubarb."

"Are you giving me a crash course in parenting?"

"I'm offering a few tips. Just in case."

"I'm not taking her" - Martin buried his face in his hands.

"I understand. But maybe one day my advice will come in handy. They're free. It took me a while to figure out how to deal with a picky eater. First of all, you serve smaller portions. A plate piled high with food doesn't necessarily look appetizing - I remember that from childhood. Mom always packed on tons of food, and the worst was the blob of spinach. It would spread out and look like cow dung..." - Joanne trailed off.

"Ugh."

Martin couldn't help but laugh at the memory.

"But a small cutlet, a spoonful of potatoes, and some carrots are different. And you try to make the meals look fun and colourful. You make faces with cucumber or ketchup on sandwiches, slice apples into wedges and arrange them in a rosette, shape the cutlet into a duck. Culinary creativity is a very effective method."

"Jo, this sounds like a nightmare. What culinary creativity? What cutlet duck? Please!"

"I want Else to grow up as a happy girl. So there's no bitterness, sadness, disappointments, or regrets in her. I know those are necessary too, and you can't completely avoid them, because..."

"Because they show that you've been hit, even if it was unjust?"

Joanne bit her lip.

"Kids sometimes get kicked for no reason. And it hurts for a lifetime, even though the bruises have long faded. I'm afraid Else will never let go of her grief. That her life will be filled with fear and that kind of melancholy that I carried within me for a very long time."

"Because of me."

"Stop it. Most of the things you did were unconscious, because I don't believe you wanted to hurt me. Our parents probably didn't want to either, although their injustice hurt the most. And the realization that, despite what people say, you can love one child more than another."

"Is that why you didn't want Else to have siblings?"

Joanne thought for a while.

"They say that in adulthood, we repeat the same mistakes our parents made. And even though we promise ourselves that we'll be different, certain things come back to us like a boomerang. Suddenly, we're speaking our mother's words, raising our voice like our father, being just as unfair, just as hurtful. Maybe I wanted to avoid that, so I wouldn't have to confront the past. I wanted only Else. And to focus solely on her."

"What else should I know about your daughter?"

"When I put her on a swing, she demands to be swung high, fast, and without limits. At home, she does everything at a dizzying pace, and she's everywhere. She climbs on the sofa, tries to open kitchen cabinets, rolls around on the floor. An hour without movement, running, and noise is a wasted hour. She also thinks there's nothing better than jumping on the bed and landing on soft pillows. Or the carousel. In activities like these, Else concentrates all her senses on exploring the world around her. She touches it, tastes it, smells it, and experiences it. I used to be like that. Once. But then something locked me in a cage."

"Me" - Martin said reflexively.

"I'm telling you again, it wasn't your fault. Stop beating yourself up. You were a perfectly normal brother. It's just that at some point, I started nitpicking everything and only saw the bad in you."

"I found something else here" - Martin tapped the blue notebook with his finger. "A story about cat therapy."

Joanne shrugged.

"I copied that from a magazine."

A seven-year-old boy was afraid of everything - tests at school, sports, homework. His parents had piled too many responsibilities on him, and he didn't want to disappoint them. It got to the point where fear dominated more and more areas of his daily life. The boy didn't want to go shopping, was afraid of the crowds in the city, and of moving cars. During therapy with the school psychologist, he was scared of a small cat named Kiki. Fortunately, Kiki wasn't very trusting either. - She's afraid of you - said the psychologist. When he tried to feed her a cookie, she hissed but didn't come closer than a few

"Were you scared too?" - Martin asked.

"When you were born, our parents told me that you were more precious than a diamond. But at the same time, very fragile. And that I had to be careful and learn to do many things on my own, because they wouldn't have much time for me. They had to take care of you, especially since you spent the first few weeks in the hospital in an incubator. Then it didn't get any better. Mom would jump up at every sneeze, every cry, every sound you made that seemed suspicious to her. When I forgot to tell her there was a party at preschool, I simply didn't go because she didn't have time to make me a costume. And I wanted to be the Winter Princess, in a white dress, white shoes, and a sparkling silver crown."

Martin clenched his teeth.

"Jo, but I didn't know any of this. I thought you didn't like me because I was younger, stupid, because I was always bothering you and forcing you to play with me. Jeez, that story about the kitten is so telling..."

"It wasn't that I didn't like you or didn't want us to do things together. It's just that almost every time, it ended in some damn misunderstanding, and I was the cause. Over time, I started writing down and collecting in a jar all the accusations that were thrown at me. I'd write on little notes that I was 'selfish,' 'not doing well in school,' 'destroying my brother's toys,' that I had 'some kind of destructive nature.' I only threw that jar away when I met Ebbe. Then I realized that I didn't have to be afraid anymore, I didn't have to prove anything, and that the way I was, was enough for him."

"And until then, you were like that seven-year-old boy trying to tame Kiki?"

"And Kiki him" - Joanne confirmed.

"Does Else speak Polish?"

"Of course she does. She even knows a few poems by heart and quite a few songs. And she dances beautifully."

"Just like you" - Martin reminded her.

"I was just fooling around in front of the mirror. But she puts her whole heart into it. And she loves rhubarb."

"Ah yes, you mentioned that" - he recalled.

"There aren't many things she likes to eat, that's true, but she loves rhubarb. She once told me it reminds her of magic wands, and if she eats it, she'll gain magical powers. And then she'll conjure up an entire field of rhubarb."

"But does she like it raw?"

Joanne looked at him with pity.

"Have you ever tried raw rhubarb? Of course not. We usually eat it as a compote, jam, or just as an addition to cake. Can you bake?"

"No. If I want something sweet, I just buy it."

"You'd have to learn. There's a lot of magic in baking too, and chaos, especially when you're doing it with a child. But it tastes twice as good then."

Martin didn't look convinced.

"I know what I'm talking about. If you're going to buy rhubarb, remember that the redder it is, the less sour it will be. And you know, it's technically a vegetable? Although apparently in the States, it's considered a fruit."

"Since it mostly ends up in cakes or jams, I guess that's fair?" - Martin noted.

"Kind of. On the other hand, you can make a cake, even a pie, out of carrots or nettles."

"Sure" - Martin shook his head in disbelief. "But let's agree, I won't be experimenting. I can get a piece of rhubarb pie at the bakery. Or at least a pastry."

Joanne winked at him.

"The baked one is the healthiest. And it tastes best until the end of June" - she added.

December twenty-third, 8:20 a.m.

"I don't want you to disappear again."

"I don't have to. But that's entirely up to you."

Martin looked up at the brightening sky. The snow was falling evenly, and the flakes seemed to be swirling faster and faster.

"Can you imagine how Catherine would react if I suddenly told her I was going to have a child? It could be a shock for her."

"But I know she'd be very happy. Believe me, I'm on the other side and have better information."

Martin looked at his sister one last time.

"Is there a nickname for Else?"

"That's up to you."

"I'll call her Furby."

"Beautiful."

"Jo?"

"I have to go. Have you made your decision?"

Martin nodded, and then he broke down and cried like a child.

The Hour of Flowers

Marriage is a perpetual conversation.
Betty Jane Wylie

She was fat.

The allegory of a doughnut and a porpoise, combined in one. Anna tried to be objective, but no other comparison came to mind. Fat, short, with a somewhat pleasant face, sure, but men usually look for slim, youthful women with firm bodies, right? Until now, she had believed that all men sought affairs for the same reasons - they were after what they lacked at home, reaching for something previously unavailable. New tastes, new scents, new experiences. After all, why would anyone choose something similar to what they already had? Or worse?

Anna watched that woman from a distance. She felt a bit ridiculous in her baseball cap and sunglasses, especially since it was cloudy. But she didn't want to show her face, and no other disguise came to mind, though the

189

chance of the woman knowing her was practically non-existent. Anna stared and tried to understand. She had been following the woman for over an hour.

Fat. Just fat.

It's natural for boredom to creep into any relationship after a while. At first, it's tiny, no bigger than a bacterium, but over time it grows, fed by indifference, until it swells to monstrous proportions. It rises, dominates, and eventually devours the last remnants of love that remain, because only hard work can piece them back together. Some people realize it in time and rise to the challenge, while others sleep through the moment, and when they finally wake up, it's usually too late. That's how it was with Anna and Matthew. The only comfort was that they both fell into the same kind of indifference, so neither of them suffered. They lived side by side, drank coffee together, although each prepared it for themselves. In the morning, they left the house, only to meet again in the afternoon, exchange a few words, sometimes a few sentences, and then retreat, each into their own domestic space.

Matthew on the couch in front of the TV or in the garage, and Anna in the kitchen or the bedroom. Over time, they had learned to cleverly avoid each other, rarely getting in each other's way. When they met in the evening, they greeted each other like strangers on a train.

"Good evening."

"Good evening."

If someone looked closely at many marriages, they'd find that a significant portion of them function in a similar way, though most would vehemently deny it. You can get used to anything. After all, it's hard to live in constant admiration and sigh at the sight of your partner changing their socks.

"I'll be back later tonight. The client can only view the apartment in the evening" - Matthew said.

Anna just nodded, signalling that it wasn't a problem. She'd be at her flower shop until five anyway, and if she went to the cinema afterwards, it would likely be by herself. She even thought for a moment about mentioning the cinema, but she just waved it off.

Goodbye. Goodbye.

And that's how it had been for the past five, maybe six years. Then suddenly, the flowers appeared.

Roses are beautiful and full of contradictions. They smell sweet, yet they prick. Though relatively easy to care for, they also require patience.

Some people are a lot like these flowers. They're charming, beautiful, almost perfect - no wonder everyone enjoys their company. But they can also hurt, especially when they feel betrayed. A rose person needs emotions to bloom fully. They need warmth, care, and attention. They are proud and confident. They detest deceit, disloyalty, betrayal. A rose has a strong backbone (a firm stem with sharp thorns), which means it's not as fragile as other flowers and can endure a lot. In pivotal moments of life (a breakup, a divorce, losing a job), it still someone to lean on. It's tough, sometimes titanic, but that doesn't mean it can handle problems alone. A rose thrives in the company of others, wilts when left unwanted. It's dominant, sensual, and quick to react. One must know how to handle it. In friendship - loyal, honest, trustworthy. You can always count on it; it's not afraid to speak the truth.

Anna had run her flower shop for seventeen years. She used to be an art teacher, but when her school reduced staff, she started helping her mother in the flower shop. It was a tiny business, a small booth rented for next to nothing. Anna quickly found her place in this floral world, though she never imagined she would stay in it for so many years. When her mother passed away, Anna considered selling the shop but soon abandoned the idea. She realized that she loved all the asparagus ferns, baby's breath, ornamental cabbages, boxwoods, sedges, cordylines, and miscanthus.

"This is your place" - Matthew had told her then. And he was right.

After so many years, she knew almost everything about ornamental plants and treated them like people. Customers came not only for bouquets, but sometimes also for advice, asking Anna what flowers to choose for their mother, a friend, or a loved one. And Anna was happy to help, applying floral psychology, even if some thought it didn't exist.

"I'm looking for something for my mother-in-law. She's energetic, loud, and hard to impress."

"I'd suggest peonies, all in one colour, with no embellishments. Arranged in a white basket."

Peonies - full, fragrant, incredibly decorative - were perfect for mature and decisive women. For shy and modest women, she recommended lilies of the valley or freesias in pastel colours, arranged in small drop-shaped bouquets. For the elegant and slightly old-fashioned, she combined white with silver or beige with gold, all in the form of muffs or cascades. Extravagant women could expect fan or ball-shaped bouquets made of orchids or black tulips. Anna always hit the mark, which was why customers kept coming back. Over time, she couldn't imagine doing anything else.

"I'd like to buy some beautiful flowers." - The man standing at the counter blushed deeply.

"Stupid request, I know, I'm in a flower shop, after all. It's just that this woman is special, so the bouquet should be special too. - He stumbled over his words."

Anna smiled.

"What's her name?"

"Michelle" - the man brightened up. "She's delicate but also confident. She's always slipping away from me, like a rainbow. I know it sounds horribly cheesy, but what I mean is that you can never catch a rainbow. You can only admire it from afar" - he finished clumsily.

"Eustoma" - Anna said.

The man looked at her questioningly.

"Take a look for yourself" - she pointed to the delicate flowers ranging from white to pink to blue. "They're dainty, intricate, resembling roses. And a bit like poppies too. It's hard to believe their homeland is the prairies, from Nebraska all the way to Texas. They're some of the most interesting flowers in my shop. Subtle, unique, different from the rest."

"Yes." - The man smiled. "That's exactly like Michelle."

"And your name is?"

"Alex. Thank you very much. This is exactly what I was looking for" - he said, his face lighting up.

***

Anna didn't receive flowers from her husband, after all, she was surrounded by them every day. So it startled her when, one day at the end of February, or maybe early March, Matthew brought her roses for no reason at all.

"What's the occasion?" - she asked.

He shrugged.

"I don't know. I was at the market for tomatoes, and I just bought these roses from a sweet old lady. She said they were from her garden. They're kind of miniature, aren't they?"

She nodded.

"Yes, it's a dwarf variety of Chinese rose, *Rosa chinensis*. It blooms all season and is quite easy to grow since it's resistant to disease" - she said more to herself.

"Uh-huh" - Matthew agreed, though he had no clue about flowers.

His world was real estate. Renting, selling, and brokerage. He was a popular agent because, like Anna, he understood his clients and didn't treat them as mere transactions. He enjoyed talking to them, listening to their various problems, advising, and always trying to find the best solution.

Anna wondered why her husband had suddenly brought her flowers. If he had bought pickled frogs, she would have been less surprised.

Then came the lavender. A potted plant.

"Apparently, it was wintered outdoors, and it's sure to take root" - Matthew said.

She looked at him in astonishment, but he didn't notice her gaze, as he turned and walked to the bathroom. So she stood there with the pot in her hands, unable to move for a few moments.

Lavender. It smells divine, soothes the senses, heals. In natural medicine, it's used as a calming agent for insomnia, nervous palpitations, and anxiety. Just a few sprigs of dried lavender can enrich and enhance the flavour of any dish.

Dried lavender is often placed in wardrobes to make clothes smell wonderful.

The lavender woman is a good spirit. Always ready to help, full of energy. She loves helping others. It doesn't matter what you ask - taking care of a dog while you're on vacation, helping with a move, going shopping together, or offering support in tough times, lavender will always be on your side. She's uncomplicated, doesn't know what jealousy is, and doesn't hold grudges for no reason. She doesn't expect constant admiration or adoration. She's content knowing that others appreciate her help. People love spending time with her because they feel better around her.

All these thoughts flashed through Anna's mind, but she didn't feel any calmer. Matthew rarely gave her flowers. When he proposed (lilies of the valley) and when she gave birth to their son (lilies). Then there were the roses, but this time without any occasion. And now lavender. People generally like surprises, as long as they don't disrupt their status quo. When something unexpected happens, it can cause unease. Not everyone enjoys being caught off guard.

She decided to clear things up, for her own peace of mind. She made dinner, and though they hadn't eaten together in a long time, she called Matthew to the kitchen.

"What's this?" - he asked, surprised.

"I made dinner for us" - Anna was equally surprised that her husband was asking such an obvious question.

"Should I sit at the table?"

"Yes, please" - she said.

Husband and wife can drift so far apart that even a shared meal feels strange.

When they sat down, an awkward silence fell. Anna tried to break it but had no idea where to start. They hadn't been good at small talk for a long time. They were better at exchanging plain, dry information. Simple messages.

"Tasty?"

"Yes."

"It's salad."

"I see that, yes."

"Romaine and lamb's lettuce."

"Oh wow."

"What?"

"Nothing, why do you ask?"

"I thought something was wrong."

"Everything's fine. Lamb's lettuce is the one with the smaller leaves?"

"Exactly."

"And romaine?"

"That's the other one."

"Right."

The rest of the evening passed in silence because Anna decided she no longer wanted to ask about the lavender. Maybe he got it from a client, or found it in a house rented out today, and didn't want it to wilt. That had to be it. There was no point reading too much into the lavender. People sometimes work themselves up for no reason, ending up with a stomach-ache and a whirlwind of obsessive thoughts.

After dinner, they dispersed without meeting each other's eyes, and then Matthew said he was going to tinker with the old *Polonez* (he refused to sell it, preferring to turn it into a fascinating piece of automotive art), while Anna began clearing the table, even though all she wanted was to retreat to the bedroom with a book or simply crawl under the covers and sleep. Her mood had completely soured.

She glanced at the lavender plant she had placed on the windowsill. It needed to be planted. March was the perfect month; even a frost wouldn't harm it because, having been wintered outdoors, it was grown in harmony with its natural growth cycle and was resistant to various shocks. Unlike Anna.

One day, at the beginning of April, an orchid appeared in the kitchen. When Anna returned from work, the orchid was sitting on the table. She didn't know where it had come from or if it intended to stay. It was a fascinating work of nature, even for those who weren't particularly fond of it. Anna touched its soft petals.

"Phalaenopsis" – she said.

An orchid is an incredibly beautiful and unique flower. It demands immense patience and a delicate hand. It is temperamental and difficult to cultivate. One variety prefers sunlight, another moisture, and yet another requires a special place to fully blossom. Their patterns and colours are nearly countless.

In Anna's view, an orchid woman knows she is special and is happy to emphasize it. She loves being cared for, and she thrives in the spotlight. She always puts herself first, her own well-being above all. She chooses unconventional careers and exotic hobbies...

She infects others with her originality and knows how to inspire. It's the orchid who will drag you on a rafting adventure, persuade you to go on a balloon ride, or whisk you off to Barcelona in search of the Cemetery of Forgotten Books. Her ideas are often surprising, but that's what makes her so special. It's impossible to get bored with an orchid. She refuses to let life slip through her fingers or shrink to the size of a kitchen. She wants more and reaches for it without hesitation. However, you must never force her into anything or bombard her with advice. The orchid flower dislikes too much sun, too much water, and frequent repotting. The orchid woman despises unsolicited advice, excessive criticism, and attempts at dominance. For her, freedom and uniqueness are paramount.

Anna sold orchids quite often, especially after she developed their psychological profiles and shared them with clients, half-jokingly. Some would smile, while others took her words very seriously.

"Oh, you're right! This is perfect for my friend, my mother, my aunt, my relative, even my mother-in-law" - they would say, pleased with their choice. This little personalization trick made the flowers seem like the perfect gift.

When Matthew came home from work, it was already dark. Anna was sitting in the kitchen, still staring at the orchid. He turned on the light, startled by her silence.

"God, you scared me! Why are you sitting here alone in the dark?"

She looked at him without smiling.

"I'm sitting alone because, besides you, no one else lives here with us. I didn't notice when it got dark. Why are you bringing me flowers?" - The question came out of nowhere, and Matthew was visibly thrown off balance.

"What do you mean?" - he asked, confused.

"Exactly what I said. Why have you been bringing me flowers since February? You've never done that before."

He shrugged.

"I thought I'd make you happy. Plus, I liked the colour. I know you're surrounded by flowers all day, but this is something different, right?"

"That's true. But I've been working in a flower shop for years, and you suddenly decided you should start buying me flowers?"

He raised his hands helplessly.

"Are you saying I should have always done that?"

"No. I want to know why I'm suddenly receiving flowers."

Matthew opened his mouth as if to say something but sighed heavily instead.

"It was spontaneous. You're hard to please."

"That's not an answer."

"I don't have a differenrt one. I wanted to be kind. That's it."

She forced a smile.

"Then thank you. Would you like something to eat? There's some leftover tuna pasta."

"I ate out."

That answer shouldn't have surprised her, yet Anna felt something different in the way he said it. She had also stopped at a sandwich bar earlier that day, one run by an old friend of her mother's, Theresa, who had been trying to persuade Anna to take over the business for some time now.

"Annie, are you sure you don't want to change your career? I'm slowly losing my energy and drive. I think I'm finally ready to retire. I fought it for a while, but a person has to rest at some point. And that doesn't mean giving up, just moving into a well-deserved state of blissful idleness. I've certainly earned the right to lie down and relax. Or at least just lie down."

"Tessie, I still have my flower shop."

"Aren't you tired of it yet?"

Anna laughed.

"I love flowers. I can't imagine loving sandwiches as much. The flower shop is one-third of my life, and it's also a keepsake from my mother."

Theresa sighed heavily.

"But promise me you'll at least think about it."

"Fine. You've planted a seed. We'll see if it grows."

***

Anna pushed away thoughts of the sandwich bar and reached for the orchid, carefully removing it from its pot.

"What are you doing?" Matthew asked, surprised.

"I need to repot it. The soil is compacted, and the new growth has less and less room. It's time for a new home."

"But do you like it?"

She looked at him coolly.

"Yes, I like yellow orchids."

"Did you know that a few years ago, an orchid was sold at auction for over a hundred and sixty thousand pounds?"''

Anna just smiled.

"*Shenzhen Nongke*. It took passionate horticulturists from China quite some time to cultivate. The orchid blooms once every eight years, but they say it's worth the wait to experience its fragrance."

"Well, I knew I wouldn't surprise you."

In this, however, he was slightly wrong. What surprised her was the conversation itself. They hadn't exchanged so many words in months.

Next came daisies. These flowers grow quickly and are relatively easy to cultivate. They love sunshine and water. Without watering, they wilt fast, and their petals begin to brown.

A daisy friend wants to be the most important person in your life. She enjoys it when you give her lots of attention. If she feels special to you, she'll be loyal and devoted. Daisies don't like being pushed into the shadows or forgotten. The key moments in their lives are their friend's wedding and the birth of her child. During those times, they feel like they're fading into the background. They stop talking, stop calling, avoid meetings. It takes great patience to convince them that they're still important and needed.

***

Anna sat down in front of the mirror in her bedroom and turned on the lamp. She gazed at her reflection, deep in thought. She was fifty-two years old, and it suddenly struck her that half her life was already behind her. Maybe even more than half. She was, for the most part, satisfied with what she had achieved. She was proud of her son, who was studying in Spain, of her flower shop, of the modest house that was almost paid off. She liked herself. Even her marriage seemed reasonably successful, despite the silence that had filled the last few years.

"Am I missing something? Or am I longing for something I can't even name?" - Anna wondered.

Happiness is hard to define because its algorithms are ever-changing. But if she had to answer right now, staring at her reflection in the mirror, without witnesses, without embellishment, honestly and bluntly, her answer would have been:

"No, I'm not missing anything" - she said aloud.

And that surprised her the most.

The worst part was that Matthew's flowers only confirmed her feeling that something was wrong. Something was beginning to awaken her from a strange slumber. With each new gift, it dawned on her that she wasn't happy, or at least not in the way she wanted to be.

A person should smile in their sleep. They should wake up with a smile and find joy in the small things. To appreciate the smell of coffee, the sunlight streaming through the window and lighting up the room, the quiet in the kitchen as the world slowly wakes and rubs its sleepy eyes. To rejoice in each day. She had been doing everything automatically, without even considering whether she enjoyed what she was doing. She had become like a machine, responding to commands. In some ways, this applied to her work as well, a fact that suddenly hit her with terrifying clarity. Yes, she loved flowers, loved arranging bouquets, but was this truly her passion, or had it simply become a routine? Perhaps everyone has their own threshold for satisfaction. For fascination. And once they reach it, they can no longer feel the same excitement. The vessel is full. Some people react immediately, seeking out new vessels. Others don't even notice that the water has been overflowing for months. Sometimes for years.

Anna realized that she had long since lost her sense of happiness. The question was: what now?

It was the beginning of July. Outside the window, the air smelled warm and rich. People were eating ice cream and dipping their feet in fountains. They were going on vacation or returning from it. They rested on benches, strolled lazily through parks, while she sat in front of her bedroom mirror, thinking about her life and how she wasn't happy. In the background, a bouquet of daisies was visible.

Some decisions are made spontaneously, without weighing pros and cons, without much thought or consultation. Sometimes, you just have to listen to your inner voice, even if someone on the outside might think you're crazy.

Anna reached for the phone and called Theresa.

"Hi Theresa, listen, do you still want to hand over your business to good hands?"

Teresa felt relieved.

"Girl, you're heaven-sent. I was just about to put my little shop up for sale, but I gave myself two days for a sign. Not even one day has passed, and here it is. Let's meet at my place."

Anna applied a bit of blush to her cheeks and put on some mascara. She wanted to highlight the importance of the moment, so she did it in a feminine way: makeup, a dress instead of a worn-out tracksuit, and her hair pinned up high. She couldn't remember the last time she looked like this. She usually went to work without makeup, in jeans and a comfy T-shirt. She was quite slim, though her stomach and hips had been bothering her a bit lately. She had even thought about running in the evenings, but gave up after the first session. She actually liked her body, even though it wasn't as firm as it used to be.

The sandwich bar Theresa ran wasn't very large and wasn't exactly inviting either. Black and white tiles on the floor, a few tables - all rather nondescript and quite dull. On the walls hung pictures of famous people from restaurants and bars around the world: Paul Newman devouring pancakes, Elton John with a huge sandwich, Cindy Crawford leaning over a salad. Although Theresa's sandwiches were tasty, Anna already had an idea on how to diversify them.

„Do you think I could add edible flowers to the sandwiches?"

„Darling, you can even add edible beetles and caterpillars if that's your vision. I'm thrilled you've finally made up your mind! And what about the flower shop?"

„I'll sell it" - Anna said calmly, and it didn't even hurt much.

„Does Matthew know?"

Anna shook her head.

„I haven't talked to him about it yet, but it's my flower shop, and I don't think he'll mind. I'm simply swapping one business for another. I think Mom would have understood."

Theresa scratched her chin.

„You know, this bar might not be a gold mine, but it was enough for me. Besides, I believe you'll manage to turn it into something more. After all, each of us sees the same things differently."

She is often called the queen of ornamental plants: the camellia. In the past, in Europe, its blooming sprigs were the perfect complement to formal attire. Ladies would pin them to their dresses, and gentlemen wore them in their buttonholes. Camellia flowers are elegant, multicolored, and majestic. They dislike frost and cold, preferring light and a bit of moisture. When strong wind blows, rain falls, or the sun shines too brightly, the camellia stops growing and its petals fall off.

A 'camellia woman' doesn't like change. She feels comfortable when her life is filled with rituals. She's not fond of unexpected visits and dislikes canceled plans. Winning over a camellia woman requires patience and calmness. Once she feels safe, she will fully bloom, showing her best qualities: loyalty and devotion. But it's important to remember one thing: if you ever betray a camellia, you may never regain her trust.

The camellia was the last flower Anna received from Matthew. It was the end of August, warm, green, still full of the scents of summer, though on that particular day, it decided to rain.

„I'm going to a client's plot" - Matthew said.

„Why?" - Anna asked. „It's Sunday."

Matthew looked at her with surprise, though he seemed a bit pleased - or maybe it was just her imagination.

"Do you really want to know?"

In truth, Anna wanted to talk about the camellia, to make Matthew finally say something, and maybe also to tell him that the sandwich bar was actually a very good idea, even though he had initially reacted quite sceptically to the change.

"Yes, I do want to know" - she confirmed, nodding her head.

"My client started building a house, but unfortunately lost his job, so he can't repay the loan. Now he wants to sell the plot with the already laid foundations before winter" - Matthew explained.

"Matthew…"

"I have to go now. I'll be back in the evening" - he waved goodbye.

For a moment, she thought he might kiss her on the cheek - husbands usually do that when they say goodbye to their wives - but then she remembered they hadn't done that for years. Someone had stopped at some point, and it just stayed that way. She realized she even missed it, but she wasn't sure if she longed for her husband's closeness or for any touch at all. Until now, she hadn't thought about other men. She couldn't imagine starting over, that slow process of getting to know someone and growing close. Besides, she had never thought about leaving the flower shop. One needs to mature to embrace change.

She brewed some coffee, flipped through a few newspapers, wandered around the kitchen, and then went out to the garden. The rain had finally stopped. She enjoyed these lazy Sundays, even if she spent them alone. She liked the feeling of a free day - baking a cake, trimming bushes and flowers, lounging in a hammock, gazing at the sky, and enjoying a peaceful evening. And then she thought that doing all of this together with someone else would be even nicer, and maybe next weekend she and Matthew should start with a coffee together on the terrace. Who knows, maybe it would bring them closer.

But in the evening, the police arrived, and the officers, somewhat chaotically, explained to her that there had been an accident. The road was more slippery than usual, though it was the driver's fault for an unnecessary overtake. Unfortunately, Matthew fell victim to this recklessness. He died before the ambulance arrived. The other driver also perished in the crash. Luckily, the passenger who was with Matthew only suffered minor injuries that weren't life-threatening. She was taken to the hospital on Szwajcarska Street. Her name was Jeannette Dobraniecka.

Anna watched the policemen in silence, their words reaching her with a certain delay:

Slippery…

Overtake…

Recklessness…

Died… '

Died before the ambulance arrived…

On Swiss Street…

Jeannette Dobraniecka?

The camellia is a temperamental plant, but when treated well, it rewards you with beautiful blooms.

Well-tended and properly cared-for orchids rarely fall ill, though they are sometimes attacked by viruses, fungi, or bacteria.

The daisy is the princess of summer - charming, white, and endearing.

Roses always have an odd number of leaves.

In the tomb of Tutankhamun, opened in 1922, lavender was found that still retained some of its scent, despite having lain there for over three thousand years.

The world swirled, and Anna with it.

***

Of course, she had suspected something, but every time, she pushed those thoughts away. Maybe she simply preferred not to know, afraid of how she might react? It's one thing to extinguish love for your husband; it's another to discover that someone else has rekindled it in him. Until now, she had felt contempt for women who accepted infidelity, unable to understand the humiliation they willingly endured. For what? Out of shame? Fear of being alone, living a life that might not be as comfortable or convenient? A person should have enough pride to walk away from a place where they're no longer wanted.

But when she smelled the scent of another woman on him, she understood that it was possible to live with it, as long as you didn't lose your own sense of self. That it was possible to somehow come to terms with it, gently accept it. You just had to refrain from speaking it aloud and avoid opening the door wider than your dignity allowed.

She and Matthew shared a son, a mortgage, a marriage contract, habits, and one electric toothbrush with two heads. Red for her, blue for him. And their shared bedroom, which, however, had nothing to do with sex. The last time they had made love was seven years ago, and since then, neither had attempted to initiate anything. They had replaced their shared blanket with two smaller ones, thus creating a barrier, insulating themselves from each other, from the warmth of their bodies and the touch they once knew. After a while, they stopped missing it, though Anna sometimes felt the chill of her own skin and wondered if the extinction of love was precisely that - the sadness of an untouched body.

Her suspicions really began when the yellow-petaled orchid appeared on the kitchen table. From that moment on, she discreetly observed Matthew - not stalking him, not eavesdropping or rummaging through his phone, but watching him a little longer than usual. She quickly noticed subtleties that someone else might have overlooked. Marriage, after all, is all about the subtleties, the small things, the trivialities, and you need to be deeply involved to catch the slight shifts in colour that tint any relationship.

When someone starts shaving more frequently than usual.

Lingers in front of the wardrobe, selecting clothes.

Puts down the phone when they know you're watching.

Comes home later than usual, and then begins adding an extra hour, sometimes two, to that later.

When their eyes shine a little brighter.

And when they start bringing flowers.

At first, she wanted to be brave, modern, and tolerant. Calmly ask, have a conversation, maybe even make a joke. But she couldn't. The thought that another woman was touching her husband, that she knew the map of his body, where his moles were, where he had a tiny scar from falling off a bicycle, filled her with a strange fear. She felt something was ending, and it was happening without her involvement. It is much easier to close the door yourself than to be pushed out of it.

She decided to focus on her new project, pushing away the thoughts about what was happening in her marriage. Initially, she hadn't taken Theresa's proposal seriously - after all, it was just some small sandwich bar. A café, maybe a restaurant, even a bakery - that would be something, but a bar?

"Surprisingly, I've built up quite a loyal clientele here, and they're particularly attached to their favourite sets, their usual days, and even their regular tables. I'm never bored, and that's the key to this business." - Theresa winked at

Anna and showed her the back room. "You've got everything here. Two months ago, I even bought a new fridge that talks to you."

"What? Why?" - Anna asked, startled.

"Relax, it's no magic. It just lets you know when something's nearing its expiration date or already expired. It also has a 'zero-degree' compartment, a special drawer between the fridge and freezer, and it generally looks quite space-age. Let me tell you, we became fast friends."

Anna laughed.

"I hope I can make friends with it too."

Theresa winked again.

"Do you ever change the menu?" - Anna asked.

"Every now and then I add something new, though lately, less so. Humans are creatures of habit, and when they like something, they'll eat it nearly until the day they die." - Theresa chuckled. "My late husband was obsessed with these particular candy bars. Basically, they were the only sweets he ever ate. When he found out they were being discontinued, he bought up all the remaining stock in the local stores. Then he started driving around town, stockpiling them. He even ordered some online, and for weeks, we kept receiving packages of candy bars. He sorted them by colour and arranged them in boxes. He liked the ones in silver-green wrappers best. Least of all, the silver-blue ones. He ate two a day. And you know what? After eight years, they finally ran out. He died two weeks later. Sure, officially it was a heart attack, but I know he didn't want to live without his candy bars anymore." - Theresa smiled nostalgically. "I figured he must've eaten about six thousand of them in those eight years. Can you imagine? Six thousand candy bars. He was proof that once someone gets attached to something, it's hard to let go. Unless, of course, it's for someone younger. "

Anna swallowed hard.

"Six thousand candy bars" - she repeated, though in her head, Theresa's last sentence still echoed: "Unless it's for someone younger."

Lately, everything seemed to remind her of the same thing, as if the world was sending her signals, poking her and saying, "Are you really that blind?"

"But I can introduce new sandwiches, right?" Anna asked after a while.

"Sweetheart, you can sell pickled nettle leaves or dried tarantulas if you want. This place will be entirely yours."

"I'd like to add some colour."

"Colour?" - Theresa looked surprised. "What do you mean?"

"I'd like to paint the tables and chairs in different colours. Like a rainbow. And if someone orders a sandwich at the orange table, they'll get it wrapped in orange paper."

"Brilliant!" - Theresa exclaimed in approval. "And I bet you'll have matching napkins too?"

"And the glasses as well. I've seen sets in all the colours of the rainbow. I'll make seasonal sandwiches, too. In spring, I'll use fresh vegetables, in autumn, kale and beetroot, and in winter, pickles. And I'll give them their own names."

"Personalized sandwiches?" - Theresa laughed. "I love it. Who knows, maybe you'll turn this place into something truly special. I really hope so."

"And what about you? What will you do now?"

Theresa brewed a strong cup of coffee, and they both sat by the window.

"I think I've come to realize that life is made up of stages. And that each one is necessary, though of course, the final stage is the hardest to accept. Because no one wants to admit they can't keep up, that their breath is shallow, and they don't want to get out of bed as often. Or that when they do get up, they first have to stretch their stiff, rusty bones. Or rather, crumbling bones. Old age is very unattractive, but perhaps it's necessary. It's about reaching the point where you realize it's time to let others take the stage. That there's no longer any need to prove anything to anyone. And with that comes peace."

"But you're not dying, are you?" - Anna asked, suddenly alarmed.

Theresa took a big sip of coffee and puffed out her cheeks comically.

"No, I'm not going anywhere just yet. But I do want to slow down and indulge in some well-deserved laziness. Long, unhurried walks without constantly checking the time, home-baked cakes - I love cakes but always deny myself, as if I'm preparing for a contest to have the smallest waistline. I'll let myself sleep longer, forget to take a bath some evenings, have breakfast - or even lunch - in bed, and finally read all those books I've been stacking up for years. I think I've got about eighteen of them, but please, don't tell anyone. Did you know I've never read *In Search of Lost Time* by Proust? I've always been too busy." - She laughed. "Running this place has been fun, but it's started to wear me down. I think I've lost my spark."

"Are you saying you'll disappear under a blanket, reading literary classics and snacking on Pavlova?" - Anna asked in a conspiratorial whisper.

"Worse. I'll also read romance novels because I enjoy cheesy love stories where the hero is always perfect and loves her more than life itself, which, as we know, is nonsense. I'll have a bucket of coconut macaroons on the right side of my bed and a caramel cake on the left. And the best part? Even if I forget to brush my teeth at night, it won't matter because I have dentures anyway!"

Now they were both laughing, fully and freely.

When a loved one dies suddenly, the natural response is grief. Sometimes, denial intertwines with a pain so intense that it seems to tear a person apart from the inside. Other times, there's an eerie numbness, a kind of paralysis, as if nothing truly registers.

But Anna felt a growing fury. Matthew hadn't been heading to a meeting with a client; he was going on a date. And though she had no proof, she knew with absolute certainty that his passenger was "the other woman." The one who had quietly slipped into their marriage some time ago but now had a name, a face, and a personal history. At this very moment, she was lying in a hospital bed with a broken wrist and a possible concussion.

"You bastard!" - Anna spat the words aloud as she stood in front of her husband's closet. At first, she wanted to throw everything out - burn it, donate it to the homeless - anything to rid herself of every trace of this godforsaken marriage that had ended in the worst possible way. Matthew's death was suddenly insignificant, eclipsed by her rage. Anger consumed her, leaving no room for sorrow.

She reached for his sweaters and swept them onto the floor in one swift motion. Then the shirts, suits, and trousers followed. But suddenly, her strength gave out, and she collapsed onto the floor, crying like a little girl.

"Why can't I grieve like a normal person? Why can't I mourn you and go through this pain like everyone else?" - she thought.

All she felt was hate - raw, unbridled fury at being deceived. That he had turned her into the unwanted wife, old and irrelevant, someone who had bored him...

But deep down, Anna knew she was wrong. Matthew had never made her feel unattractive. It was she who had avoided closeness, who no longer wanted to take walks together, to talk, let alone have sex. It was she who had set the boundaries, who had bought separate blankets. And yet, she still felt betrayed.

Was Jeannette Dobraniecka twenty years younger? Did she have long, shapely legs, firm buttocks, and luscious, kissable lips? Did she make love to him every time he wanted it? Who was she? What did her voice sound like? How did she move? What did she like to eat? Did freckles appear on her nose in the summer? What did they do in their spare time - did they reach for the stars, or was it just the mundane - walks, conversations, dinners?

For two days, Anna moved through life in a daze. She couldn't recall whether she had eaten, brushed her teeth, or slept. It felt like she was stuck in a half-dream, aware of what was happening around her but also seeing flashes of the past. The first flowers Matthew had ever given her, and that last potted camellia; the walk along the beach and the seagull that had attacked their waffles; the dinner under the open sky in the park and her reaction to the sight of the scallops she didn't dare to eat; meeting at the bus stop in the rain, herself heavily pregnant with a belly so big she could hardly walk, and Matthew… laughing, saying she looked like a giant sun with arms and legs attached. And then there was the swim at sunset in the lake. It had been so cliché, yet so beautiful.

After two days, she realized she had been lying in bed the entire time. There were several missed calls from Theresa, a few from other friends, and four from her son. She swallowed hard and dialled his number, forcing her voice to sound calm.

"Yes, the funeral is this Saturday. I'm sorry I didn't answer earlier; I've had so much to deal with. Of course, I'll pick you up from the airport. I love you too. Everything will be fine."

She downed a glass of ice-cold water and dialled Theresa's number.

"Yes, the funeral is on Saturday. I'm sorry for not picking up earlier; it's just been overwhelming. Thank you for taking care of the bar. And for helping with the funeral arrangements. I love you too. Everything will be fine."

Then she got up and stepped into the shower, letting the water wash away the remnants of those lingering half-dreams. She wanted to return to the world of the living because, after all, she still belonged there.

Three days later, while sorting through Matthew's closet, she found the letters. This time, though, she remained calm. The anger settled quietly at the bottom of her soul, watching her closely. She knew it wasn't done with her yet, but for now, it was dormant. And that was fine. That was very fine.

She carefully folded Matthew's clothes and packed them into boxes. The letters lay beneath the T-shirts, tied with a green ribbon. She touched the cream-colored envelopes, and though she already knew what was inside, her heart began to race. Now everything she had suspected was about to be confirmed in black and white - or rather, cream. Desires, thoughts, longings - all laid bare across a dozen or so pages. Despite the simple, somewhat melodramatic language, they brutally intruded into a world that had once belonged only to Anna and Matthew. She felt as if someone was stealing pieces of that world, understanding it better with each passing day, drawing closer, and loving it more deeply. From Jeannette's words emerged the Matthew Anna had fallen in love with years ago: kind, quiet, caring, with a passion for old cars, a love for white chocolate, raspberry ice cream, and coffee table books filled with the world's most magnificent architectural works. Matthew, who loved foraging for mushrooms and pickling them afterward. Who had that funny little birthmark above his right ankle that looked like a balloon on a string.

It hurt Anna deeply that someone else had noticed all these things too. That they knew about them, admired them, and even cherished them. Just because she and Matthew hadn't spoken honestly in years, using only pleasantries and neutral phrases, didn't mean they weren't still connected, still one. Now Anna felt as though someone had suddenly severed an electric circuit of which she had been a part.

When too much current flows through a fuse, the wire burns and melts, breaking the circuit and halting the flow of electricity. Jeannette was that "too much current," both literally and metaphorically.

Anna read all the letters and felt as if Matthew had died a second time. Suddenly, the car accident seemed less horrific. She also knew that nothing could stop her from meeting Jeannette. She needed to see her, to hear her voice, and to try to understand why Matthew had been with her.

When you look at me, I can feel it, even with my eyes closed. And I turn toward you like a fern unfurling in the sunlight...

Anna closed her eyes. And then she began to scream with all her might. It lasted for several long minutes before she finally collapsed onto her knees and rolled onto her side.

She slept for eight hours straight. She dreamed of blackness.

***

"Here, take this" - Theresa handed Anna a joint.

"Marijuana?"

"Yes, but don't overthink it. Don't worry about whether it's right or wrong. Just take a couple of puffs - two or three, no more. The idea is to numb yourself a little. Right now, you're like an egg without a shell; it won't take much for you to crack."

If it hadn't been for Theresa, Anna wasn't sure she would have been able to keep it together at the funeral. And all the while, she kept wondering if Jeannette would show up. Would she stand off to the side, mourning her lover? Or would she sit in the church, pretending to be a mere acquaintance?

"I'm scared she'll show up" - Anna whispered to Theresa. "And that she'll be this strange, additional source of guilt. Though maybe I'm just rambling."

Theresa wrapped her strong arm around Anna.

Anna didn't want to tell anyone about Matthew's affair, at least not at first, but she knew she wouldn't be able to keep it a secret for long. She needed to unload it, to scream her anger, to finally confide in someone who would understand.

Since her mother's death, Theresa had become the closest person to Anna. Twenty years separated them, but Theresa had never told Anna that certain things were off-limits, that there were rules to follow or norms to uphold at a certain age. In her eyes, norms were shaped by life's experiences, making them flexible, varying for each individual.

"Do you know who she is?" Theresa asked.

"No, but I know her name. And I have to see her. Maybe then I'll understand, maybe even forgive him - or at least come to terms with it. The worst part is that I can't fully grieve. Because all I see is him with her. And the flowers… he brought them because he felt guilty and wanted to justify himself." - Anna buried her face in her hands.

Theresa took a deep breath.

"But you do realize that infidelity doesn't just come out of nowhere, right? There's no neat division between saints and whores; sometimes, the roles simply reverse."

Anna shrugged.

"I know. But that knowledge doesn't help. And yes, I know I'm partially to blame, but right now, I don't give a damn how much. Because it was still me who got deceived."

Theresa stroked her hair.

"You have every right to be angry, even furious. And I agree, you should see her. It might have a therapeutic effect- hopefully in a good way. Sometimes, these meetings can bring clarity because suddenly, something just clicks. I don't know; I've never been in your situation, but I think I'd want to know who my husband's lover was. If you don't see her, she'll haunt your thoughts forever."

***

She was fat.

236

A cross between a doughnut and a porpoise. Anna wanted to be objective, but no other comparisons came to mind.

Two weeks after the funeral, when she had finally started to think clearly again, to eat breakfast, even to brew her own coffee, she decided to confront her rival. Perhaps not directly, since she preferred to observe her from a distance first, but she knew she was ready. All of Jeannette Dobraniecka's details were in Matthew's notebook - address, phone number, email, workplace. It hadn't been hard to find her on Facebook, and it was just as easy to track her down in the real world.

I watched you slice onions. It was such a beautiful thing.

Jeannette Dobraniecka was fifty years old, divorced, with two children. She hadn't graduated from any prestigious university, nor was she a distinguished writer, painter, or high-powered lawyer. She worked in suburban greenhouses. She was ordinary, but she was capable of being enchanted by Matthew slicing onions. She thought he was exceptional and that he had finally brought peace to her life. She had written to him that he had rearranged her world and that he was a tiny piece of the cosmos she had been lucky enough to find.

What nonsense. It was like a bad romance novel come to life.

Anna clenched her jaw. It wasn't the affair that bothered her most - it was the damn onion slicing. Sex was one thing - hotel rooms, cars, even at her place, anywhere really. Secret dates, stolen weekends - those were expected. But slicing onions? That meant intimacy. It crossed a boundary far more personal than sex ever could. And it was, perversely, much more intimate.

"Have you found out anything about her?" - Theresa asked her some time later.

Anna lowerd her head.

"Yes. And you know what the worst part is? She's not better than me. Not younger, not prettier, not even thinner. And to top it off, she works in a similar field. She spends all day in greenhouses. She's surrounded by flowers. God, the irony. Why would he want someone so much like me? Someone so... ordinary. And fat."

Theresa laughed.

"Were you expecting a leggy blonde who could wrap her legs around the earth?"

"More or less."

"With grapefruit breasts, luscious lips, and lashes like butterfly wings?"

"Yes, that's exactly what I had in mind" - Anna admitted. "Even her name fit."

"And now you're disappointed?"

"I'm surprised. And now I understand even less. The worst part is that I can't even ask him anymore. Sometimes I look at his picture and wait for him to start talking. I stare at it intensely, as if I could will him back to life. I know it's insane…"

Theresa shook her head.

"No, I get it. But maybe it's better that she's ordinary. If she had legs longer than both of ours combined and lips that could wrap around a zucchini, you'd feel even worse. Inferior. Uglier. Worthless."

Anna thought about it for a second.

"Maybe. Right now, I just feel robbed, as if someone's stolen a part of me, and there's no place where I can report it. And no way to demand justice."

"So what will you do?"

"I don't know. For now, I need to focus on the bar. I've only just started; it'd be stupid to give up after four weeks."

"Remember, I'm here to help" - Theresa reminded her.

"I know. But I have to do this on my own. I need to stop thinking about everything that's happened, because it's worse than poison. I feel like something has spilled inside me, attacking my organs one by one. Sometimes I wake up with pain all over, and I know no pills will help. I just have to grit my teeth and wait it out."

"Are you drinking?"

"Believe me, I tried. I even bought a few bottles of wine and pulled out the whiskey from the cabinet. But it's not for me. I don't like alcohol. I only managed to get drunk once, and then I threw up for hours. I wanted to numb the pain, but it had the opposite effect."

In the weeks that followed, Anna threw herself into work. She paid attention to every detail, bought colourful napkins and plates, came up with new menu ideas, and even contacted an advertising agency to design a small campaign for the bar. She worked hard to push thoughts of death from her mind, and to stop thinking about the fact that Matthew's second duvet was stored away in the chest, or that his favourite blue mug, the one he always used for coffee, would never be touched again. She didn't want to think about Jeannette anymore, either, but occasionally she would check her Facebook profile, hoping to find something, anything. What exactly, she wasn't sure - maybe a mention of Matthew? A snippet of a letter Jeannette had written to him? Some kind of goodbye?

But Jeannette hadn't posted anything for weeks. She had vanished, retreated from the online world, as if she wanted to process her grief in solitude.

Anna was tempted to write to her, to signal that she knew, that she had always known, and that Matthew would never have left her. That Jeannette had only been a lover, even if he had sliced onions for her.

"Let it go" - Theresa advised. "It won't change anything, and you're just winding yourself up. Focus on what's here and now. And on what's ahead. The past is just a memory, and you can't change it."

Anna knew Theresa was right. For a while, she really did try not to dwell on the past. Matthew was dead, and with him had died this new love that Anna couldn't reconcile with.

Yet after some time, the impulse returned. It happened one Saturday morning. Anna woke after another restless night filled with strange dreams and nighttime terrors.

"I need to see her again. And maybe again after that. I want to see more than just her face and body" - she said aloud.

She simply had to do it, though she couldn't explain why.

In the afternoon, she called Theresa.

"If I ask you to help with the bar for a while, will you do it without asking questions?"

"Just promise me you're not planning anything foolish."

"That depends on your point of view. But I need to do this.

"Alright. Do what you need to do. Just come back soon" - Theresa replied, nodding as if she understood everything.

***

On the morning of December twenty-third, a light snow began to fall, as if cautiously announcing heavier flakes to come. By Christmas Eve, everything would be covered in a thick, white blanket - the kind people loved most, the postcard-perfect kind you saw in beautiful holiday movies.

Anna woke up unusually early. She sat up in bed, wrapped herself in the dark green duvet, and gazed out at the swirling snowflakes.

Of course, it wasn't going to be a happy Christmas Eve. If not for Theresa, who had dropped by unannounced as usual, Anna

243

probably wouldn't have had any cheesecake, or poppy seed cake, or even cabbage with mushrooms.

"Wait for me on Christmas Eve. My daughter and son-in-law will drop by in the early afternoon, and then they're heading to his parents. I'll pack everything up in containers and show up at your place like Santa Claus - though without the beard, but with a gift."

"That's really not necessary" - Anna tried to protest, but Theresa waved her off.

"Of course, it's not necessary, but I don't know how to be any other way. I'm infected, cursed with the holiday tradition, and nothing can cure me of it. People have tried, but it's always ended in failure."

"But I don't have anything for you" - Anna whispered.

"Perfect. I much prefer giving gifts to receiving them. I never know if I've thanked someone enough. And I have a bit of a complex because my late husband - by the way, you can say 'my late husband' now, too" - Theresa winked at Anna – "always gave me the most horribly tacky gifts. You can't imagine the feeling when you unwrap a crystal vase in a colour that's somewhere between ultramarine and emerald, and you have to smile and exclaim, 'I've always dreamed of this!' even though your aesthetic senses are screaming, 'No!' And just when you think it can't get worse, the next year you receive a jewellery box made of seashells. Your eyes burn from the sight, but you bravely lift your gaze and say, 'I'm overwhelmed with joy.' So trust me, it's better that you didn't get me anything. We'll avoid those awkward moments and fake smiles."

Anna hugged Theresa, and Theresa patted her on the back.

"It'll be alright, you'll see. The first Christmas Eve like this is always the hardest, because we're not used to having a second empty chair at the table. I'll admit, after Walter died, I made Christmas Eve dinner for myself. I could've gone to my daughter's, but I decided to face my fear. I had to change the room and buy new dinnerware so it wouldn't feel like a broken copy. And so I had Christmas Eve in the kitchen."

"And did it work?" - Anna asked.

Theresa thought for a while.

"Looking back now, I think it did. I asked my son-in-law not to say the usual wishes, but to speak them collectively, into the air, so that everyone could catch them without the face-to-face confrontation. That way, we could hold onto the wishes for a moment, then sit down and focus on serving the food that I could barely swallow."

"I think it'll be the same for me tomorrow."

"Possibly" - Theresa agreed. "I won't push you into anything, but just so you know, I made a cheesecake-poppy seed cake with caramelized oranges on top, and I doubt you'll be able to resist it."

Anna smiled at her gratefully.

On December twenty-third, at seven-twelve, she got dressed and went out to the garden to look at the first snow and feel the cold, just enough to appreciate the warmth of a hot cup of coffee and the dark green duvet she planned to return to. She loved her garden. It wasn't large, but it charmed anyone who had the chance to visit. It was designed in white tones, simple and a bit whimsical. Anna had always believed that white gave it an air of elegance. Throughout the season, all the plants bloomed in white, from low rock-garden perennials to shrubs and trees. Anna carefully chose the species and varieties so that the flowers would bloom one after another, allowing her to enjoy white blossoms all season long. First came the crocuses and snowdrops. Then, forget-me-nots, fragrant lilies of the valley, candytuft, and pasqueflowers joined the scene. There were tulips, hyacinths, freesias, daffodils, gladioli, lilies, and, of course, anemones. Along with bellflowers, alpine saxifrage, edelweiss, and blazing star. Now the garden lay asleep, as if covered with a white cloth woven from snowflakes.

Beneath the white dogwood stood a bench. She and Matthew had spotted it years ago at a flea market and immediately thought it would look beautiful in their garden. How many years ago had that been? Twelve? Fifteen? They had brought it home on a trailer borrowed from their neighbours. The bench was black, made of metal, though now the paint had begun to peel away.

Anna sat down. Despite the December chill, she felt warm and comfortable.

She closed her eyes.

"How much time do we have?" - she whispered softly.

"An hour" - Matthew replied.

He was dressed in a grey wool blazer, matching trousers, and a light-coloured shirt. He wasn't wearing a tie, just a burgundy scarf. Anna had given it to him once. He liked it because it was made from soft wool, the kind that didn't scratch but rather gently brushed against his chin.

"Why?" - she asked simply.

He didn't answer right away. He seemed to be weighing every word and its meaning. An hour could be an eternity or painfully short if there wasn't going to be another one after it.

"I wanted to feel like I used to. To see admiration in someone's eyes again, hear someone laugh at my jokes, feel someone's touch on my body. To believe I was special, the only one, desired and dreamed of."

"You wanted to feel like someone better?"

"I wanted to be noticed. I once read that the worst kind of home is one where nothing happens. You talk out of obligation, about nothing, look at each other with disdain, and avoid touch. And that's the kind of home we built for ourselves."

Anna swallowed. She had known it was like that, but hearing Matthew say it out loud made the sadness of those words hit her. Nothing much had happened between them in a long time. The house didn't live - it just existed. It had walls, rooms, a lovely garden. But there wasn't a family inside.

"And I want to tell you that a lot of that was my fault," Matthew admitted. " It wasn't just you who shut down. I went silent too, over time. I gave up. I see now how absurd it is that I put so much effort into restoring that old Polonez, but I let our marriage fall apart."

"We both let it fall apart" - Anna said. "Like we didn't care anymore, like we'd run out of colours to paint with."

"Do you still love me?" - Matthew asked suddenly.

"Of course, after all, we are… well, we were married" - she responded reflexively. " It just kind of unravelled, drifted in different directions, but we were still together. Until… until Jeannette showed up."

Matthew nudged her shoulder.

"Are you jealous?"

She nodded.

"And you know that's exactly what I wanted?"

"What do you mean?"

"I was waiting for your jealousy. I wanted it to hurt you. I was hoping you'd come to me furious and start shouting at me. I was even ready for a fight.

"Are you crazy?"

"Did you notice I bought three new shirts recently?"

"That was supposed to clue me in?"

"You always bought them for me before. Then I started coming home later from work. But that didn't get to you either. It wasn't until the flowers that you reacted."

"Weren't they meant to ease your guilty conscience?"

Matthew spread his hands.

"I wanted you to start suspecting something. I wanted you to react. And once, we almost had that conversation, remember? When I brought home the orchid. But you cut it short. I had hoped you'd become more suspicious after that. And that eventually, you'd crack. Honestly, I don't even know what I was expecting. Some sign that you still cared about me. I know, it was like walking on thin ice, but I couldn't think of anything else."

Anna shook her head in disbelief.

"I don't understand. You made up the affair? You didn't love her?"

"It's not like that. Not exactly. When I first met Jeannette, I wasn't thinking about cheating at all. She was looking for a small apartment after her divorce, and we spent a lot of time viewing different places together. We became friends over time."

"You must've been quite close if you were slicing onions for her" - Anna muttered.

"How do you know that?"

"It doesn't matter."

"Remember when I used to make you that mushroom and onion stew with cream and fresh cilantro? Your favourite."

Anna bit her lip.

"For her too?"

Matthew didn't answer. He caught a snowflake in his hand.

"I've always been fascinated by these little works of art. From a chemical perspective, they're just clusters of ice crystals. But look closely at them."

"Hasn't it melted yet?" - Anna asked in surprise.

Matthew smiled.

"That's one of the perks of being on the other side. I can hold a snowflake as long as I want. A little magic trick."

Anna leaned in to look at his hand.

"It really does have six sides. And it doesn't even seem flat. It looks like a tiny prism, transparent too, even though I always thought snow was white."

"White is just the reflection of light in the ice crystals."

Anna gazed at it in awe.

"Do you remember, twenty-seven years ago, when I was enormous with our son in my belly, and you built me that igloo in your parents' garden? You even brought blankets and pillows, and we spent the night in it. We lit a candle and told each other stories about the future. About what our son would be like, and how we wouldn't give him chocolate so he wouldn't fall in love with sweets too early."

"It seems like my mom ruined that plan. She gave him so many candy bars for his first birthday that he could've shared them with half the daycare. He managed to eat two before we could even say the word 'no.'"

Anna laughed.

"And from that moment on, he was always demanding sweets, and your mom kept saying we were crazy for raising a child without chocolate, that he would grow up miserable."

Matthew smiled at the memory and looked at Anna.

"Aren't you cold?"

"I'd say I feel rather warm. Strange."

"Are you still angry with me?"

"A little, yes. Tell me, honestly - did you fall in love with her? I need to know."

***

Matthew hadn't planned for an affair. He had always been honest, with principles, and he loved his wife - or at least, he thought he did. But when he met Jeannette, he realized just how much was missing from his life. It wasn't material things or the allure of a young, beautiful mistress. What he lacked was everyday life - conversations, cooking together, sitting on the couch and dozing off while she watched a movie. The simplicity of mornings with coffee and the radio, aimless walks, and sharing one blanket in the marital bed. Jeannette gave him all that without questions or expectations. She gave him her whole self, knowing full well she'd always be the second one. But sometimes, it's better to enjoy a homemade pie than wait your whole life for a wedding cake.

Two years ago, she had gone through a painful divorce, and for the next two years, she lived with her mother, who couldn't forgive her for the failed marriage.

"Mom, but he left me."

"You must have given him a reason. I can't see it any other way" - her mother would reply. After hearing that for the hundredth time, Jeannette decided it was time to move out.

She spent months looking for a small, affordable apartment that felt even slightly cozy and didn't require too many aesthetic compromises. That's when she met Matthew, one of the few real estate agents who immediately understood what she was looking for. With a smile on his face, he showed her different places, understanding perfectly when she shook her head.

"I know, this place just feels sad" - he'd say.

And then he found her a charming attic apartment at a good price, though it needed a little work. The moment she saw it, she said yes. An open space, a bedroom partitioned off by a partial wall, and a relatively large bathroom. Stone, wood - simple, but with character. It was exactly what she had been searching for.

"If you'd like, I can help with the renovations" - Matthew had offered, and to her, it sounded like poetry.

It sounded like poetry for months after that because she fell in love with him so deeply that sometimes it took her breath away. It was a love that was somewhat dishonest, one-sided, with little hope for a future together, but she embraced it fully, eyes shining with happiness. Matthew tasted that happiness more cautiously, approaching it with care, rather than diving straight in. Yet over time, he visited her more often, his presence becoming more and more tangible. Once, he even left a sweater at the apartment and later told her it didn't matter - she could just hang it in the closet. That had meant more to her than any declaration of love.

"I'm so glad you're here" - she had told him once, and Matthew realized just how much he needed to hear that.

***

"I did something awful" - Anna said now.

"You?" - he asked, surprised. "You've never done anything awful or bad. You never could."

"But I did." - She smiled slightly. "I followed Jeannette and found out what car she drives."

"The red Corsa?"

"Yes."

"But wait - what do you mean, followed her? Why?" - Matthew asked, confused.

Anna shrugged.

"I don't know. I guess I had to see what she looked like and why you chose her. I wanted to step into her world - don't ask me why. I was surprised that she's... well, a little plump - she finished quickly."

"You were expecting a long-legged waif?"

"I was expecting someone better" - she admitted honestly.

Matthew chuckled softly.

"It's not about size, or breast shape, or even wrinkle-free skin."

"Then what is it?"

"It's about the smile, the attention, the interest. It's about feeling like you're needed. Everyone's a little selfish, a small centre of the universe when it comes to their own needs. They want to feel important, noticed. And, you know, we even want someone to cry for us after we're gone. You have to admit - that's pretty egocentric."

"In a way, yes" - Anna agreed. "Although, it's normal to cry for someone you knew."

Matthew snapped his fingers.

"But I'm not talking about situational crying, triggered by the atmosphere of the funeral. I mean real longing for someone who's just signed off for good."

Anna opened her mouth, but the question wouldn't come out.

"Go ahead" - Matthew encouraged. "This is really your last chance."

"Did you fall in love with her? Answer, because I feel like you're dodging the question."

He sank into thought.

"And don't lie" - she added.

"Why would I?" - he protested. "Besides, you can't lie over here. Something about this side forces you to tell the truth."

Anna let out a soft laugh.

"At first, I was captivated by her being captivated. I was electrified."

"Excuse me?" - Anna looked at him, bewildered.

"Positively charged. I came across the term once. It's about the way electric charges affect each other, how they can electrify objects around them. I thought it fit me. I felt like I'd been jolted with electricity, but in a good way. It brought me to life."

"And then came love?"

He shook his head.

"In matters like this, I'm old-fashioned. I believe in one love for life, even if it gets shattered into a thousand pieces along the way."

"But did you fall in love?" - she pressed.

Matthew winked at her.

"Before I answer, you have to tell me what awful thing you did to Jeannette. Or rather, to her car, I'm guessing."

Anna lowered her head and whispered:

"I wrote 'Bitch' on it. With a marker."

"Jesus! - Matthew exclaimed. - On the hood?"

"No, on the back, near the exhaust. Just a tiny word, almost unnoticeable. But I felt better afterward. Though now, I'm ashamed. It was really stupid and kind of low. And it didn't even help."

It was a reflex. Anna truly wasn't the type to seek revenge, hold long grudges, or harbour hatred toward others. In that way, she and Matthew were alike. They liked people, trusted them, and always tried to give everyone a second chance. But this time, Anna acted on a surge of strong emotions. That Saturday, when she felt the impulse, she went to Village Street and stood outside the building where Jeannette lived. She knew Jeannette rented the attic, what car she drove, when she left for work, and when she returned home. For the next two weeks, Anna followed her almost every day. She noticed that Jeannette preferred to wear wide skirts and tunics that somewhat concealed her broad hips and belly. She paired them with long sweater-coats and comfortable flat shoes. When it rained, she put on rubber boots and a puffy, waterproof jacket in the colour of spring grass. It was the only brightly coloured thing she wore. The rest of her wardrobe was confined to blacks and greys. Those colours didn't quite suit her, but Anna knew it was part of her mourning for Matthew.

In truth, Jeannette led a rather dull life. Repetitive, routine. No evening outings to the city, no guests. Work, home, sometimes grocery shopping. She had light hair, which she usually wore in a messy bun or loose braid, rarely wore makeup, and smelled faintly of something citrusy. Anna noticed the scent when she stood behind her in line at the grocery store. Jeannette had bought a few apples, some vegetables, chicken wings, dark chocolate, a packet of hazelnut wafers, and two kilograms of flour.

"Yes?" - Anna finally realized the cashier had asked her a question and was now glaring at her with raised eyebrows.

No wonder. Anna hadn't picked up a basket, hadn't put anything on the conveyor belt, and was just standing there empty-handed in sunglasses. It was November.

"Sorry" - she muttered and quickly headed for the exit. "This is pointless" - she whispered to herself as she got into her car.

And yet, she didn't drive home. Instead, she parked by Jeannette's building, waited until it was dark, then got out, walked up to the red, worn-down Corsa, and wrote the word "Bitch" with a black marker. Though the word was barely visible, Anna felt as if she had spray-painted the entire Palace of Culture.

She drove home and decided that she would never follow Jeannette Dobraniecka again.

"You know, I was so furious with you then, and it didn't fade easily."

"Really?" - he asked.

" Yes! That anger blinded me, but now I understand you so much better" - she admitted quietly. "And I've been thinking, you don't need to answer whether you fell in love. When someone is deprived of feelings, they fade. And when they have the chance to regain some light, they reach for it without hesitation, without second thoughts, without fear. It just happens, like when you throw a dry twig into a dying fire. I think I might have reacted the same way - with gratitude that someone still cared enough to ignite a spark. With hope that I could glow again."

"I like your sandwiches" - Matthew suddenly changed the subject. "Did you know I used to send a taxi driver to pick them up for me? I had to try each one and even made a list of my favourites."

"Why didn't you just come?" - Anna asked, surprised.

"Because you never invited me. I know I'm your husband, and maybe you think I didn't need an invitation, but I was waiting for one. But… should I even be saying this in the past tense?" - he pondered, wrinkling his nose.

Anna felt a little embarrassed.

"I'm sorry, I didn't think… I just assumed it was natural for you to drop by whenever you wanted. But you're right, I should've made it clearer. Especially since we hadn't been doing much together lately. I didn't even ask for your opinion on the flower shop. I just sold it." She lowered her head. "Which sandwich is your favourite?" she asked after a moment.

"The one with beets and sheep's cheese, the 'Red and White.' Great name, by the way. And the 'Purple Fantasy' with grilled eggplant. I've never eaten anything so good. You should also make one with pickled mushrooms, which I love. Promise you'll think about it. You've probably got regular customers by now?"

"Yes, many. Martin comes most often. He's about thirty, an IT guy, always in a rush, but I kind of like him. And then there's Tamara, though I haven't seen her in a while. She's a few years younger than me. She doesn't talk much, just smiles sometimes. She always came alone, but once, she was with a guy. They barely spoke to each other, just stared, almost devoured each other with their eyes. Then she started crying, and he left. I thought maybe it was a failed romance, but they didn't seem like a couple. He was a lot younger than her, but that's not a scandal these days. I'll ask her the next time I see her. I think she's waiting for someone to speak to her first, but lately, I haven't had the headspace for that. Everything's been focused on your passing. And on Jeannette.

Matthew adjusted his scarf.

"You've always liked observing people. You've got a knack for it. I remember when you softened my mom up with that bouquet of wildflowers. You spent so long deciding what to pick, and then suddenly, you told me to stop the car by a meadow, and you went out to pick cornflowers, poppies, and those yellow flowers that smelled so strong."

"Mullein" - Anna confirmed. "And there was also pink sainfoin and woolly woundwort, which you refused to help me pick because you thought it was nettle."

"I remember it perfectly! I thought my mom would chase us away with that bunch of weeds, but she was delighted. You somehow knew she hated roses, lilies, and especially orchids. No wonder she fell in love with you immediately. Just like I did. Remember?"

Anna laughed.

It had been a very ordinary meeting at a bus stop. And a very ordinary situation - the bus just didn't show up. It was raining, and they stood there getting soaked because the stop didn't even have a shelter.

"That day, when we were standing there, completely drenched, you suddenly asked if we could dry off together at Hortex and eat a 'Brzdąc Cake.'[1]

____

[1] "Brzdąc" cake – traditional Polish chocolate-cream cake

"A Brzdąc Cake!" - Matthew exclaimed with delight. "The perfect little cake with sponge and tons of coffee-flavoured cream."

"Chocolate. Or rather, cocoa."

"Really? It wasn't coffee?"

"The coffee one was the 'Wuzetka Cake.'"

"Ah, that's right" - Matthew agreed. "We ate two 'Brzdąc Cakes' each. I felt a bit sick afterward, but I was thrilled you weren't one of those girls constantly on a diet."

"I was starving" - Anna admitted.

"And you were wearing that grey coat, which got completely soaked."

"We must have sat there for four hours. You told me about your childhood and how you saw the sea for the first time. You really cried when you saw it? The vastness scared you?"

"I was babbling anything that came to mind because I didn't want you to say, 'I have to go now.' I wanted to stretch that moment out as long as possible."

"I remember when I got home, my mom was furious. I forgot to do the shopping, and she wanted to pickle cucumbers. And I didn't bring her any cucumbers or dill."

"But you gave me your address."

"And you showed up the next morning with sandwiches with cottage cheese."

"And radishes" - Matthew remembered. "From my parents' garden. They were fiery hot."

"And then we couldn't stay apart anymore."

"Because that was love. That really was love." - Matthew smiled at her broadly, and Anna felt her anger dissolve, her fury evaporating, replaced by the peace she had always felt when they were together.

"I'll ask you one last time. Do you love me?" - Matthew gently lifted her chin.

Anna looked straight into his eyes.

"You were right when you said love sometimes shatters into a thousand pieces. But that doesn't mean it disappears. Some part of it stays with us until the end, even if it's no longer the love it once was. Now, I see that I probably didn't love you the way I should have or the way you deserved. My jealousy came from selfishness, just like you said. Even from arrogance. A baseless certainty that you would always belong to me, even though you got nothing in return - or very little, at least. But that wasn't love. Just a tiny fragment of it."

"And I believe you'll find your soulmate yet. And feel butterflies again." - Matthew smiled.

"I don't know if I'll fall in love again. Certainly not like I did with you. I also don't think anyone will get to know me as well as you did. You were part of me, perfectly fitted. You have no idea how much I'll miss you. I already miss you, even the silence between us. I wish your scent could stay with me forever. And all those memories that make me a better person." - She paused for a second. "But who knows, maybe I'll give myself another chance. It will be a different love, shaped by all we've been through, but maybe not a worse one?"

Matthew leaned in close and whispered:

"We had a lot of great years together."

She had no choice but tu agree.

"Many couples would envy us."

Anna smiled softly.

"And I always thought you had the most beautiful breasts in the world.

This time, she laughed out loud."

"Thank you" - she whispered, grasping his hand.

"And tomorrow, you're going to eat a piece of that Poppy Seed Cheesecake that Theresa's bringing, just for me."

"I promise."

"And one more thing."

"Yes?"

"Name the sandwich with pickled mushrooms and caramelized onions 'Mateo's Special.'"

The Hour of Friendship

It takes many years to find a friend; just a moment to lose one.

Stanisław Jerzy Lec

It all began in kindergarten. Alexy and Fabian became friends thanks to their distinctive names, which those Tommys, Petes, Jacks, and Andys found simply amusing. In this situation, Alexy and Fabian had to stick together to face the jeering and idiotic remarks. Together, they definitely felt stronger. The older kids' group had a watering can in its logo, the middle group had cherries, and the youngest - a teddy bear.

The first teasing remarks appeared in the charming "Colourful Crayons" preschool, where Alexy first arrived after moving from another town, and Fabian joined three weeks later. Until then, his grandmother had taken care of him.

"We need to form a gang" - Alexy declared one Tuesday, after once again failing to join a group of three Tommys and five Jacks for their rug-car race. How many times had he missed out on those races?

Fabian had it even worse; his mother made him wear red tights and felt slippers embroidered with a watering can. Grandma's handmade work was treated as art at home, but in preschool, it wasn't necessarily seen the same way.

"Fafa-fafa-fafa," the kids called him, snickering nastily and asking if he'd lost his pants somewhere.

"Alelelele" - they'd say about Alexy, which always made him fume.

Fabian agreed to form a two-person gang, which, as it turned out, lasted for many years - exactly thirty-two. It was a true male friendship. It wasn't spoiled by silly arguments, sulking, or minor misunderstandings that often become real dramas between women. Alexy and Fabian were above such nonsense. They built their bond slowly but surely. It started with a toy excavator that Alexy wanted to play with but which somehow always ended up in the hands of Big Pete, who was quite large for a six-year-old and had a habit of hitting indiscriminately and, unfortunately, often accurately. For breakfast, he could eat three rolls and still be hungry. Taking the excavator from him by force wasn't an option. A cunning plan was needed, and two pals. So one November Thursday, Fabian distracted Big Pete with a whistle-lollipop, while Alexy seized the excavator and proudly placed it on the table. Big Pete tried to protest, but thankfully, Ms. Lucy, their teacher, stepped in, announcing firmly:

"Alex was first. You'll get a turn once he's done."

Big Pete was defeated - at least for one afternoon.

Over time, Alex decided he preferred to go by "Alex," shedding the ending "y", and Fabian became "Fabi." It sounded a bit like a nickname and eventually caught on with everyone.

Alex and Fabi.

After years of silly comments, their names finally became original, unique, and attention-grabbing.

They say a child's imagination starts forming around the time they begin to speak. Young children who like to daydream tend to use a richer vocabulary than those who prefer activities that don't require much thought. They use complex words, assumptions, adverbs, and adjectives. A simple doll becomes a fairytale princess, a wizard from another planet, or a forest spirit. A matchbox turns into a little car, a dollhouse for tiny creatures, or a dwarf's bed. As they play, they mutter under their breath, creating their own stories. And they laugh more often. Meanwhile, the TV generation uses what we call "prepackaged language." They speak in phrases from cartoons. They don't want to listen to fairytales; they can't draw from their imagination. Instead of books or a walk in the woods, they choose TV. They wait for ready-made stories, avoiding the trouble of creating their own.

Alex and Fabi belonged to the first group, shaped by the everyday life of preschool. Excluded by their peers, they created their own stories, taking on the roles of superheroes battling an unfriendly world. Though they didn't yet understand the words "ostracism" or "rejection," they subconsciously felt they didn't fit in with the other children. It wasn't just their unique names. There was something else - Fabian's distinctive clothing and the fact that Alex had no father.

"And you don't have a dad!"- their peers would shout.

"He must've run away from you!" - they taunted.

It's no wonder that, in time, Alex and Fabian gradually withdrew from those who teased them. This bound them together far more than the watering can in the older kids' logo. While their friendship may not have faced significant tests, it was no less meaningful than the bond between Sam and Frodo from *The Lord of the Rings*. The most important thing was that they had each other.

Male friendship is about action. There's no exclusion, no pouting, no countless threads to unwind, pull, and explain. Men don't have to say much to show support. They don't need to reassure each other of their friendship or promise they'll always be there. They simply know it. They don't judge each other by shortcomings, deficiencies, or mistakes. They accept more, tolerate more, and understand more.

"I'd like to open a bar" - Alex said.

"That's a dumb idea" - Alex's mother replied.

"I'll help you" - Fabi assured him.

Such understanding is only possible between men and close friends. Concrete, straightforward, and essential.

And then she appears.

Michelle, aged thirty-three. A woman with an unusual background: she ran away from the altar, having previously married and divorced in rapid succession. Michelle was indecisive, a little lost, and romantic, which made many men want to care for her. Alex and Fabi did, too.

They fell in love with her almost simultaneously and with equal intensity. It's hard to navigate such a situation unscathed. It's difficult to curb one's ego, give up on one's feelings, and still pat a friend on the back. Maybe it works in movies. Or books. But in real life, very rarely.

***

The idea of opening a coffee bar wasn't original. It was more about fulfilling a dream than making a profitable business or securing a retirement fund. Alex had studied economics and worked as an accountant in a construction company for several years but always dreamed of something of his own, something that would bring him satisfaction - a place that smelled of freshly roasted coffee, where he wouldn't have to wear shirts and ties. People have different visions and desires, but they're often stifled by "good" advice and harsh reality. We succumb to others' whispers, and ultimately, fear wins. After all, no one likes uncertainty or the fear of missing loan payments. Alex wasn't the type to leap into the unknown. He carefully weighed the risks.

Fabi was a copywriter - confident, dynamic, sometimes impulsive. He worked for a large ad agency and had no shortage of work or money. He understood Alex completely: his vision of a bar, flexible hours, laid-back lifestyle, a scruffy beard or even a full beard, late-night chats with customers, and listening to cool music. It was a masculine vision of life with no room for a wife, a child, baby food, or diapers. To start, there was a dog that Alex took in one spring.

The dog wandered around the garden plots and didn't respond to any name, though Alex tried the whole canine alphabet, from Azor, Burek, Carlos, and Jack to Egon and Fuks, all the way to Pimpek, Rambo, and Zgredek. Nothing.

"Fine" - he finally said. "I'll call you Kayden."

All he was missing now was a bar, so when the opportunity arose to buy a small place near the Old Town for a decent price, Alex knew it was fate. Too bad he didn't have enough money to take it on.

"But I do" - said Fabi.

That's how he became a partner, though he didn't intend to get involved, as he simply didn't know a thing about coffee.

The bar was named "Coffee," simple and to the point. Wood, glass, metal, a stone counter, a large espresso machine, benches covered with grey paper, black-and-white photos on the walls of plantations in Vietnam, Brazil, Colombia, and Indonesia. From the ceiling hung a dozen or so light bulbs on red cords and mugs on metal hooks.

And above the counter hung a glossary for coffee tasters, which quickly became a favourite read of the café's patrons.

"Aroma: animal, smoky, medicinal, chocolatey, nutty, grainy, almondy, winey, woody

Taste: bitter, acidic, slightly sweet, astringent, salty

Mouthfeel: balance, harshness, strength, intensity."

Fabi nodded approvingly.

"This is exactly how a guy's place should look. No pink pots with tulips, lace doilies, or floral sugar bowls. This is a good place. And I'm not saying that because I'm a chauvinist who despises pink or feminine touches. I just think places like this are worth their weight in gold" - he explained. "You don't even need to advertise it; any guy can see it right away."

Alex agreed.

The café brought in a moderate income, but it was enough for a decent life, provided "decent" didn't mean a hybrid car, the latest iPhone model, designer clothes, and vacations in the Seychelles.

Alex was happy. He woke up every morning with a smile, took a shower, ran his fingers through his hair, threw on a random outfit, and headed to "Coffee" with genuine pleasure. They say that if you do what you love, you never have to work a day in your life. Alex completely agreed.

"Initially, coffee was treated as medicine, which justified its high price" - he would explain to interested customers, who came in waves.

The first one would arrive around eight in the morning, the next at ten, then another around lunchtime, and finally in the evening. Alex had a colleague who covered shifts, but he sometimes stayed longer because he enjoyed the place more than his two-bedroom apartment.

"The first European coffeehouse was opened in Venice in 1683, though some sources suggest it might have been even forty years earlier."

Fabi soon decided he didn't want to be a partner anymore and proposed a lifelong deal to Alex.

"Listen, Alex, in exchange for the cash for the place and decor, I don't want any shares or cut of the profits - just unlimited access to coffee. Deal?"

"But that's absurd! Even if you hadn't put a single penny in, you'd still be my non-paying customer. That's no arrangement at all. I should at least pay you something. You were supposed to be my partner, and a partner always gets a share. Agree" - he insisted, "I'd feel better about it."

"I don't want anything" - Fabi shrugged. "I make good money, and helping you out makes me happy. It's not about the money, you know that. But let's do this. If I ever lose a leg, you buy me the fanciest prosthetic there is. Swarovski crystals, if you like. Okay?"

"Dumb joke" - Alex just tapped his forehead. "All right, let's agree I'll send you a small monthly sum. You never know when you might need it. Besides, that feels fairer."

Fabi shrugged and winked at his friend, then pointed to the silver contraption on the counter.

"What is that?"

"A Neapolitan flip pot."

"I love you, man. No one else would buy one. And certainly not remember the name."

"Oh, I know what that is" - said a young guy sitting at the counter. "Though probably because I go to Italy a lot, and I have the same one at home."

Alex and Fabi laughed.

"How's the coffee?" - Alex asked.

The guy smiled.

"I've had far worse in Italy" - he replied. "Besides, if it were bad, I wouldn't be here so often."

"True" - Alex agreed. "Sorry I don't serve food. I decided to focus exclusively on coffee in all its forms."

"No problem. There's a sandwich shop nearby, so I stop there when I'm hungry. And here, I drink." - He smiled and reached out his hand. "Boris."

When he left, Fabi shook his head in disbelief.

"Incredible. I now know two guys who own a Neapolitan flip pot, know what it's for, and actually use it. Guess I need to catch up. A man should be able to impress even himself. Or maybe especially himself?"

***

Mario Puzo wrote in *The Godfather* about the "Sicilian thunderbolt" that upends even the most reasonable lives and "boils the blood in your veins." Passion is said to be a constellation of emotions so intense it's hard to control. On one hand, it unleashes euphoria; on the other, it stirs anxiety, jealousy, and longing. Sometimes just a glance, a scent, or the wave of a hand is enough to fall in love despite logic. Even brief separations cause physical pain, and longing disrupts focus on ordinary tasks. Passion is a trance where you shape reality to match your dreams.

Something like that happened to Fabi when he first saw Michelle.

Love always knows how to surprise. Sometimes it's thoughtful, long-awaited, a consequence of friendship; sometimes, it takes just one look. Fabi had always considered himself a stoic who kept reality in check, and then, one day, he stepped into the office elevator, running a bit late for a client meeting. A few seconds later, she walked in. And that was it. Fabi was gone.

Maybe it was her scent or the blend of pheromones with citrus shampoo, or perhaps her gaze, not quite flirtatious but so magnetic he couldn't tear his eyes away. Perhaps her smile, maybe her mouth, or maybe everyone has a moment when reason stops? Had anyone asked him in the elevator what was happening, Fabi would have said without hesitation: It's love.

Michelle seemed equally smitten, agreeing to meet him for coffee the very next day. Their conversation flowed so naturally that he found it pleasantly surprising. No awkward silences or long pauses that get so uncomfortable they make you sweat. That first meeting wasn't the last, and Fabi understood what it meant to "grow wings."

"Alex, I know it's real" - he told his friend over the phone, and two days later, he brought Michelle to "Coffee." And that was a mistake because his friend reacted to her the same way Fabi had in the elevator.

A cascade of misunderstandings, sneaky manoeuvres, and mutual resentment ensued, though not right away. Alex tried not to show his feelings and hoped his dreamy expression and softened gaze didn't give him away. He kept himself in check and only offered a brief: "Yes, she's charming."

Why did this happen to them? It was as if someone wanted to test the strength of male friendship and see how much it could endure. Would it prove to be a house of dominoes where a slight nudge sends everything tumbling?

And yet, everything began to topple, and nothing could stop it.

Suddenly, Alex and Fabi's friendship felt stifling, intense, too overpowering. Both felt they needed a break from each other, though they were fully aware of the reason - or rather, who the reason was - behind that decision. Besides, each had their own life, one they now longed to share with a woman.

Just to remind you, I met Michelle first - Fabi would say. - I brought her to you because I wanted you to meet the woman I fell in love with, who's turned my world upside down. I never asked you for anything, but now I have to say it straight: stay the hell away from her!

That's how Fabi reacted two months later, after hearing Alex say, "Yes, she's charming," and realizing exactly what lay behind those words.

Alex had never intended to stand in his friend's way, nor had he wanted to fall in love. But that "Sicilian thunderbolt" had struck him too, and perhaps even harder, with more force.

"I can't" - he replied, choosing to be honest with his best friend, even though it would cost them both dearly.

Fabi clenched his jaw and his right fist.

"You want to hit me?" - Alex asked.

"You have no idea how much. But I'm holding back."

"So, how about a duel?" - Alex looked at him with irony. He understood Fabi's fury, yet he couldn't handle his own feelings. He was falling for Michelle like a lovesick puppy, like a young boy seeing a princess for the first time. Not some spoiled diva, a sleeping beauty, or some Cinderella in glass slippers, but a real princess: witty, beautiful, with a contagious smile and a love for coffee. He'd never had such easy, flowing conversations with a woman, nor felt so at ease and relaxed with anyone before. If Michelle hadn't shown any interest in him, he would have suffered in silence and maybe even cheered Fabi on.

But she didn't know what she wanted. She was somewhat overwhelmed by the attention of two men, each offering up his heart almost at once. Sure, women like confident men, but not necessarily two at the same time. Especially when both were genuinely intriguing, with surprising ideas that made choosing the "better" one nearly impossible.

No, Michelle wasn't calculating. She genuinely couldn't decide. And then, when everything tangled into an inescapable mess, it was simply too late to choose.

***

First, there was the picnic.

It was a bit spontaneous and chaotic - no basket, no paper plates or cups. No checkered blanket, no breaded pork chops. Michelle arrived at "Coffee" that Saturday at nine. She didn't quite understand what had drawn her there, maybe curiosity to see how things would unfold, maybe the rush of adrenaline. She had been through a failed marriage, one she'd leaped into after only six months, choosing the first available slot at city hall. The marriage was fraught with all those small and large issues that grew each day like yeast until it all boiled over in infidelity. He had cheated on her, but in truth, it no longer mattered.

"I don't want to be your wife anymore" - she had told him then, and he'd only shrugged and said, offhandedly:

"Yeah, I'd gladly walk away from this marriage too."

The separation went smoothly, without any mudslinging. Michelle had briefly considered wallowing in self-pity but ultimately let it go. Sometimes freedom is worth far more than pointless bitterness.

A few months later, she met Steve, and once again, she fell too fast. The next marriage never stood a chance; she knew it but gave in when he pressed her, figuring maybe she owed herself one more shot, even though she wasn't eager to start a family and wasn't even certain of her feelings. Her epiphany arrived as she walked down the church aisle in a white dress to the sentimental strains of Ave Maria.

"No! Just no!" - she declared aloud, then unpinned her veil and walked out of the church. She felt as though she'd woken from a deep sleep, realizing at last that happiness could be found elsewhere - not necessarily in another marriage.

She resolved to be open to new relationships but wouldn't let herself be caught and locked into another cage of love too quickly. She wanted to sample various flavours first before settling on just one. She wanted to learn how to be alone, to embrace solitude and enjoy her own company in bed. Was that dishonest?

Perhaps a little selfish, maybe even narcissistic, but Michelle had no ill intentions and didn't want to hurt anyone. She liked them both - Fabi and Alex. The former was decisive and witty, the latter romantic and sensitive. Yet in their own way, they were very similar.

And maybe she'd sent the first signal to Alex without realizing it. He responded just as he should.

"Beautiful day" - she said, smiling at Alex that Saturday when she came to "Coffee" alone. Fabi didn't know.

Alex reached under the counter and pulled out a bouquet of lovely pale blue and pink flowers.

"Oh my gosh, they're beautiful!" - she exclaimed with genuine delight.

"Lisianthus" - Alex said.

"What?" - she replied, a bit confused.

"Apparently, it's native to the prairies from Nebraska all the way down to Texas."

"This is one of the most gorgeous bouquets I've ever received" - she said, still smiling. "Though I've never heard that name before."

"Feel like going on a picnic?" - Alex asked, surprising even himself with the invitation.

She hesitated for a while.

"Do you know a good spot?"

"Absolutely, but it's a surprise. You'll see."

Alex packed a thermos of coffee, two cups, a few cookies, two apples, and two small bottles of orange juice he'd brought. He grabbed a sweater from the back and asked the other barista to cover his shift. Then he and Michelle got in the car and drove a full thirty kilometres out of town before stopping.

"Can you tell me what a 'Neapolitan flip' is? Fabi mentioned you have something like that in the café."

He laughed.

"It's a simple two-chamber pot where you boil water in the lower section and then flip the whole thing upside down. The hot water filters through the coffee into the upper chamber, which is, of course, now on the bottom. Hope that made sense. I'll show you sometime."

Michelle leaned on her elbow.

"And what kind of coffee are we drinking now?"

"Colombian Medellín Supremo. Prepare yourself for an unforgettable blend of fruit, chocolate, and caramel."

Michelle lifted her cup to her lips.

"Delicate, but very aromatic."

"Can you taste the chocolate?"

"Maybe? Hold on, let me close my eyes."

Alex wanted nothing more than to taste the leftover coffee on Michelle's lips, but he knew that would likely ruin everything. Besides, he felt he shouldn't. Even if Michelle wasn't officially Fabi's girlfriend yet, there was no denying his friend's intentions toward her.

"You're right; I think I can sense a faint hint of chocolate" - Michelle agreed. – "Is this Arabica?"

He nodded.

"Do you know why it's called Medellín?" - he asked. "It's a small town located in the central Andes. There's a small company there known worldwide for its high-quality coffee production. The coffee cherries are harvested from September to December, and fermentation takes place at night. I don't know how it affects the flavour, but they clearly know what they're doing. It's one of the best coffees I've ever had."

Michelle licked her lips.

"Can I kiss you?" - Alex suddenly asked.

She chuckled, tossing her coppery, slightly curly hair back over her shoulder. The stronger the sun shone on it, the more it gleamed in shades of gold, orange, and chestnut. Her eyes, flecked with dark spots, were a soft green. She looked at Alex in a way that made him immediately understand her answer. He also thought that maybe this picnic was a turning point, a sign, and a hint for her.

Sometimes people lose their way and wander, and it only takes a small sign to find the right path again.

Mistakes in love happen... or so Alex believed.

But then came the ice-skating trip. Skating, on the other hand, was Fabi's idea - just as spontaneous and slightly wild. It was as if a child had suddenly awakened in him, one with that wonderful knack for instantly fulfilling its own whims. He didn't know, of course, about the picnic or the kiss. Nor did he yet suspect that anything might have transpired between Alex and Michelle. Surely, he thought, with so many women out there - and especially those who frequented Alex's café - there was someone out there who'd caught his friend's eye.

He never guessed it might be Michelle.

"I can't skate" - she admitted.

To be honest, that's exactly what Fabi had hoped. He wanted to help her, hold her, catch her as she wobbled, and teach her the ropes. He pictured them skating hand in hand, laughing and clinging to each other, maybe even inviting her back to his place afterward for some mulled wine. Sometimes dreams don't come true, no matter how carefully laid out, but that night, every detail unfolded perfectly, and he even got a few bonus moments. Michelle drank her mulled wine at Fabi's apartment, then had another. She shed her sweater, her pants, and sat on the couch in her tank top and underwear. Then Fabi took off the rest, and they made love three times in a row before finally falling asleep on the floor together. But this wasn't a fairy tale, where you only sleep with the one you love and remain faithful to them forever. Two days later, Michelle slept with Alex too.

And she still didn't know whom to choose.

Neither of them realized they were fighting for the same prize.

Of course, it came out by accident - as things usually do. Or perhaps it wasn't an accident. Maybe Alex was ready to confess. Talking to Fabi about Michelle had lost its charm. He didn't want to hear about their dates, what they did, where they went, or what they ate for breakfast.

Though breakfast was actually the tipping point.

"Michelle loves mango with…"

"… oatmeal," Alex finished without thinking.

Fabi looked at him, first with surprise, then with growing fear, and finally, with anger.

"I don't even want to know how you know that" - was all he said.

Alex began setting cups on the shelf, clinking them together too loudly and too hard. It was no surprise when two of them cracked.

"How many breakfasts have you shared with her?" - Fabi asked through gritted teeth.

Alex shrugged.

"I haven't been counting. But each one is like a holiday."

"You son of a bitch."

Alex started breathing heavily through his nose, rubbing his forehead nervously.

"I love her" - he forced out, struggling to admit it.

"You!?" - Fabi shouted.

"Yes. Me too. Do I not have the right?"

"I'm not giving her up."

"She should decide that, shouldn't she? She's not your property."

"I don't care. I'm not giving her up, even if it means the worst."

Alex grabbed a cup and threw it against the wall.

"Do you think it's easy for me? That I planned this and am enjoying it?"

Fabi walked up to Alex, grabbed him by the collar.

"I don't care if it's easy, hard, or hell for you. I'm not giving her up."

Then he left.

Since that fight, they barely saw each other. Each tried to act like they had things under control, but each continued to see Michelle. Both hoped that some decision would come soon. It was not a good time. Alex missed Fabi - missed their nights at the café when it was empty, and they'd talk until late. Sometimes they'd comment on the latest episodes of *Game of Thrones* or *House of Cards* with Alex's snoring dog in the background, reminiscing or just sitting and sipping wine after the café was closed to customers.

"I have a beer campaign on my plate, and here I am, drinking wine. This has got to be a bad idea" - Fabi laughed.

"Who knows?" - Alex replied. "We get about the same pleasure from either one."

"Wine is more refined, though - it doesn't leave you with a burp" - Fabi noted.

"There's a thought. Maybe we should convince people that beer is refined and sophisticated too. That drinking it doesn't have to mean you have a beer belly and eat greasy sausages."

"Do they have beer experts who test flavours? You know, like coffee has baristas and wine has sommeliers."

"There's someone like that" - Fabi raised a finger. " A *cervesario!*"

Alex laughed.

"Brilliant. A *cervesario,* a beer taster and connoisseur who opens up the world of hops for you."

"Perfect" - Fabi agreed. "I'll go exactly with that. I'll tell the client that every beer has a unique story, its own colours, foams, tastes, aromas, varieties of malt, and pouring techniques. Drinking beer can be a sensory experience. Thanks, old friend - you never let me down." - Fabi patted Alex on the shoulder, and the two of them finished the bottle of wine, from which an excellent beer campaign was born.

But those days were over. Now, with Michelle in the picture, Alex forgot about the whole world, thinking only of how he could win her heart.

And how to surprise her next Saturday.

Maybe with a speakeasy bar? Alex had heard about them before but had never been to one. Fortunately, a café customer who loved his espresso with ground cardamom so much had tipped him off to a "place for insiders only" as a reward. It was the perfect idea for a memorable night - one where he could impress Michelle, show her something original, and take her on a unique date. Maybe it would give him an edge.

He knew this competition was foolish, pointless, childish. And that Michelle's choice shouldn't be a matter of successful dates, better gifts, or clever courtship. Yet he couldn't stop competing, as if he needed to prove to the world that if he wanted something, he could win it.

"What's this place?" - she asked, smiling in a way that immediately made Alex lose his head. It was probably those dimples in her cheeks.

"A bar with good wine. They only take in about forty people, but it's rare to see that many at once. They don't advertise, no press releases, no sponsored articles. It's the kind of place only a few people know about. It's all word of mouth."

"How's that?" - Michelle looked at him curiously.

"These are hidden spots. You only get in if you meet certain requirements or know the special password."

"And you meet the requirements?"

"The requirements? I don't know. "- He laughed. "But I know the password. And I have a rough idea where it is." - He winked.

"So, does the entrance to these places also stay disguised?"

"Indeed. Some have entrances through tattoo studios, basements, or Vietnamese restaurants. For others, you might go through a barber's shop. Not sure if they have secret labyrinths or puzzles, but it could be interesting."

Michelle bit her lip.

"Well, lead the way. I'll admit you've piqued my interest."

She looked stunning tonight. She wore a white top, a black skirt below her knee, white sneakers, and a canvas backpack. She was part innocent girl, part confident, attractive woman - a combination that many men would die for. Alex was one of them.

But so was Fabi.

Tonight, however, she was with Alex, and he would do whatever it took to make it unforgettable. The mysterious bar was located near an old, unused slaughterhouse. First, they had to pass through a few empty rooms, then squeeze through a narrow opening in a wall, and finally come to a staircase leading down.

"It's a bit gloomy here, but I guess that's the idea" - Michelle whispered.

Alex squeezed her hand tighter in silent reassurance.

"You'll like it" - he said with a confidence he didn't quite feel as he had no idea what to expect. But when you want to impress a woman, you sometimes have to stick your head in the lion's mouth.

"Password?" - asked a tall man dressed in black.

"Piglet" - Alex replied.

The man opened the door for them.

Alex walked in first and let out a sigh of relief. Inside was a large room with leather sofas, plush armchairs, and metal tables, all bathed in a smoky glow and softened by low music. In the centre there was a round bar with a giant espresso machine and a massive samovar. But the walls were the real highlight - some were lined with shelves filled with books, while others held recessed shelves displaying rows of aging wine bottles. As they entered, the guests didn't even glance their way. Everyone was engrossed in their own world.

A waiter appeared shortly after and led them to a table by the wine wall. Michelle sank into the plush armchair and reached for Alex's hand.

"I love it" - she said, and he felt the same blissful warmth he had felt when he'd first tasted Nutella pancakes.

There was an inscription on their table: *"Wine is the loveliest smile on a table."* They ordered Gewürztraminer, a semi-dry white wine from Alsace with notes of lychee, passion fruit, pineapple, mango, rose petals, orange zest, ginger, mint, cloves, and pepper.

"Where did the idea for these places come from?" - Michelle looked around, curiosity glowing on her pleasantly flushed cheeks, her lips moist from the wine.

All Alex could think of was kissing her.

" It all began during Prohibition, which had one main benefit - it was the golden age of bartending and clever ways to hide alcohol in drinks with the strangest names. Of course, these drinks were enjoyed in bars that few people knew about and could only enter by referral or secret password."

"And the name, *speakeasy*?"

"That has its own story. Legend says it was coined by a bartender named Kate Hester, who ran a bar near Pittsburgh. When her customers got too loud, she'd hush them, saying, 'Speak easy, boys! Speak easy!'"

Michelle was thrilled, and Alex was simply happy.

But a response wasn't long in coming.

Fabi scoured every possible website and blog for ways to impress a woman and finally settled on an urban game with Poznan as the board. Some mental effort, a little physical exertion, sparked curiosity, and a dash of adrenaline - part flash mob, part scavenger hunt, part video game, and part adventure trail. He knew it could captivate even those new to it. Though urban games worked best with larger groups, Fabi preferred a two-person team. They would create the tasks for each other, and the winner would get to decide on the prize.

"Give me your phone; I'll download a start card for you. It'll help us on our hunt, but the rest is up to you." - He winked at her.

Michelle was immediately hooked. They spent the entire day chasing after Otto III's stolen crown, which would have prevented the coronation of Bolesław the Brave, retracing the steps of the Greater Poland Uprising, following the sculptures of the Castle District, and finally making their way through Ostrow Tumski, the birthplace of Poland.

"I'm exhausted" - Michelle admitted that evening as they reached Lake Malta and sat by the shore.

"A good kind of exhausted?" - Fabi asked.

"I never realized how interesting this city could be. I've lived here for a while, but my knowledge was mostly limited to the Old Market Square and the goats" – shew admitted honestly. "It's been a really good day". - She smiled at him warmly, and they kissed, lying on the grass until the first hint of cold nudged them up.

Of course, Michelle went back to Fabi's place. After all, they were adults with no obligations, and her indecision didn't need to interfere with natural, healthy intimacy. Yes, she had a twinge of guilt, but she quickly silenced it, reasoning that a final decision needed a strong foundation. She had endured too many disappointments. One wrong choice was understandable, but making the same mistake over and over only proved that you were blind and hadn't learned a thing.

She decided to approach this like buying a new car. After all, everyone takes a test drive and tries out different models before settling on the one they want.

Summer had passed, September had come, but nothing changed between Alex, Fabian, and Michelle. Their world had become a bubble of unspoken thoughts, unanswered questions, unsettling feelings, and the hope that things would somehow resolve themselves. It was an odd triangle where each of them was, in some way, both happy and unhappy. Laughter mixed with tears, good days with restless nights - or maybe it was the other way around.

Michelle was sitting on a park bench while Fabi stood in front of her, reenacting movie scenes for her to guess.

"I have no idea… *Silence of the Lambs*?"

"Exactly, my dear. You're absolutely unbeatable at this. How about this one?"

Fabi stood with his legs apart, giving Michelle a sombre look. He narrowed his eyes, then suddenly lifted his hands as if reaching for something behind his back, miming a weapon.

"I take it you're fighting someone?"

He nodded.

"You're the good guy?"

Another nod.

Michelle squinted.

"You're good, but you seem rather gloomy. You don't smile. Someone from *Game of Thrones*?"

He shook his head.

"Not enough clues" - she said.

He flexed his muscles and placed a scarf on his head.

"Is that supposed to be hair?"

He smiled.

Oh, so you have long hair. Could you maybe make a sound? Just a little something?

Fabi let out a deep "Hmm," and Michelle clapped her hands and burst out laughing.

"You should have started with that. *The Witcher.* "

Fabi's mood darkened suddenly.

"What's wrong?" - Michelle asked.

"Just tell me - why are you seeing Alex, too?"

She blushed.

"I like him."

"But it's messed up, don't you think? You can't see two guys at once!

"Why not?" - she replied, a hint of challenge in her voice.

Fabi was momentarily stunned.

"Because… because I was first!" - he finally managed to say, a completely hopeless argument.

Naturally, she burst into laughter.

"Because we're monogamous" - he tried again.

"We? People?" - she was astonished. "We're not. It's more of a wish than reality."

He shook his head.

"Damn it, this can't go on forever. You have to choose someone!"

Michelle stood up.

"I'll let you know when I've made my decision, I promise" - she said through gritted teeth, adding that he didn't need to walk her home.

Fabi kicked a rock lying in front of him with all his might.

The next morning, Alex called her.

"I've prepared a special blend of three different coffees with some orange zest and dark chocolate shavings."

"That sounds so good; I want to try it right now. Are you at "Coffee"?"

"No, still at my place."

"Can I come over?"

That's exactly what Alex was hoping - for a breakfast together, a coffee together, and maybe more. Michelle was thinking along the same lines. She liked mornings like this with men who were willing to make her a special coffee, run out for fresh rolls and strawberries. They were a little smaller and less red now, but they still tasted like summer. The best part was the feeling of being someone longed for, someone anticipated. When Alex looked at her, the world closed in around that look. And she could see it. But then, she'd meet up with Fabi again, and her mind would spin all over.

Both men were different from anyone she had known before - especially from her ex-husband. Alex and Fabi were genuinely fascinated by her, without any pretence, clumsy pickup lines, or awkward jokes. Sometimes she felt they were like one entity split into two. They thought alike, saw the world in similar ways, even smiled in a similar way. She used to think choosing between twins would be the hardest. Fabi and Alex were even more complicated. They looked in the same direction and shared each other's feelings. She knew the situation couldn't last forever, but she had no idea how to resolve it. Fabi had every right to be angry, she knew that. But making a choice was just too hard, maybe even impossible.

Because Fabi and Alex were like a word you just couldn't break into syllables.

What will they do when they learn the truth?

***

September, almost unnoticed, slipped into October - slightly damp but still rich with autumn colours. It was a Wednesday afternoon, a routine day that had started with light rain but finally cleared up around four.

Fabi burst into "Coffee" just before three, practically tumbling through the door like a snowball. It had been a while since he'd shown up, so Alex was all the more surprised, but he immediately realized this wasn't a friendly visit.

311

"This whole situation is completely messed up. Back off" - Fabi said, not even bothering with a greeting.

"I can't" - Alex admitted. "I tried, but I can't."

Fabi slammed his fist on the counter.

"I met her first, and since she can't decide, it's up to us. If one of us backs off, the problem's solved."

"You could back off, too."

"No" - Fabi shook his head.

"See?"

"Damn it, man, let's stop playing games here, seriously. Let's act like adults. I was first. She can't decide, so you back off. Do you hear me? Back off! "-Fabi shouted.

Alex turned away, pretending to clean the espresso machine. Deep down, he knew that Fabi's proposal was the only reasonable solution and that he did, after all, want his friend back. But he couldn't, he just couldn't. If everyone says that love is the foundation of the world, then why should he give it up willingly?

Wasn't friendship supposed to be based on loyalty, not fear or blackmail? Why should he give up just to go back to watching *Game of Thrones* together?

"No" - he repeated, clenching his fists.

Fabi stormed out of "Coffee" at 3:20 p.m., resolved to end this damn friendship, and that from now on, he wouldn't play fair. You have to choose the right weapon for the battle. Meanwhile, Alex decided he'd go to Fabi's place that evening and calmly explain his side. Even if it meant they'd never see each other again.

That was his plan.

That same day, at six, Alex sat frozen on the hospital floor, unable to move. "Time is muscle," the doctor had told him. The longer an artery stays blocked, the more heart muscle dies, and there's only so much time to save it - two hours, maybe five. After that, the heart stops. The doctor had also mentioned that, in Poland, nearly two hundred thousand people die of heart attacks every year. This year, Fabi was one of them.

Two months had passed, yet the world wasn't the same. Not for Alex, and not for

Michelle either. Time moved on, sometimes slowly, sometimes quickly, with days and hours blending into an indefinite blur. Alex went to the café daily, functioning on autopilot - he talked to customers without really hearing their questions, brewed coffee, cleaned equipment, took orders, and meticulously tidied up each evening. He wanted as little free time as possible so he wouldn't have to think about his friend, whose last words to him were: "Back off!"

If only he'd known the day, the hour… if only someone had whispered, "This is the last time you see him."

"And what would I have done?"- he asked aloud. "Shut my mouth and been nice? Hugged him? Said something meaningful?"

The worst part was the guilt and the ache of knowing that nothing could be explained anymore. Fabi had vanished from his life in an instant. And then Michelle had vanished, too - although that might have been his subconscious wish. Maybe he blamed her. Maybe he thought that if it weren't for her, for her hesitation and indecision, everything would be different now.

Or maybe they were both to blame and instinctively avoided each other to ease the hurt.

Alex tried to relive every moment of that last meeting with his friend. To remember what Fabi looked like, what he was wearing. Was it a jacket or a coat? Sneakers or slip-on loafers?

"Probably a black puffer jacket. And black jeans" - he whispered in his sleep, then repeated it in the morning, squeezing his eyes shut so tightly it hurt, hoping to remember every detail.

But that day had been filled with anger, and anger almost always wears black. Alex slept worse and worse, and when he finally drifted into half-sleep, he saw images from childhood. The red tights, the toy excavator, the watering can, the pastries they ate for dessert, the old jungle gym in the yard, whistle lollipops, colouring books, and the imported markers Fabi's aunt had sent him from Germany. Then the playground with wooden swings and the cemetery where they'd go to collect chestnuts. They weren't bad dreams, but when he woke, Alex couldn't shake the crushing pain in his chest. Like something was pressing him down, stopping him from breathing.

He'd take a cold shower, down an espresso, and try to get through another day. Twice he dialled Michelle's number and twice hung up before she answered. He didn't know what he wanted to say to her, wasn't even sure he wanted to hear her voice. Avoiding her was safer, although he sometimes missed her like mad.

And he immediately punished himself for it in his thoughts. Now even more than ever.

In the café, it was quiet. No surprise there. It was the day before Christmas Eve, Saturday, seven in the morning. People were still in bed or out walking their dogs in the early light. Alex stared at a wooden plaque hanging on the wall, one of five that Fabi had given him as a gift. Each was inscribed with a coffee fact, which Alex had once thought was a brilliant touch.

And he still did.

"In 1511, coffee was banned in Mecca. People believed it incited radical thought and idleness."

And on another:

"Beethoven was such a devoted coffee lover that he counted out sixty beans per cup before brewing."

He thought for a while.

How is it possible that one moment can undo everything? People hate surprises; they prefer to have the last word. If he'd known it would end like this, would he have tried to change things? Could he have willingly given up Michelle?

"Good morning, are you open so early?" - A woman stood at the café door.

"In December, yes. Hard to believe, but lots of people come by even before seven," Alex replied out of habit, though it wasn't true. "As if they can't sleep.

The woman smiled slightly and ordered a vanilla drink."

"Should I add cinnamon?" - he asked, then threw in a cinnamon cookie for good measure. "On the house."

Of course, cinnamon. After all, it was almost Christmas.

Fabi sometimes drank coffee with cinnamon.

"What's your name?" - the woman asked.

"Alex."

"You look like something's weighing on you...?"

"More like eating me up. But..."

Was it that obvious? He didn't want to talk about it. He didn't want to talk to anyone about it.

The woman smiled, as if she understood his thoughts, took her drink and cookie, and quietly closed the door behind her.

Alex considered for a moment whether he should close "Coffee" for the day; he didn't feel like letting any more customers in, talking to them, or pretending to be excited about the holidays. Christmas Eve could disappear for all he cared. It would be best if someone could erase it from the calendar, move it, or even remove it altogether. How could people feel joy in those lights, trees, gingerbread, and dumplings floating in borscht?

✳✳✳

He could still see the funeral in his mind. Initially, he hadn't wanted to go, thinking he would say goodbye to Fabi in his own way. But he'd ended up going to the church, sitting in the last pew, and zoning out completely. He didn't want to hear stories about someone he knew better than anyone else there. He didn't want to participate in the sorrow, regret, and grief, in those pompous speeches over the black urn that didn't suit his friend at all.

"Honestly, Fabi, you really thought this one through. Damn heart" - he muttered under his breath when everyone had already left, driven off, and said their goodbyes to Fabi at that miserable cemetery.

Michelle hadn't come. He even understood. And he was glad to finally be alone, to stand under a tree, talk to himself, curse, yell, until eventually, in a very unmanly way, he simply broke down and cried. He really didn't care anymore. And what bothered him the most was the fact that every question he'd had for Fabi would now forever remain unanswered.

319

"You messed this up, man. You can't just walk out of life without leaving a full stop. Couldn't you give me a heads-up? Somehow let me know we didn't have as much time as we thought? You were my best friend, and you took off as if we were strangers. As if you were someone I never knew. Damn it, how could you do this to me?"

Alex walked over to the door and locked it. He lowered the blinds, turned off the radio and the espresso machine. He also turned off the lights. The café would be closed. Most people were already immersed in cheesecakes, gingerbread, dumplings, and beet soup anyway. If anyone wanted coffee, they'd have to look somewhere else.

He glanced at the wooden signs.

"In ancient Arab culture, a woman could divorce her husband only if he disliked the coffee she made."

He smiled sadly, throwing on a jacket over his black sweater.

He walked to the back and yanked open the door, stepping outside. The air felt thick, almost stifling. The café was tucked behind a small square, just a patch of grass, a few barberry bushes, and a single tree - a birch.

A bench stood beneath it. Metal, a little chipped, black. He sat down and stared at the first snowflakes falling from the sky. He missed Fabi. And Michelle. But he couldn't bring himself to call her, and she had remained silent too.

Everything fell quiet, as if the whole world had suddenly hushed - even the traffic.

But someone was there.

"Hey, Alex. We've got an hour. I don't know if it'll be enough, but it's more than nothing - said Fabi, who had taken a seat at the other end of the bench."

Alex swallowed.

"Good entrance. I have to say, you surprised me. I don't even know where to start. Should I launch into an epic on friendship or maybe an elegy on death? None of this should've happened in the first place" - he said quietly.

Fabi shrugged. He was wearing black jeans, a black puffy jacket, and blue sneakers.

Wasn't that the outfit he'd been wearing the day he died?

"And why not?" - Fabi asked now. "We're not the first guys on this planet to fall in love with the same woman. I think our story is actually pretty ordinary, even predictable. For us, it was a traged - Shakespearean even - but to anyone else? The world has seen much worse."

"I could've backed off" - Alex whispered.

"Or I could have. But neither of us knew I'd get this damned heart attack as a parting gift from life. I never even had heart issues. Then again, I'd never been to a cardiologist either. You don't go to the doctor unless you're actually suffering. At least, that's how it always was with me. Remember when I nearly died from a toothache? Finally had to face my fear and go to the dentist. No other option. - He laughed. -But a heart? That never crossed my mind."

Alex tried to smile, but it came out more as a twisted grimace.

"Will you see her?"- Fabi asked suddenly.

"I can't. She hasn't reached out to me either. Maybe we both feel guilty."

"That's pretty stupid. My heart attack was caused by damaged plaque, not by us liking the same woman."

"But it stressed you out. And that meant your heart didn't get enough oxygen. Everything has a starting point. One small pebble can trigger an avalanche, you know that."

Fabi waved it off.

"Not always. And I don't think my heart attack had anything to do with it. Look, I was pissed at you - no, I was properly furious. I wanted to punch you, but I knew it wouldn't change anything. I think we just went a little crazy. Somehow, we both wanted this competition. We each wanted to prove we were better. There had never been any conflicts or grudges between us before - nothing. Maybe that's why we ended up going for each other's throats, to see who had the sharper teeth. Did I tell you I took her ice skating? The last time I skated was in elementary school. But I wanted to impress her, show her I was this amazing alpha male, and that with me, she could do anything -

jump, dance, fly, swim. My calves were sore for two weeks, but it was worth it."

"I took her on a picnic to the woods. With coffee, birds chirping, and the sound of the trees. We even found a little stream, and we waded in it, holding hands. Like something out of a Fałat painting. I almost started reciting poetry."

Fabi snapped his fingers.

"And I took her on a city adventure game. We racked up tens of thousands of steps around Poznań, running through the trails of the Greater Poland Uprising and hunting down sculptures. We even found old wall fragments that once marked a moat filled by Bogdanka ice rink. Ever heard of that?"

Alex shook his head, raising his brows in surprise.

"Never would have thought of that. Did she enjoy it?"

"A lot. I did too, and I'm hardly a history buff. But with her, everything felt different."

"I took her to a *speakeasy*."

Fabi whistled in admiration.

"Where's that place?"

"Hidden in an old slaughterhouse."

"Huh, I have to admit, I'm impressed" - Fabi said. "I'd always wanted to try something like that, but I didn't know where to look. Too bad we never went to a place like that together."

Alex lowered his head.

"Yeah, too bad…"

"What else did you guys do?"

"We took a cooking class, too."

"No way!" - Fabi exclaimed. "As far as I know, Michelle's not exactly a whiz in the kitchen."

"Well, she's gotten a lot better now. We stuffed pasta shells with homemade pesto. From sun-dried tomatoes and an insane number of herbs I didn't even know existed. We also made chicken breast with a raspberry sauce, stuffed with spinach and blue cheese. It looked amazing on the plate - red, green, and golden-brown chicken."

"Mmm" - Fabi smacked his lips.

"Wait…you still feel hunger?" - Alex asked, surprised.

"No" - Fabi replied thoughtfully. "But it sounded really good. No wonder she wanted to keep seeing you. I'd invite myself to a dinner like that. I, on the other hand, took her to a rather unusual photo shoot. None of that fake studio posing; it was spontaneous, start to finish. We went to an abandoned factory in Wilda. I brought some old cardboard, tacked it up on the wall, and drew a plane, a car, a palm tree, a deck chair - even a speedboat. Then we arranged ourselves to look like we were lying under a palm tree or sitting in a car. I haven't had that much fun in ages. No money spent, no fancy dinners at upscale restaurants."

"Nice" - Alex admitted. "I bet she loved it."

"It was the first time I had so much fun with a woman. And while planning each date was sometimes stressful, it was worth it. Much better than the usual parties, coffee dates, movies, and city strolls - except for that urban game, of course. And for the first time, I felt like I genuinely cared. Like I was doing it, not just to impress her or get a compliment, but because I actually wanted to be with her."- Fabi said.

"It was the same for me" - Alex admitted quietly. "Remember Doris? I think I was the closest I'd ever been to falling in love with her, but something always bothered me. I couldn't fully accept her; she often annoyed me until I started finding excuses to avoid our dates. I thought it was something wrong with me, but after I met Michelle, I understood what unconditional love really was. Not for something, not because of anything in particular, but despite all her flaws and quirks. With Doris, I forced myself to accept things that annoyed me. I didn't like her laugh, the way she wolfed down popcorn at the movies, or her constant complaints about how boring soccer was. I couldn't stand her pet fish either, with those ridiculous names - Isabella, Marcella, and Donatella."

Fabi burst into laughter.

"I remember you hid from her in my bathtub. I think you pretended to be dead"- He winked at his friend.

They were twenty-three then. Alex had started dating a girl from university, mainly because she'd been so persistent. He'd figured it was high time he fell in love, experienced romance, maybe even sex, and perhaps entered into what people called a "relationship." Doris was uncomplicated, cheerful, and talked nonstop. But that had its charm because he didn't have to worry about the conversation. Usually, she'd chatter away while he quietly zoned out, minute by minute.

After a while, though, he realized that even though the intimacy was good and Doris was lovely, he felt stifled in the relationship. He needed breathing room. Once, he'd actually hidden out at Fabi's place, going completely off the grid for three days. Doris eventually came looking for him, naturally starting with his best friend's place. The moment Alex heard her voice, he darted into the bathroom, locked the door, climbed into the tub, and lay there motionless until she left to search elsewhere.

"Man, I told you there was no future there," Fabi laughed half an hour later, just for fun, turning on the cold tap.

"I wanted to kill you" - Alex admitted. "I was already cramped from lying in that rock-hard tub, and then you doused me in freezing water."

"But to make up for it, I went and talked to Doris. I told her you weren't cut out for everlasting love and that you might even join the priesthood. That's when she finally let go, though she really wanted to know if you had a specific order in mind."

"What did you tell her?"

"That you were leaning toward the Camaldolese monks since it's a cloistered order. You know, no going outside the monastery walls, no TV, no phones, no outside world. She figured you were totally unhinged and moved on to a guy a year ahead of us."

Alex looked at Fabi with admiration.

"I had no idea."

Friendship is sometimes absurdly fascinating. A boundary between grotesque and drama.

Fabi sniffed and glanced at his friend.

"We've been through a lot together, so I'll tell you this: you can ask anything of a friend, but deep down, we both know what can't be asked. I had no right to demand that you let go, but I did because it pissed me off to see you going after something I thought was mine."

Alex started to tug at the edge of his black sweater.

"We both got completely twisted up" - he finally admitted. "We put our friendship on the line without hesitation. And before this, we were solid. We had each other's backs against all those jerks in preschool, learned to ride bikes together, built forts, accidentally set the rug on fire, and even went through puberty at the same time. That bonded us more than any war."

"I remember that rug" - Fabi brightened up. "Didn't we cut it to shreds first, or am I getting things mixed up?"

"Pretty much. We were building a bird feeder in your apartment, and for some reason, we cut all the wood on top of the rug, practically turning it into a giant puzzle. Then, to cover up the cuts, we figured we'd set it on fire. Seemed like a solid plan- except that if your dad hadn't stepped in, the whole apartment might've gone up in flames" - Alex recalled.

Fabi chuckled.

"Lucky for us, he put it out with pickle soup."

"Indeed" - Alex laughed too. "He thought filling a bucket with water would take too long, so he grabbed the first thing he could find - a pot of soup - and poured it right over the rug."

"When Mom saw it, she was sure we'd lost our minds. She swore she'd sooner eat a rat than leave us alone again. But she liked the bird feeder, and we avoided any punishment because everyone thought it was just a freak accident."

"We never confessed" - Alex noted.

Fabi drifted into thought.

"Guess we should be proud of keeping our friendship strong all these years. Women would've argued a hundred times by now, made up, and still thrown each other the occasional jab. Men just don't work like that. And we managed to destroy it."

"Did you ever try to talk to Michelle about it?" - Alex asked.

"You mean, did I ever ask her why she couldn't choose? Why she went back and forth between us? - He shook his head. - Honestly, I was afraid of the answer. I figured maybe she just needed time, so I tried to keep myself in the running, hoping she'd pick me. And I didn't want to push her. I just started doing things for her."

"You painted her kitchen?"

"And you fixed her shower."

"You built her a shoe rack."

"And you transformed an old fence into a bookshelf. I actually liked that one."

"You planted tomatoes together?"

"And you rigged up that hammock on her balcony. Hats off, you pulled it off" - Fabi admitted.

They looked at each other and burst out laughing. It all seemed funny now, though back then they'd been desperate, scoring as many points as possible with Michelle.

"Total high school stuff" - Fabi sighed.

"If we told anyone about this, they'd think we'd lost it. They'd assume Michelle was playing us, but she wasn't. We were the ones who turned it into a duel, like two roosters fighting over one hen. A rooster drama in two acts."

"Would you believe I even considered adopting a dog from a shelter? – Fabi asked. "Probably just because you had one, and I didn't want to fall behind."

Alex looked at him, surprised.

"You've never even liked dogs. You barely ever played with Kayden. I remember once you threw him the Frisbee three times, and when he came back the fourth time, you tried to explain to him that he was crazy and you were exhausted."

"Exactly. I'd have no time - or patience - for a dog of my own. But I figured she'd find it touching. I even planned on adopting an old, sick one." - He covered his face with his hands.

"On one hand, that's pretty noble; on the other, it's kind of calculated. What happened? Why didn't you go through with it?"

"He died before I could arrange things with the shelter" - Fabi admitted. " It was selfish of me, honestly. I wasn't really thinking about the dog, only about how Michelle would react. I wanted to impress her, to show I could care for something, that I wasn't just a selfish jerk. The dog's death felt… symbolic, like even he was trying to tell me something. That's when I realized I was just going in circles, all to prove I was better than you."

"You had worthy competition. I was out there fighting for the gold, too. We weren't just roosters - we were like two dancing blackcocks. Someone watching from the outside would've had a good laugh. All those silent battles, these ridiculous romantic-comedy stunts. But without a happy ending."

The snow began to fall more heavily, turning the once-green park and the small berberis bush and birch tree completely white. It was like a dreamlike stage set for a lost hour.

Fabi gazed at the swirling snowflakes.

"I like snow. Remember the competition for the most interesting snow sculpture? That was second grade, I think. Everyone went for snowmen, castles, and igloos, but we made a crocodile" - Fabi recalled.

"A crocodile mother and her baby. It had a long tail that curled around three times. We really impressed them; we got everyone's votes. That was probably the first time no one made fun of our names, and they let the usual jabs go. We were heroes for the rest of the day. And as a reward, we got excused from two homework assignments. I don't remember if I even took advantage of that because I think I actually liked homework" - Alex said thoughtfully.

"I definitely did. I'd rather play instead. You have to admit, though, I was the Mastermind champion. No one could guess the colours and peg positions like I could."

"I beat you once, but that didn't end well; you swallowed a peg out of shock."

"The red one" - Fabi remarked. "I know because it eventually… made a reappearance."

They both laughed.

"Did you know there's a town in Norway called Hell that freezes over almost every winter?" - Fabi asked.

"And I heard about a frog that freezes in winter - its heart stops, blood flow ceases, and its eyes go white. In summer, it defrosts and starts living again" - Alex added.

For a moment, it felt like the old days. Before everything had gotten so ridiculously tangled. Before she had appeared.

* * *

Michelle worked in the same building as Fabi, just two floors down. He was at the advertising agency; she was a secretary at a consulting firm.

"You know, I have always dreamt of this job" - she once told Alex. "As a little girl, I'd sneak staples, hole punchers, notebooks, and thumbtacks from my mom and pretend I was the lady managing all those treasures. I didn't even

336

know there was a name for this job. Some people think it's low ambition, but I love it. I actually have a bit of mini-authority. I decide meeting times, and I can order as many staples as I want, in whatever shape I like. Recently, I bought some in the shape of animals. The most important documents are held by dog staples, the less urgent ones by cats, and the ones you can forget about for a while by parrots."

Alex found himself captivated by her voice. Calm and low, without a trace of squeak or shrillness. Michelle had a natural serenity that was hard to ruffle. She claimed that even her husband's infidelity and their subsequent divorce didn't hurt as much as they should have. When her lawyer explained her rights, she realized she didn't need any of it. She didn't want the house, the furniture, the kitchen island, or even the groomed garden. Unlike her husband's new partner, who had already moved in before Michelle had time to pack her things. There wasn't much - just a few boxes, two suitcases, three bags, a bike, and an old crystal chandelier she'd inherited from her grandmother.

"All right" - she had simply said. "All right."

A quick marriage, a quick divorce. A quick love that didn't work out.

She rented a small apartment in Jeżyce and immediately hung the chandelier, which was a bit too large for the space, but at least it gave her a sense of security.

Life felt just as it had before, running along as if on the same track, though Michelle knew she sometimes lost her way and didn't know how to get back without a compass. And then she met Fabi and Alex and lost herself even more.

It started with watching. Sometimes one, sometimes the other, comparing, assessing, weighing pros and cons. But when a decision can't be made, living two intimate lives begins to feel like straddling two parallel worlds. And you can't split yourself, dividing yourself into now and later, here and there. Sooner or later, the two worlds will intersect, and a choice will have to be made.

She knew that, yet couldn't bring herself to act on it.

Some say love is like a mirror. When everything flows harmoniously, the mirror is smooth, without cracks or scratches. But each crisis, each failure, every tragedy causes the mirror to shatter into pieces. In each shard, you still see yourself, but you can no longer piece the mirror back together as it was, as if some fragments are missing. Eventually, you realize you need different experiences and multiple loves to reassemble yourself. Maybe only then can you regain a sense of wholeness. But there will come a time when only one person and one love will define you, even if longings remain for things unfinished.

"Is there a dream I could make come true for you?" - Alex once asked Michelle. Two days later, Fabi asked her the same thing.

She didn't know what to say or whose vision of fulfilling dreams she liked more. She looked at each of them through the lens of past relationships; the less they reminded her of her exes, the better she felt. Yet she still couldn't mark either one as the clear winner.

Maybe neither was the ideal.

Or maybe both were.

When she discovered she was pregnant, she couldn't find the words. She had no idea who the father was, and, in truth, didn't want to know. She kept seeing both men, wondering how she could break the news to them - or if it wouldn't be better to just disappear. This would be her child, and hers alone. When you have two choices and can't decide, sometimes the third path turns out to be best. So that day, she packed a suitcase and resolved to move to the coast. Just like that, on a whim. Like a woman she'd once met on a train. They were alone in a compartment and simply started talking.

Tamara? Yes, Tamara.

She moved from place to place, refusing to stay put.

"Doesn't it tire you?" - Michelle had asked, astonished.

"Stagnation wears me out. Traveling lets me see everything from a different perspective."

That was exactly what she needed now - a fresh perspective. She wouldn't tell them. And she would never find out which of them was the father.

It was Wednesday afternoon. A regular day, beginning with a drizzle, but around four, the sky cleared.

And then Alex called...

Michelle listened to his message, then removed the SIM card from her phone, tossed it in the trash, and walked out, closing the door behind her with a resolute click.

***

"Did she ever tell you she loved you?" - Fabi asked.

Alex shook his head.

"No, never. But sometimes, she'd look at me in a way that made me feel extraordinary. In those moments, I was sure it was love."

"Same here. Sometimes I thought she'd finally chosen me. But then she'd go to 'Coffee,' you'd make her an espresso or a cinnamon cappuccino, and then show her this whole other world of yours. I'd feel her slipping away again, like I'd done something wrong, and I didn't know how to keep her from going back to you. There was something mesmerizing about her elusiveness, even though I knew I couldn't keep living like that. Every evening, I'd tell myself it was over, that I had to talk to her, and then by morning, I'd lose my resolve again, terrified she'd pick you after all."

"So we both just kept sinking deeper into this, letting anger and frustration build. I knew it was a bad path, but I couldn't stop" - Alex admitted, lowering his head.

Friendship between two grown men isn't as carefree as it is for kids. They both knew that well enough; they often marvelled at how seamlessly they fit, like knife and fork. Lock and key.

"Remember the day I forgot my sleeping bag on that camping trip?" - Fabi pointed a finger at Alex.

"How could I forget? We had to share one, and as natural as it seemed, I still had some issue with it - having to sleep snuggled up to another guy!"

Fabi laughed.

"The worst part was no one believed we weren't a couple. I was furious, especially since it ruined any chance of picking up girls."

Alex smirked.

"There were two nice ones there, friendly and pretty open-minded, remember? Every time we tried to chat them up, they'd just laugh and suggest a group manicure. I felt like an idiot."

"I think we handled it perfectly" - Fabi chuckled. "We accepted that for the duration of that trip, we were unofficially gay. At least it kept people off our backs. The upside to my absent-mindedness: we saved a ton since we didn't have to buy drinks for anyone!"

It had been one of those classic student trips: camping, low-budget, with cans of luncheon meat and backpacks, one of those unforgettable adventures that would always feel nostalgic and full of memories, even before they were over. That was when they'd promised each other their friendship would endure, that nothing and no one would tear it apart. If they could pretend to be an odd couple then, they'd survive anything.

"You know, the thing with love is that it overtakes you entirely. It drains out past promises, makes you forget the vows you made. Love's greedy because it truly takes everything. It doesn't hold back or play soft" - Alex hugged his knees, leaning forward. "In truth, that's how it should be - no second thoughts, no doubts. But it came at our expense. We gave up something we'd built for years in no time. I feel like a fool." - He looked down.

"I feel even worse. And, as it turned out, my heart literally gave out. Irony at its finest - like some cheap romance. But let me tell you something: I want you to keep seeing her. Our Michelle" - Fabi lowered his voice.

Alex shook his head firmly.

"Stop that, or you'll sprain your neck," Fabi teased, pretending to reach over to pat him on the back. "I'm serious. It's not about being magnanimous, or your feeling grateful. It'd be ridiculous to pile misfortune on misfortune just because of some stupid guilt trip. From where I am now, I can tell you with certainty - love is what matters, along with those days you feel happy, feel like dancing and singing, even if we look like fools doing it. Even if we're off-key and can't keep time. Because love is simple, and we're the ones who make it complicated. And besides… I love you, too."

Alex laughed.

"So, a gay love, then?"

"No, more like love for a best friend, the one you've always been."

Alex bent down and started packing a snowball.

"If I throw this at you, would you feel it?"

Fabi laughed.

"Don't dodge the question. But no, I wouldn't feel it much at all. I think you could set off an avalanche on me, and I'd probably just smile. It's a perk of this place - you don't die twice."

" I wish you were here."

"I am."

"For how long?"

Fabi looked at his watch.

"A good twenty minutes."

"And after that?"

His friend shrugged.

"Then you'll have to figure things out without me. And something tells me you'll be okay. Just don't get stubborn about it - call her."

Alex swallowed hard.

"I can't…" - he whispered.

"Then let me do it; just hand me your phone."

"You know that's not the point."

Fabi sighed.

"Alex, consider it a Christmas wish. Or a gift. Did you factor me into your holiday plans this year?"

Alex nodded.

"I was going to buy you a telescope for stargazing" - he admitted after a while.

"Ah, now that actually sounds nice. But I'm afraid it's not going to be of much use anymore."

"I hadn't ordered it yet."

"Then don't. Just call Michelle. Tomorrow's Christmas Eve; you've got the perfect excuse. Just wish her a Merry Christmas. Start out normally, you can even ramble a bit, but she'll get what's between the lines. That'll take you to a whole new level of conversation. Just don't bring me up right away - if you two start crying, nothing's going to come of it. After some time, you can both visit me at the cemetery."

"Dark humour, I get it. I usually like that, but this one doesn't work for me."

"That's because you've got a cultural hang-up on death."

"Fabi?"

"Yeah?"

"You know…"

"I know. After all, I'm your best friend."

The Hour of Stolen Moments

*A mother not only gives birth to a child but
is also born through her child.*

Gertrud von le Fort

Boris sat across from the woman, unsure how to begin the conversation. He had arranged to meet her at his favorite sandwich bar, a place that felt cozy, neutral, and homely.

Although, "homely" might not have been the best word to describe the situation they were in. What did home mean to her? Did she even understand the concept?

He studied her intently. She looked different from her photos - more tense, her lips pressed tightly together, and her eyes avoiding his. She seemed subdued, burdened with guilt, unsure of what to say, and perhaps even wondering if she should speak first at all. And yet, she had been the one to suggest this meeting. Or was he being unfair? Perhaps his own anger, bitterness, and belief that none of this should have ever happened clouded his judgment.

She was beautiful. Dark hair, dark eyes - just like his. Long, slender fingers with nails painted a deep shade. Her face still carried a youthful glow, though up close, he noticed faint wrinkles. Her lips were soft, full, naturally tinted in a pale red hue. A scattering of freckles adorned her nose. She wore a dark navy dress and brown lace-up boots, giving her an almost timeless appearance, as though she had wandered here from another era and wasn't entirely sure of her place.

They sat at a green table. Boris had ordered two sandwiches with smoked white cheese and sun-dried tomatoes, but neither could bring themselves to take a bite.

At last, she looked at him, attempting a smile. She didn't seem scared, more curious - and perhaps a little hopeful.

He clenched his lips.

His mind teemed with questions that now sat tangled within him, unsure whether they should see the light of day. Sometimes, assumptions, imaginings, and personal interpretations are far easier to bear than the truth. But he had to know.

He picked up the sandwich, then set it back on the plate.

Tamara in her navy dress.

And now what?

Was he supposed to call her "Mom"?

What is a home to a person? What do words like "nest," "family," or "community" truly mean? How significant are roots, that place you can always return to? Is home just a building, or is it defined by the people who inhabit it?

Boris held a master's degree in architecture and was ready to bring his dreams to life. He wanted to create, design, and let his imagination take flight.

"A graduate with a second-level degree is prepared to independently work as a designer in architectural and urban planning firms, local government offices, state administration, or research institutions."

In practice, it wasn't that simple. The market was fiercely competitive. Grades and diplomas carried little weight compared to experience and the ability to sell oneself. But Boris managed, thanks in part to his mother's connections in architectural firms. Finding a job had been only a matter of time.

"I'll help you," she had said matter-of-factly. "But don't think of it as me building the bridge for you. Let's call it just one span of the bridge." She had smoothed his hair affectionately.

At first, he resisted. He wanted to achieve everything on his own. But after months of fruitless searching, he accepted her help. Sometimes, you needed a ladder to reach the cherries on the tree. Sure, you could climb the trunk slowly, but sometimes it wasn't worth the risk - better to grab those cherries before the starlings got to them.

Besides, he was good at what he did. He knew it. Sooner or later, he'd prove to everyone that he was worth the job. After all, his mother was a respected architect herself, so talent was in his genes.

Well, not entirely. But not everyone needed to know that.

Boris had fantastic parents. He had never heard them argue, never witnessed unpleasant scenes, never felt unwanted. While his classmates often complained about their families, Boris had to invent problems so they wouldn't think his home life was unrealistically idyllic.

"My folks won't let me get a dog", he would sigh, nodding meaningfully.

It wasn't entirely true. His mother was allergic to pet hair but had told him there were breeds that didn't trigger allergies. If he wanted a dog or cat, they could find one.

"I found a breeder of Chinese crested dogs and some Peruvian hairless ones", she had shown him pictures. But Boris dreamed of a big dog - a real dog, furry and strong.

"No, Mom, not now, but thanks for thinking of me," he had kissed her cheek, silently hoping she wouldn't surprise him with a Peruvian hairless mutt.

He decided then that someday he'd get a dog. Big and black as night. He'd call it Raven.

Another time, he skipped a school party to claim the next day that he'd been grounded. At least he earned a bit of sympathy and didn't feel like the odd one out with his picture-perfect family.

Sometimes, he wanted to rebel, to scratch the pristine image. But he never mustered the courage. He never got drunk, smoked, or tried weed. Once, he ran away from home but came back before anyone noticed. He was fourteen then and wanted to do something out of the ordinary - something that might make the news or be mentioned on the radio.

He boarded a train to Kutno but got off in Konin and took a bus back home. He didn't go to school that day, but his parents never found out.

"How was school?"

"Fine, same as always."

And that was it.

Deep down, he felt a sense of gratitude he didn't quite understand. No one demanded it of him, and no one rationed affection based on his behavior. He was their only child. Their pride and joy. Their most precious treasure.

Theirs - though not biologically.

***

Nomadism is a lifestyle defined by constant movement.

It's the way of life for some African tribes that relocate based on the availability of water or Asian communities following pastures for their livestock. The Romani people also embrace a nomadic existence. There are, however, modern nomads who reject the traditional framework of owning a home, a car, and holding down a stable job. They choose independence, adventure, and nonconformity. This doesn't mean they abandon the idea of family - at least not all of them. Some travel alone, while others journey with a partner.

From what Boris had managed to piece together, his biological mother traveled alone. She often changed where she lived, moved between cities, and switched jobs frequently. She had been a hairdresser, a waitress, and even a secretary. For a time, she ran a small shop in a rural village. Yet, every time she seemed to establish herself, she would abruptly abandon it all and move somewhere else.

Was she searching for something? Unable to put down roots? What drove her to live that way?

Boris learned about his adoption when he was five years old. He was still too young to grasp the gravity of the revelation, but old enough to comprehend it in his own way. He had two mothers. One gave birth to him; the other raised him. One carried him in her belly; the other fed him, changed his diapers, and sang him lullabies. It was strange, a little confusing, but not necessarily bad. After all, having two chocolates was always better than just one.

"You are the best gift we've ever received from life," his mother, Emilia - the one who sang him lullabies - told him with a trembling voice, while his father, overwhelmed with emotion, wiped at his eyes.

His father's name was Ben, which always made Boris think of bedtime cartoons.

"From now on, we'll celebrate your birthday twice a year. Actually, we've always done that, though you probably didn't understand why you got presents on the fifth of August.

That's the day we officially became your adoptive parents. We still consider it the most important day of our lives," they often reminded him. Boris would nod enthusiastically, glad to see how much it meant to them.

In truth, he didn't understand the word "adoptive" or much else from their emotional speech. What he grasped was that he had two mothers. But what did words like "identity," "origin," "personal history," or "roots" even mean? He decided not to dwell on such thoughts. After all, he'd received a bicycle, a cake with candles, and an overwhelming sense of importance. He was special.

As the years passed, his understanding grew. Eventually, he fully absorbed the reality of having a biological mother who had given him up and an adoptive mother who raised him. Sometimes, he felt a chill of unease, a strange fear, but he quickly learned to shake it off. Adoption wasn't a dark or difficult topic for him - it was more like a mysterious, yet ultimately positive, part of his life. He had a home. He had parents. Not all children were so lucky.

Over time, the subject faded, neither stoked nor questioned by anyone involved.

But winter's sleep doesn't last forever.

When Boris turned thirteen, he boldly asked about his biological mother for the first time. He wanted to know her name, who she was, what she did, and whether she was still alive. His curiosity had been stirred by a documentary about adoption - about children who were abandoned or had lost their biological parents. It spoke of disrupted love and the possibility of finding it again, though in a different home. It told of mothers who didn't want, couldn't have, or had no choice but to let go of their children.

"Will you tell me my biological mother's name?" he asked Emilia, fixing his dark gaze on her.

"Tamara", she replied. "When she gave birth to you, she was still in school. She was underage. She's alive but constantly on the move, as if she can't settle anywhere. It's like she's a nomad. From what I know, she's lived in the mountains, by the sea, in Mazury, and Podlasie. She's lived in Wrocław, Kraków, and spent a few months in Warsaw, but she's most often in small towns. She also frequently changes jobs."

Boris wanted to ask more, to dig deeper, but he noticed his mother growing increasingly tense. Her hands clenched nervously, reaching for her glass of water every few moments. Her breathing became quicker, uneven. The sight unsettled him. He didn't fully understand the reason for her reaction, but he decided not to press her any further - for now.

One day, they would revisit the topic. Or maybe he would ask his father. Perhaps Ben would be more forthcoming.

"Like a nomad", he thought.

He liked the term, though he couldn't quite explain why.

When Boris grew older, he too began traveling extensively. He loved discovering new scents and flavors. He enjoyed imagining that, under some far-off latitude, someone was breathing air thick with dust and grit, while a few hundred kilometers away, someone else stood in the rain, watching bubbles form in puddles. He loved studying houses - their designs - and wondering what had driven people to make those particular choices. Why did they want to live on islands, in stone houses, or aboard houseboats? What inspired the Japanese architect to create the Nakagin Capsule Tower? Boris was fascinated by that thirteen-story structure with interchangeable living modules - residential capsules.

Or the Wooden Gangster House in Arkhangelsk - the tallest wooden building in the world, with thirteen floors reaching half the height of London's iconic Big Ben. People sometimes referred to it as the eighth wonder of the world. Then there were treehouses - whimsical, fairy-tale constructions in which people could actually live - or the portable, foldable, single-person micro-homes.

The house Boris lived in was white, metal, and glass. Beautiful, modern, and tastefully furnished. He liked it, though it didn't quite match his idea of "cozy." He often marveled at how he preferred chaos to order, how clutter didn't bother him, and how he longed to do something spontaneous - something entirely out of character for his family and upbringing.

His parents seemed almost too symmetrical at times, too balanced, too perfectly attuned to reality. They loved to plan, break things down into details, and predict the potential outcomes of every situation.

Calculation. Planning. Programming.

When they went to the seaside, they were prepared for any weather. They even brought a hand-crank generator in case of a power outage. It was both amusing and exhausting, yet it always gave a sense of security.

"You have to be prepared for anything," they'd say, as if on repeat. "Especially when you have such a treasure in the house." Then they'd wink at him.

And yet, over time, Boris grew tired of celebrating the fifth of August. He didn't want the cake, the gifts, the memories, or the reminders of his second birthday, the day he was "born again." Wasn't once enough? He preferred to forget that date and celebrate like everyone else - once a year. But he could never tell his parents that, especially Emilia, because he knew how much it meant to her.

Tamara.

Who was she really?

How old was she?

Where did she come from?

Did she have a dog?

Did she even know about his second birthday?

He asked all these questions when he was seventeen.

His parents couldn't offer much help - or perhaps they didn't want to. They didn't know her current address either.

"Maybe here, maybe there. We're not even sure if she's still in Poland," his mother had said, and he pretended to understand.

"Why do you ask?" his father wanted to know, but Boris couldn't give him an answer. "I'd love to help, but I really don't know how," he added.

But with today's technology, the internet, and omnipresent social media, it wasn't difficult to find someone. He knew her name and surname

- all he had to do was type it into a search engine...

But then what?

On one hand, he felt he should meet her, see her at least once in his life, ask her a few questions. On the other, he was afraid. She might tell him something he wasn't ready to hear. And in some way, it would feel like betraying his parents - and that was something he didn't want to do.

"We've booked a Nile cruise," his mother announced one evening. "And next year, we're planning Sri Lanka. We know you've always wanted to ride a real elephant."

Boris thought to himself how lucky he truly was.

And once again, he shelved the subject of Tamara, like an unfinished book he wasn't ready to read but knew he'd return to someday.

Maybe after Sri Lanka.

***

Secrets and deeply buried questions don't disappear just because they've been mentally sealed away. Their significance doesn't change, nor does their weight diminish. The fact that they lie dormant doesn't mean they'll never awaken. And when they do, they hit with twice the force.

At a conscious level, you can control them, restrain them, manage your emotions. But the subconscious? It's far stronger. And nearly impossible to tame.

Eventually, Boris reached a point where anger began waking him more and more often. These were no longer the calm, colorless, uneventful dreams of his youth. Now they irritated him, poked and prodded, stabbed at him with blunt truths. There was no diplomacy here - just raw, unvarnished clarity. What had been buried for years was clawing its way to the surface.

Everything has its time. Some people need more of it; others refuse to wait.

Boris lost his inner peace when he was twenty-six. He grew irritable, his temper short, his tone increasingly cynical. Work became a struggle - he couldn't concentrate, and frustration seeped into every interaction.

"I asked for the latest version of the project printed," he barked through clenched teeth at the office secretary, furious at how long it was taking.

Seven minutes. He'd waited seven minutes.

He found himself zoning out during team meetings, then fuming afterward when he realized he'd missed key decisions. He'd spend hours staring at sketches, unable to come up with anything.

"Do you need a few days off?" his boss asked one day. To Boris, it sounded laced with sarcasm. It stung. He'd only been at the firm for a year. Sure, he had good ideas, but he wasn't in a position to sulk. Yet he couldn't seem to get a grip on his emotions.

"I'll take two days," he muttered at last, retreating to his apartment, where he spent hours reading stories about adoption online.

"Adoptive parents aren't extraordinary. They didn't do anything remarkable. They simply found their child because they had an enormous capacity to love."

"These kids aren't imaginary, perfect children. An adopted child isn't a 'replacement' child. They're ours, just like any other, brought into our home by a different path. But you have to accept that they come with their own story. That story might not be easy, but it's part of the package."

"What's the meaning of my life if the essence of a woman's life is to be a mother?"

Boris slammed the laptop shut.

He stretched out on the couch, pulled a blanket over himself, and tried to fall asleep. But he couldn't. He didn't want to understand how someone could give up their own child. There were no guarantees that he'd end up with kind, loving people who would treat him as their own. There was never any certainty. The risk of something going wrong was Immense.

After all, she hadn't wanted him.

As his dreams grew more restless, as his mind circled endlessly back to the past, Boris realized he couldn't ignore it any longer. Everything unfinished eventually demands attention. The human memory plays cruel tricks.

The harder you try to forget, the more impossible it becomes to escape your thoughts.

It was time to leave the side paths. Time to step into the open.

"Alright, man", he muttered to himself. "Brace yourself. Take the hits. Maybe they won't kill you. Maybe they'll just graze you, and you'll shrug it off like it's nothing."

The next day, he called work and asked for a few extra days off.

"Sure. Take a week, even two," his boss replied. "Sort out whatever's weighing on you and come back with a clear head."

Boris had to admit - his boss had nailed it.

It was time to clean house.

He didn't want to ask his parents for anything anymore. He couldn't bear the expressions on their faces. But there was such a thing as a full birth certificate - a document that included the biological parents' names, the place of birth, and the court case number associated with the relinquishment of parental rights. With that case number, he could petition the court for further information.

It didn't take long. Soon, he had the name: Tamara Kowalov.

It was Thursday, 3:00 a.m. Once again, he couldn't sleep. He woke up every few minutes, seething with anger. He got out of bed, wandered into the kitchen, and gulped down a glass of icy water.

To hell with it. He was an adult man. He'd finished prestigious studies, landed a good job, and for a long time, everything had seemed to be falling perfectly into place. He even had tickets booked for trips to Malta and Spain next year - because he liked having concrete goals. Like his parents, he'd tried to plan everything.

He typed her name into the search bar.

Tamara Kowalov.

Three results. Just three.

He recognized her almost immediately from the photo. They had the same eye color, the same hair, the same expression, and a similar smile. He didn't need any other proof. The woman looking back at him was undoubtedly his biological mother - there was no question about it.

But he didn't learn much from her Facebook profile. Most of her posts were private. He couldn't even see her friends list. In one photo, she was standing beside an old Citroën - one of those iconic "lemons." In another, she was winking at a goat.

It actually made him laugh. The goat looked pleased, and so did Tamara.

She liked U2, Simply Red, and the Harry Potter books. She had a fondness for Lewis Carroll and *Through the Looking-Glass*. She'd liked the page for the film *Inside Out,* so she'd probably enjoyed it. And there was *Jabberwocky,* which he'd never heard of.

There were photos of a field of yellow rapeseed, a beach, a river, a meadow bursting with colorful flowers, and a large black dog. He smiled reflexively at the sight of the dog.

In one picture, she was standing in front of a hair salon. In another, she was cooking something. And in yet another, she wore a wig and an outfit straight out of a Fredro comedy.

That was it.

For the next several days, Boris kept revisiting her profile, but nothing much happened on it. A few times, he even considered sending her a friend request, but something always held him back.

What if this was Pandora's box?

Maybe it was better to leave some things unnamed, not to unearth old wounds, not to peel away more layers.

A while ago, he'd watched an online tutorial about watercolor painting. He liked the initial stage - a few irregular, seemingly random brushstrokes. He liked the second stage, too, when the colors began to blend and form abstract shapes. He even liked the third stage, when figures and objects started to take shape. But then, something always went wrong. Suddenly, everything became too literal, too perfect, with vibrant colors and smooth brushstrokes. The final painting rarely matched the intrigue of its early promise.

Boris feared that meeting Tamara might turn out to be like one of those overly polished paintings. As long as he only imagined it, as long as he spun hazy visions in his mind, the whole thing felt mysterious and beautiful - even with the anger he carried. But confronting reality? That could ruin it all.

And there was one more thing.

Tamara was forty-one years old. Which meant she'd had him when she was just fifteen.

***

It was more than certain that her father would fly into a rage.

He hated when things happened without his knowledge, but he hated it even more when people talked about him, mocked him, criticized him, and pointed fingers. It was bad enough that he had "Russians in the family" - a constant source of endless jokes and stupid jabs. Her name sometimes drew snickers too, but she didn't mind. She actually liked it. It couldn't be softened into a childish Sophie, Annie, or Katie. She was always simply Tamara, and she felt good about it. No one else in the area had a name like hers. It set her apart, made her feel unique in a way.

"She's a whore. A goddamn little whore," her father declared now, rasping like a rabid dog. He was truly furious.

Tamara froze in the buzzing grass, alive with the hum of the first spring bees and bumblebees, straining to catch every word that spilled through the open kitchen window and floated freely into the garden. Gradually, the words arranged themselves into a whole, one that was anything but pleasant. But then again, what had she expected?

"There's no other way. We've got to get her out of the house. At least for a while, until people stop gossiping and poking their noses where they don't belong. I never thought this little brat would bring us so much trouble. As if life wasn't hard enough already. Whore", he repeated, slamming his fist on the table.

Her mother, usually silent and almost always in agreement with her husband, chimed in hesitantly.

"Maybe it'll blow over?" she said, with all the conviction of someone expecting Robert

Redford to land a helicopter on the roof and propose to her.

The screech of a chair being shoved back sounded to Tamara more threatening than a hurricane.

"It'll blow over? Bullshit! You know damn well she's already been expelled from school - so she doesn't 'corrupt' the others. That bastard will have to be given away. And she? We'll send her somewhere else, maybe to my sister in the city. Less shame that way. And I don't understand how you didn't notice earlier. For God's sake, she's about to pop. You can see that belly from a mile away."

Tamara was terrified. First, she was scared of the pregnancy itself, the baby she hadn't planned, and the future that now seemed so far removed from her dreams. She was supposed to graduate high school, maybe even go to university afterward. She didn't know yet what she wanted to be - a teacher, perhaps, or a doctor. But she definitely hadn't planned on becoming a mother. Not now, not while she was still a child herself.

The worst part was that the boy she'd been with was just some passing guest, someone who'd given her a fake phone number and made promises that were doomed from the start. She'd called him dozens of times before realizing what "this number is not in service" actually meant. At first, she wanted to believe she'd written it down wrong, maybe mixed up the digits, but after a few months, it became painfully clear - she'd never see that boy again.

She was alone, her heart shattered, weighed down by an overwhelming sense of shame and growing fear. At fifteen, she was pregnant by a stranger and had no one to turn to. She'd hidden her belly for as long as she could, praying silently that the problem would somehow resolve itself. Twice she climbed a tree, intending to jump, and twice she lost her nerve.

When the truth became undeniable and painfully obvious, her mother took her to a gynecologist.

"Seven months. A boy. Congratulations," the doctor said, his tone dripping with sarcasm - or so it seemed to Tamara.

Her mother barely stopped herself from slapping her right there, or at least giving her a hard shove. Thankfully, the baby served as a shield.

"Who's the father?" The inevitable question was asked, but Tamara refused to answer. She didn't know where to find him even if she wanted to. A few more times, she dialed the number she'd written down, her heart pounding as she waited for a connection that would never come.

Finally, she admitted that it was someone completely unimportant, someone who didn't know about the pregnancy and definitely wouldn't want the baby.

"Just like the rest of us," her father spat, furious at the "problem" he'd now have to handle.

Tamara had no choice. She didn't want the baby either. She wished it would miraculously disappear from her body, evaporate, or turn out to be nothing more than a bad dream. But her belly grew, as did her awareness, until eventually, a decision had to be made.

"You'll give him up at the hospital," her mother said, and Tamara just remained silent.

"We'll take care of everything. Besides, you're still a minor. Just give him a name - something after your grandfather. Boris. At least let him have that from us. And then you'll disappear for a year or two. Everyone will forget, and things will go back to how they were before."

Things never went back to how they were before.

But at the time, Tamara didn't know that yet.

***

It was a spontaneous decision, though in some way a thought-out one - nursed through days of emotional turmoil and worsening moods.

After hurling a sugar bowl against the wall one morning, Boris realized he had enough of this madness. He sat at the table, opened his laptop, and typed out a few words to Tamara. Then, he hit send and slammed the laptop shut as if afraid her reply might come instantly. He decided not to check his phone for notifications, determined to occupy his mind with something else instead.

He stood and left the office. Outside, the air was warm and carried the pleasant scent of the sun-warmed day. Boris caught a whiff of burning leaves, immediately sparking childhood memories. Chestnut figurines. Every autumn, he and Emilia would go to the park to gather chestnuts into a bag. He wanted as many as possible to create a grand chestnut army. Soon, there would be chestnut dogs, cats, hedgehogs, giraffes, and tiny people who lived in a cardboard house. He and his father built it together, meticulously planning and decorating every room, crafting beds, wardrobes, tables, and even a TV made of aluminum foil.

The next day, when the chestnut figures had lost their initial shine, Bolek had a brilliant idea: spray them with hair lacquer. It worked like a charm.

"Can we build a train too?" Boris had asked. "So the chestnut people can travel the world and everyone will admire them."

He wondered now if his biological mother would have gathered chestnuts with him, built chestnut cities, or sprayed the figurines with hair lacquer. Or perhaps she wouldn't have had the time - or the inclination - for any of it.

He stepped into his favorite café as usual and ordered a double espresso. Strong, throat-searing. He loved this place. Alex, the owner, clearly knew his craft and was obsessed with coffee in all its forms. Alex loved experimenting - grinding cardamom, cloves, or even red pepper into the coffee. Sometimes he added a spoonful of butter or homemade syrups with subtle hints of elderflower. Once, he'd even sprinkled some turmeric into Boris's cup, waiting anxiously for his feedback.

"The usual?" Alex asked now, smiling distractedly.

Boris instantly understood why.

Alex wasn't alone today. Perched on a barstool was the girl he was head over heels for -

it was obvious to anyone who looked. She had been visiting more and more often, favoring cinnamon cappuccinos. Boris envied Alex a little. He himself couldn't fall in love like that, not in a way that made the world around him vanish.

"Yeah," Boris agreed.

"Double espresso, right?" Alex confirmed. "Clean or with something added?"

"Clean."

Just then, his phone buzzed in his pocket, and Boris felt himself go rigid. It could have been anything - a random message, an ad, even a mistake. Yet deep down, he knew. She had replied.

He took a sip of coffee and slowly reached for his phone.

He was right.

"Can we meet?"

That was all. But it was enough. On one hand, he was relieved she responded as he'd hoped. On the other, a wave of anxiety crept in. Was this the right move? Did one always have to dig into the past and pry open nearly healed wounds? Wasn't there something masochistic in waking old demons, in forcing open doors that were better left shut?

Why was he doing this?

What did he want to hear?

What was he expecting?

The coffee had gone cold, and he still sat at the bar, unable to move. In Hebrew, the word for "forgive" translates literally to "wrap with a cloak." Was he ready for that? Could he meet the woman who had given birth to him and forgive her for abandoning him?

Forgiveness, he knew, would be a kind of release. But it had to be genuine. Forgiveness for the sake of obligation wouldn't bring him any peace. In some ways, he felt wounded, though he couldn't pinpoint why.

He hadn't suffered. He didn't need to cradle his inner child and soothe it - his adoptive parents had done that for him. He was loved and wanted, part of a happy family. Why did people insist on complicating things, as if unable to enjoy what they had, determined instead to ruin it?

Still, there was truth to the saying: every laugh feels fuller if preceded by tears.

"Can we meet?"

"What if I can't forgive?" he muttered aloud, then reached for his phone and typed his reply.

"Yes. When and where?"

***

The Waldspirale in Darmstadt was completed in the year 2000, making it the final project of Viennese architect Hundertwasser before his death. The building housed 105 apartments and included an underground parking lot. Constructed in a U-shape with a rising ramp structure, Waldspirale boasted over a thousand windows, each uniquely shaped and sized. Even the door handles were distinct. The corners of the walls inside the apartments were rounded, as were the building's exterior edges.

Boris sat with an album of the world's most unconventional architecture, studying it with the intensity of someone preparing to design the masterpiece of their life - something that would overshadow every other structure on the planet. He had two projects due for completion, but he couldn't focus on either. At least he had a week off to clear his head. Today, at 6 PM, he was meeting his mother.

His biological mother.

He could have stayed home, rested, but he wasn't capable of it. Instead, he went to the office, relieved that it was empty at this hour. It allowed him to switch on his computer and keep both his hands and mind occupied.

He had debated telling his adoptive parents about the meeting, but the idea of their reaction held him back. He was an adult, lived alone, and this woman couldn't possibly threaten his bond with his parents. Yet he couldn't shake the feeling that meeting her would somehow feel like a betrayal. When he turned eighteen, he had once again asked about his biological mother - whether she was still alive and whether it made sense to seek her out.

Even before he finished asking, he saw the answer. It was written in Emilia's worried gaze and his father's sharp intake of breath. And although they said the decision was his to make, he felt they believed otherwise.

He arrived at the meeting early, but she was already there. She wore a navy-blue dress and brown lace-up shoes. Her eyes carried uncertainty, a hint of fear, and a great deal of curiosity. A faint, hesitant smile lingered on her face as though unsure whether it was allowed to appear fully.

It wasn't Boris's fault that he couldn't bring himself to speak. She, too, remained silent, keeping her gaze fixed on him. At first, her stare made him uncomfortable, but that feeling soon passed. They sat there, quietly observing each other, trying to commit every detail, every twitch of a muscle, every flicker of emotion to memory.

Finally, she spoke first.

"I don't know how to say this without sounding trite, but I'm happy you wrote to me. And that I have a son like you."

He flinched at the word *son*.

He didn't feel like her son in any way, and he knew he would never call her "Mom." Some people claim that the first memories form in the womb, but that clearly didn't apply to him. He didn't remember her voice, her scent - he shared nothing with her.

Except for genes.

And again, the silence stretched on, time weaving seconds into minutes, and minutes into hours. Three or four hours might have passed. Or maybe just two. Time had ceased to matter. Boris couldn't recall ever sitting in silence with someone for so long. He suppressed the words bubbling inside him, unable to let them spill out. Then suddenly, all the anger that had accumulated over the years began to rise, swelling into his throat, attacking his tear ducts, and swirling around his mind. He felt he couldn't stay there any longer.

He shoved his chair back and bolted from the café, leaving Tamara sitting alone. He didn't care if he had hurt her feelings. He couldn't bear to look at her any longer, let alone listen to her possible justifications, her twisted explanations that she *had* to give him up, that there was no other choice.

She had abandoned him.

Given him up for adoption like a stray puppy that didn't care where it ended up, as long as it had a place to sleep and a bowl of food. People sometimes cared more about the fate of animals than their own children.

It was late, but Boris had no desire to go home. Instead, he returned to the office, turned on his computer, brewed himself a coffee, and resolved to work through the night. Then he would sleep for a few hours and get back to work, vacation or not. Anything to avoid thinking, to avoid delving into the past, to stop dwelling on memories, and to silence the anger that was beginning to take control of him.

"Calm down", he told himself. "Calm down. You met her, you saw her, you spent a few hours together, even if it was mostly in silence. And that's enough. You have nothing to say to each other; you share no memories, no chestnut figurines, no holiday baking, no paper chains for the Christmas tree. The only connection is her womb, where she carried you, only to give you away afterward."

They say men don't cry.

Or at least they shouldn't, because it's a sign of weakness.

But Boris was alone, so he curled up on his swivel chair and began to wail - part child, part helpless puppy, part grown man realizing that some yearnings can never be fulfilled.

He wiped his eyes with the back of his hand, took a deep breath, and opened his album at random, flipping to a page about the world's strangest houses.

UFO houses in Vietnam…

He turned the page.

The Bubble House in France, a completely futuristic design…

And another.

The Teapot House in Texas, which was supposedly buoyant enough to float during a flood…

What exactly is a home? Why do we need it? And why do we need family?

Is there magic in blood ties? Does disappointment, betrayal, or pain become easier to forgive when it's your biological mother? What is this overwhelming pull toward someone who didn't even want you?

It wasn't Tamara who showed him the world - it was the woman who raised him. It wasn't Tamara who taught him to push his boundaries or helped him through life's lessons.

So why the hell couldn't he stop thinking about her?

*∗∗

Tamara had been a mother for exactly one hour.

There wasn't much she could recall from that time, as the room buzzed with constant activity - nurses coming and going, questions being asked, forms being filled out. She just said „yes" to everything, too overwhelmed to do anything else. For a fleeting moment, she thought she might keep the baby after all. But her mother quickly reminded her that, as a minor herself, Tamara wasn't legally capable of holding parental rights. She was still under her parents' custody. Her situation could only change through marriage, but for that, she would need to be sixteen - and find the child's father, which seemed utterly impossible.

"It's done now; no use crying over it. What matters is cleaning up the mess you've made," her mother announced briskly before she and Tamara's father took charge of the paperwork.

Tamara stared down at the sleeping boy in his yellow swaddle. Strange emotions rippled through her - a warm, viscous feeling, as if someone had poured liquid sunlight into her chest. But alongside that warmth was a cold, sharp fear of touching him. She couldn't wrap her head around the fact that they had shared nine months together, yet now he was here, separate from her, lying just inches away.

In the last few weeks of her pregnancy, she had come to accept that what was about to happen was inevitable. It couldn't be stopped, only managed. The child deserved to be raised by someone responsible. An adult. And she needed to return to school. That's what everyone had told her. They must be right. Surely, trying to fight it was pointless…

"Hi", she whispered softly, her voice barely audible.

The hospital room held four other women. Two had already given birth, while the other two sat silently, waiting their turn, gently stroking their swollen bellies with a reverence Tamara didn't understand. They cast her occasional glances, tinged with mild mockery, but said very little to her.

That was fine by Tamara.

She wouldn't have known what to say to them anyway.

Carefully, she reached out and touched the tiny hand curled into a perfect little fist. She squeezed it lightly.

"You'll be better off without me", she said. "But maybe one day, we'll meet again. I just want you to know… I think I liked you. You smell so nice. And you're beautiful. You'll be happy, I'm sure of it."

And just like that, Boris vanished from her life.

When Tamara walked out of the hospital, she felt like a completely different person. She couldn't quite articulate the change yet, but it was there, palpable. As her mother motioned for her to get into the car, Tamara hesitated. Then, for reasons she couldn't explain, she stepped back and said, "I want to walk."

"We're going to your aunt's. Get in the car now. You've already had your little rebellion," her mother barked, tapping her temple with a frustrated expression.

But Tamara spun on her heel and bolted in the opposite direction.

Happiness largely depends on how strong we are and whether we understand our own worth. The more questions like, "Do I deserve love?" that linger in our minds, the smaller the chance of building stable relationships.

Boris couldn't fall in love, nor could he entertain the thought of creating a lasting relationship. He was afraid of commitments, promises, the shared television, and the joint bedding. He had been infatuated before but had never truly loved. When a relationship began to feel confining, and the initial fascination gave way to discussions about long-term decisions, he instinctively felt the need to back away.

"You know what your problem is?" one of his exes had asked. "A part of you doesn't believe you're lovable. So, just in case, you bail before anyone gets too close."

"Rubbish", he had scoffed. The fact that Tamara had left him had no right to cast a shadow over his life. And yet, in some way, it had. He couldn't reconcile himself with the truth that love was a right he shared with everyone else. That he, too, was entitled to it.

"Rubbish", he had repeated later in his empty apartment. He knew that a relationship was like a sponge, soaking up emotions, thoughts, and feelings. It was a foundation that provided stability and set priorities - just like family. And he had that, didn't he?

Even so, he closed himself off from love: from its grandeur, its butterflies in the stomach, its spontaneous twists, and the hope that it could last forever. But what if Tamara was the reason?

What if this wound from his past needed to be examined and healed once and for all?

He still had her number. Resolving to meet her again, Boris vowed not to remain silent this time. He wouldn't be polite, either. He would ask her all the hard questions and demand absolute honesty. She could tell him that she never loved him, that she couldn't bear to look at him, or that she never liked kids and didn't want to have one. It didn't matter anymore. It was time to know the truth.

The phone was answered, but it wasn't his mother's voice on the other end.

"I'd like to speak with Tamara," Boris said, his voice muffled, but steady.

A few minutes later, the truth hit him like a blow to the chest. She had just abandoned him for the second time.

"Tamara is no longer with us," the voice explained. "She was hit by a car while crossing the street illegally. Despite an hour-long resuscitation effort, she couldn't be saved."

Boris stared at his phone in silence, his mind numb.

∗∗∗

It was the twenty-third of December, and everything suggested that snow would fall before the day was over. The frosty air nipped at the warm tips of his nose. Heavy, dark gray clouds hung low in the sky. Boris lifted his head, and at that very moment, snow began to drift down softly.

He glanced at his watch.

Seven twenty-three.

He stood on the balcony of his apartment, dressed in navy blue pajama bottoms and a T-shirt, over which he had thrown a gray sweater. It was cold, but he didn't feel like going back inside. He sipped his coffee, which was quickly cooling, and looked down at the courtyard below, now being gently blanketed by white snowflakes.

His gaze wandered to the left. Under the tree stood a metal bench. Black, slightly battered. He looked at it again. He had never sat on it before; it was more of an ornament for the small green space - a questionable one at that. But today, he felt like sitting there. So he grabbed his hat, put on his fleece-lined ankle boots, and wrapped a green scarf around his neck.

When he stepped out of the building, he noticed someone already sitting on the bench - Tamara.

He stopped for a second, then moved in her direction. She really was there. She was still wearing the navy blue dress and brown lace-up boots. Snowflakes had formed a sort of diadem in her dark hair, and he had to admit, it looked quite pretty.

He didn't want to ask where she had come from; he only wanted to talk.

So he approached the bench and sat at the far edge.

"How much time do we have?" he asked.

"One hour. Exactly as much as I was given at the very beginning", Tamara replied.

"I don't understand."

"When I gave birth to you, we spent an hour together. Then they took you away from me", she explained.

"You gave me away", he corrected her.

She nodded.

"Reason one: you gave me away because you were too young to have a child. Reason two: you gave me away because you were told to. Reason three: you gave me away because you had no other choice. Which one is it?" He looked at her with a mixture of anger, sadness, and a flicker of hope that she might provide a fourth reason—one so obvious that it would make everything clear and easier to forgive.

"All three at once", Tamara admitted. "I didn't fight for you because I didn't even know how. I was fifteen, with parents who decided immediately what would happen to you after you were born, and with the knowledge that you would grow up without a father - because I didn't even know where to find him."

Boris grabbed his head in his hands.

"Great start. I see you weren't exactly bored in your youth."

Tamara bit her lip.

"I was naïve."

"More like foolish", he retorted sharply. "You know, some people struggle to give away a puppy. They search tirelessly for the perfect home and caretakers until they're absolutely sure the dog will live like a king. Did you do that? Did you look for the perfect family for me? Or did you just hand me over to an uncertain fate?"

Tamara began to grind her heel into the frozen ground.

"I'm sorry", she said softly after a heartbeat.

Boris wanted to run away again. To race back upstairs to his apartment, barricade himself in, or wander off somewhere far from her. But they had only an hour. The last one they were given.

"Did you look for me?" he had to ask, even if her answer would be a denial.

"I wrote letters."

He hadn't expected that.

"To me?"

"To your parents, but essentially to you, yes. Always on your birthday and at Christmas. I also sent postcards from the places I lived."

Boris didn't know how to react. He had never received a single letter, not one postcard. He looked at her darkly.

"You're lying."

She shrugged.

"Why would I? I really did write to you. It was my way of letting you know I was thinking of you and sharing pieces of my world with you."

***

Tamara's aunt, who took her in after she left the hospital, taught her one thing: the past should be buried in some remote, uninhabited place, and the present should be squeezed for all it's worth to ensure that the future is nothing but beautiful.

It was good advice. If it weren't for the nagging sense of loss, Tamara might have been more inclined to follow it. For the first three years, she focused primarily on finishing high school. She wanted to prove to herself that she could do it, that she wouldn't return to her parents defeated, and that despite the mistake of her youth, she could excel in life. Because people shouldn't be written off so easily. With each passing year, she grew more independent and self-assured. She knew she would never again let anyone decide for her. From a timid teenager who lacked her own voice, she transformed into a young woman aware of her needs, dreams, and desires. She wanted to erase the image of her former self - someone unable to make decisions, someone who allowed herself to be silenced and overpowered. She felt stronger with each passing day.

But the past had a way of returning, reminding her of itself every time she saw young mothers with their children. In those moments, the timid little girl, who no one had asked for her opinion, would resurface.

"Let it go. You can't turn back time, and the boy is happy where he is", her aunt would tell her.

"And where is that?" Tamara would ask.

Her aunt would only wave her hand dismissively.

Tamara never ended up going to university because she couldn't think of anything that truly interested her. She didn't want to do something just because it was trendy or promised good prospects.

"Go into economics. At least you'll have a solid foundation", her aunt suggested.

But Tamara wanted to try a little bit of everything. So she took courses - facial cosmetology, hair styling, cooking, and even professional payroll management. Yet she still didn't know what to do with her life. What intrigued her more than anything was where Boris was, what he was doing, and whether he was happy.

"You gave him up", her aunt said, baffled. "Let it go."

She had given him up. But that didn't mean she had erased him from her memory.

"No", she would reply defiantly. "I left him once already."

Eventually, she managed to find the address of his adoptive parents, who hadn't made much effort to keep it a secret. Even before the adoption, Mrs. Emilia had given Tamara's parents her contact information.

"We won't need it", her mother had said at the time. "The most important thing is that the child has a home. And please don't change his name."

They had promised to do everything they could to make him the happiest child in the world.

Finally, Tamara wrote them a letter. She asked how Boris was and if she could see him someday. She included her phone number, and they called back immediately, asking her not to confuse him. They told her he was happy, safe, and that they would tell him the truth someday, but not yet.

"Can I write to him sometimes? Will you read the letters to him?"

Mrs. Emilia promised that they absolutely would and said it was a great idea. But she also asked Tamara to think less about herself and focus on Boris's feelings instead.

"You'll cope with this, but a child? Please don't take away his sense of security. Don't disrupt the world where he feels so comfortable. You can write letters. But nothing more."

Tamara couldn't disagree with them. It pained her to know that she would never be a part of her son's life, but she had understood that when she agreed, years ago, to give him up for adoption. And although she had been young and somewhat naive, she wasn't so naive as to not understand the consequences of her decision. But writing - writing was something no one could take away from her.

So she wrote those letters, starting with short ones, which gradually grew longer. In them, she shared her life and the world she was trying to explore. She didn't expect a response, but every time she opened her mailbox, her heart raced.

She managed to see Boris a few times.

"Did you know I saw you a few times? And I remember every single one of those moments", she told him.

"You saw me?" Boris repeated, looking at her incredulously.

„Yes" – she whispered.

"Tell me about it."

"The first time was at the playground on Działowa Street. I followed you from your house, then sat near the sandbox. I wore a silly wig because I didn't want your parents to recognize me. You were fascinated by an earthworm you'd found in the sand. You weren't sure if you should throw it away, bury it, or give it a new chance by letting it live in a sandcastle."

"And what did I end up doing?"

"You gave it to me. You walked up and said it was a gift and that I had to take good care of it because it was alive."

"Weren't you afraid?"

"I was afraid of Emilia. She rushed over almost immediately and told you not to talk to strangers. But I don't think she recognized me. I avoided her gaze."

"And after that?"

"When you were seven and walking to school. You had a Spider-Man backpack and matching red sneakers. It was adorable. You were so excited that you didn't notice the woman who followed you all the way to the school gates and then pretended to drop off her own daughter at first grade."

"Did we ever talk?" Boris asked.

„Twice. The first time in the sandbox, and the second on the train platform, the second one. You were heading to Warsaw, and I pretended I was waiting for a train to Wrocław. I told you I wasn't from around there and that I always got a bit lost in big train stations."

Boris suddenly widened his eyes.

„I remember that. I remember you saying you felt lost. And also that you didn't like crowds. But you had a different hair color back then."

„Blonde. Platinum blonde, with fake lashes."

„I don't recall the lashes", - he chuckled. „But yes, you did ask about the train to Wrocław and told me you were from a tiny town where not everyone had even seen a train. That did amuse me a bit."

„I talked a lot, probably nonsense, but I just wanted to catch your attention. To talk for a moment, even about silly things. Later, I regretted not getting on that train, not going to Warsaw, even if it meant traveling without a ticket, just to spend three hours alone with you."

„Did my parents know you sometimes saw me?"

She didn't answer immediately.

„Please tell me."

„Emilia noticed me only once. At a fair. I told her I was there by chance, that I wasn't following you, but from her expression, I could tell she didn't believe me. I wanted to explain that I didn't do it often, that I just stole small moments, glimpses of your daily life, and then lived off those memories for a while. It helped me a lot. At the time, you were standing by a stall with balloons, and you didn't care much about our conversation. You were entirely focused on a giant inflatable shark."

Boris closed his eyes.

Did he remember that event? He had been to so many fairs and often received inflatable balloons.

„Did you buy me cotton candy that day?" - he suddenly asked, squeezing his eyes shut even tighter.

She nodded.

„But you only ate a little because Emilia immediately came over and told you never, ever to take anything from strangers. And she was right", - Tamara said, though there was a trace of sadness in her voice.

„What did she say to you then?"

„That I should disappear, let it go, and not show up in your life like some damn ghost who starts ruining everything just because they think they have the right to."

„And that's what you did?"

„Partly. That's when I started traveling. I decided the best option was to rebuild everything from scratch, in new places, with new people. And, honestly, it worked for a while. But only for a while."

"What do you mean?"

Tamara thought for a second.

„When my life began to settle, the memories returned. I couldn't cover them up with a new job, a new apartment, or a change of scenery. Those things only worked in the beginning, when I was focused on just one task. But as life fell back into its usual rhythm, you always reappeared. To forget, to not think, to stop tormenting myself, I'd pack my suitcase and hit the road again."

‚Like she was a nomad'", Boris remembered Emilia's words.

„I bought myself an old Citroën and drove it until it finally broke down from exhaustion. It couldn't be fixed anymore, so I switched to trains. I've always liked them, anyway. The clattering wheels, the monotonous rhythm of the journey. You could close your eyes and imagine the destination."

Her plan for life was simple.

Change.

And then more change, followed by even more. The more changes and challenges there were to tackle, the more paradoxically calm her mind became. Tamara wouldn't think about Boris during those times - she was too consumed with building yet another life. When her parents suggested she return to the village and "finally settle down to something normal," she simply burst out laughing.

"You can't tell me what to do anymore."

There were big cities and smaller ones. Villages, hamlets, and tiny towns. She traveled through various regions, learning to distinguish the dialects with impressive precision. In one small town in Podlasie, she even became a hairdresser. "You styled hair in Poznań, so you can cut it here," the owner of a small salon with three chairs and three vintage hair dryers from the sixties had told her.

And so, Tamara started cutting, trimming, layering, coloring, styling - whatever needed doing, she did it. She rented a tiny two-room apartment and nearly fell in love.

Nearly. Because when the time came for serious declarations, for saying she loved someone and that it would be forever, memories of Boris came flooding back. She imagined him starting school, learning to ride a bike without training wheels, or making chestnut figures for autumn projects.

The longing was relentless. It arrived unannounced and rooted itself deeply in Tamara's body, growing stronger until she had no choice but to pack her suitcase, say goodbye to those left behind, and move on. A new place, a new apartment - preferably one needing renovation - a new job, one requiring her to learn new skills, and new air to breathe, just a little freer than before.

"You won't believe what I did in Krakow", she said.

Boris looked at her curiously.

"I worked as a prompter in a theater."

"What? How?"

She laughed. "Prompters don't need specific qualifications or rigid requirements. It's all about the right skills. And apparently, I had them. I could observe actors closely and sense exactly when they needed help. I quickly mastered the art of stage whispering - it even surprised me. It was a good job with decent pay. I rented a tiny attic apartment and felt like a puppet traveling alone across the world's theaters."

"And what happened?"

"The usual. Or rather, something worse - because one night in that Kraków theater, far from home, you appeared suddenly and unexpectedly."

Boris's mouth fell open in shock.

"Me?"

"Your class was on a trip. *The Envoys of the Greeks.*"

"Oh God, I remember. It was excruciatingly boring. The teacher spent the whole ride lecturing us about the play's elegant construction and modern poetic form, while we yawned non-stop."

Tamara smiled. "I saw you from behind the curtain. It was probably the hardest evening of my life. I prayed that no one would need a prompt, that I wouldn't have to whisper a single word, because my mind was completely blank. Every line, every quote - all gone. Even with the script in hand, I couldn't read a thing. A month later, I left Krakow."

"Just because you saw me?"

"Because everything came rushing back. Suddenly, the job and my attic apartment didn't matter - only the thoughts of you. I had to leave."

"And that's how it's been your whole life?"

"Unfortunately. When I handed you over at the hospital, I told myself it was only temporary. That someday you'd come back to me. At the time, I didn't have any other choice, but I believed it could all somehow be undone. Today, I know it can't."

"What happened next?"

"Rowy. A small seaside village. I arrived before the tourist season started, so I quickly found work. I was hired at a small guesthouse near the beach. I cooked, cleaned, and took care of the guests. There were cows and goats, too, which I learned to milk. I stayed in Rowy for four months, too busy to think about you. When my duties were done, I'd go swimming in the sea, usually in the evenings, and stay in the water until every muscle in my body ached. That way, I knew I'd fall asleep immediately."

Boris looked at her in silence, thinking no one deserved such a punishment. One decision had turned her life into a kind of hell.

"You gave me up, but I was happy", he said suddenly. "And you… you took on a penance you probably didn't deserve", he added softly.

She spread her hands in a helpless gesture.

"Everyone has their own threshold for guilt. Sometimes guilt is a constructive guide, a signpost for what to do. But other times, it destroys. They say guilt comes from the nervous system, but I believe it's the voice of the soul. And you can't escape it because that would mean running from your own soul. And you can't do that."

"You've never forgiven yourself, have you?"

She smiled sadly.

"I tried," Tamara said. "I kept telling myself it was the best choice, especially for you. But that didn't help. My guilt was too bitter to be sweetened by imagining you happy. Still, I found a way to live, and I think it wasn't the worst way. Maybe a bit exhausting, scattered, and far from harmonious, but it worked, in its own way. I lived my life on the move, always balancing between good and bad, between joy and despair. Sometimes, that's better than slowly dying in sadness."

"Did you ever manage to forget?" Boris asked quietly.

"I managed to laugh", she admitted, a wistful smile touching her lips. "Like the time a seagull flew into one of the rooms at the seaside house I was working in. We couldn't get it out, and the woman renting the room was absolutely terrified of birds. I didn't know what to do first - get rid of the seagull or calm down the hysterical guest."

"And? What did you do?" Boris leaned forward, curious.

"I started talking to them," Tamara replied.

"To them both?" His eyebrows shot up.

"Absolutely. At first, I tried every call I knew for animals, but it didn't work. So I decided to speak. Calmly, like you would to a nervous friend."

"What on earth did you have to say to a seagull?" he asked, incredulous.

"That she was beautiful", Tamara said with a small laugh. "That I understood why she came in, probably drawn by the smell of the fresh-baked cake. I told her that I got it - why stick to dumpster scraps and fish when there's something sweet on the table?"

Boris raised an amused eyebrow. "And to the woman?"

"I told her it would all be over soon and that she'd get a slice of cake too."

"That sounds... surreal."

"Maybe. But it worked. The seagull gave me a long look, not exactly understanding but curious, and finally hopped onto the windowsill. I edged closer, glanced toward the sky, and waited."

"Did she get the hint?"

"She did. She spread her wings and flew off."

"Without the cake?"

"Without the cake," Tamara confirmed, chuckling.

"And the woman?"

"She ate half the cake and kept shaking for the next half an hour. Apparently, when she was a child, a group of ducks had pecked at her, and she'd been scared of birds ever since."

Boris reached out and gently touched her cheek. "You've had a strange life. Unstructured, chaotic. But there's something about it - some beauty, some magic - that I think a lot of people would envy."

***

A year ago, Tamara returned to her aunt's hometown. In a way, it was her hometown too since she had never gone back to her parents after giving birth.

"You can stay here if you want", her aunt shrugged. "It's nice to have you around."

By then, Boris was already a grown man, and Tamara had often thought about meeting him, approaching him, introducing herself, telling him who she was. But since he hadn't responded to her letters, it was clear he didn't feel the need. She didn't want to impose, step out of the shadows, or disrupt his life. So she moved into her aunt's apartment, who needed more help as time passed, and found a job at a flower shop a few weeks later.

"Do you know anything about flowers?" the owner asked her. "Because, to be honest, I don't know much myself. But I love them. I bought this place from a woman who knew everything about flowers. I used to come here often just to listen to her stories. When I found out she was leaving the business, I thought it was the perfect opportunity for me to have a place of my own. A place that smells lovely. A nice change, don't you think?"

"And where did you work before?"

"At a fish market." The woman chuckled. "I always dreamed of having my own business, my own space. I took out a small loan, and voilà - I became the owner of a flower shop, even if I'll probably never master matching flowers to someone's personality. Only Mrs. Ania knew how to do that."

Tamara quickly immersed herself in the world of flowers and plants. She was, after all, like a chameleon, perfectly adapting to her surroundings and new circumstances. It was another challenge, another subject to learn and master, providing her with a brief sense of peace.

"And? Did you learn how to match flowers to people's personalities?" Boris asked, intrigued.

"Actually, yes. Maybe not as well as the previous owner, but I got the hang of it quickly. I also enjoyed creating arrangements, bouquets, wreaths, and floral decorations. I found my place in that world of flowers, and then your message came."

"What did you think?"

"That someone had finally forgiven me. That my penance was over. And maybe I wouldn't have to keep looking for new places to momentarily drown out my longing. I was terrified of meeting you, but I also felt that something had shifted. That life was giving me a second chance."

Boris lowered his gaze.

"Our first and only meeting didn't go well. Honestly, I wanted to ask you a thousand questions, but I couldn't put them into words. I couldn't say anything because I was furious with you. And with myself, mostly for not reaching out sooner."

Tamara touched his hand.

"It's a shame you didn't read my letters."

"I don't understand why Emilia never showed them to me." He shook his head in disbelief.

"Oh, I do. She was afraid you'd want to find me. That you'd leave her and choose the mother who was never truly there."

"She had no right to make that decision," Boris said firmly.

Tamara fell silent, lost in thought for a while, then said quietly.

"I think a mother's rights are very different from those commonly acknowledged.

They're a combination of emotions most people can't fathom. They stem from love, fear, joy, and a sense of vulnerability - a mix of overwhelming elation and the terror that someone might take it all away. So yes, I understand her. But it still makes me a little sad."

"What did you write about?"

"Everything."

"Even about that seagull?"

"And my dog," she added.

"I saw him on Facebook. Big, black. Do you still have him?"

"I had him. I took him everywhere with me, and he handled it perfectly. As if he was born to travel. I actually found him on a train."

"That's impossible", Boris objected.

"It's true. No one on board had any idea where he came from. The conductor questioned everyone, but no one knew. I think someone just put him on the train without boarding themselves."

"Where were you headed?"

"To the great Warsaw. I wanted to see the capital, explore it up close, and see if it had anything to offer me. I was diving into the deep end, but it was exactly what I needed at that time. You had just turned fifteen. The same age I was when I had you."

"Did the city spit you out?"

"It tried. I felt like it was constantly testing me. For the first three months, I couldn't find work, though I was willing to take anything. But I wasn't alone, and someone always seemed quicker or better suited. I rented a tiny studio apartment, just big enough for Dynamite and me."

"You named your dog Dynamite?"

"It fit him. He wasn't explosive or aggressive, but I felt he could be if given a reason."

"I like it", Boris admitted.

"We lived together, and it was one of the best decisions of my life. Dynamite gave me stability. And finally, I wasn't alone. After three months of job hunting, I was ready to give up.

Then, as fate would have it, my dog came to the rescue.”

"He found you a job?" Boris smirked.

"Believe it or not, yes. One day, during a walk in the park, I saw an elderly woman struggling with her dog. She was calling him, trying to catch him, but he wasn’t listening. He wanted her to throw sticks, but she simply didn’t have the strength. I helped her - or rather, Dynamite did, wearing the other dog out by chasing him around. A week later, I started a new job.”

"Let me guess", Boris interrupted. "You became a professional dog walker.”

„Exactly. And you can’t imagine how many clients I had. It turned out that so many people had pets they didn’t have time to care for. It was the perfect opportunity for me and for those dogs because we spent so much time together. I’d watch them run, swim in fountains, roll around in the grass. Sometimes they’d bark at squirrels, cats, or cyclists, chase birds, or even hide from an old man with a barrel organ.“

„Seriously? They were afraid of him?“

„Not all of them, but I had a few that would cower at the sound of his organ. Maybe it was the pitch of the pipes, those specific tones? Only Dynamite was never afraid of anything. He accepted all my travels, even if sometimes they weren't very comfortable for him.“

„What happened to him?“

„He passed away from old age last year. And he did it in such a beautiful way. That evening, he dragged himself to my bed and curled up at my feet. As I was falling asleep, I felt his warm tongue licking me and then his paw resting on my stomach. In the morning, I found him in his basket. He was still warm, smelling like himself, but he wasn't breathing anymore. He had a smile on his face, and it was the only thing that stopped me from completely breaking down. I understood that he accepted death and that his time had come. That's when I decided to go back to my aunt, to the city where you lived, and to stay there forever. No matter my sadness, foolish thoughts, or depressive spirals. I decided I wouldn't run away anymore.”

Boris lowered his head.

„It's so unfair how little time we're given by fate sometimes. And how many people pass each other in life, always choosing the wrong path."

„I know exactly what you mean", said Tamara. „It's like deciding which checkout line to stand in at the supermarket. You estimate how fast people are moving, count their items in the cart, and still, every time, you choose the wrong one. Despite all your calculations, you end up waiting longer."

„Do you believe in destiny? Or do you think we weave our fate ourselves?", Boris asked.

She paused for a moment to consider.

„I think one doesn't exclude the other. That destiny is, in a way, linked to conscious choices, that one stems from the other. Destiny is like a script we come into the world with, but how its episodes unfold depends entirely on us. But I could be wrong. It could also be that we have no control over anything. She spread her hands helplessly. „I've never wanted to believe that because it would mean we're living on autopilot, that someone has just turned us on, and we're doing everything preprogrammed for us. A sad perspective. I prefer to think I made at least a few decisions myself. And surprised fate with them."

„Why did you really return to Poznan?"

„Because I realized I was slowly regaining inner peace. I stopped floundering and thought I'd try once more to fight my urge to flee. I had the feeling I finally understood what everything that happened to me was about, though, of course, I still didn't know where it was leading me. I became an observer of my own life, someone who could stand aside and start watching herself. I saw a helpless little girl running away from herself because she didn't have the courage to face her guilt. But eventually, I started looking at my actions more calmly. And finally, I realized that I no longer needed to hack my way through thickets, wander aimlessly, and punish myself for that decision for the rest of my life. That's why I came back. And then you wrote to me."

„What else was in those letters?"

„A poem" - she said enthusiastically. „From the movie *Jabberwocky*. I stumbled upon it by chance, because, you see, I usually watched romantic comedies, always the ones with happy endings. They lifted my spirits. Once, I worked for a filmmaker who forced me, once a week, to watch less popular, often strange, and certainly niche films. At first, it annoyed me terribly because I didn't understand most of them, but over time I realized that it wasn't about understanding them at all."

„What was it about then?"

„About the impact they have on you. How you perceive them. What they evoke inside you. It was another fascinating experience I could add to my own life story. That film referenced *Alice Through the Looking Glass*, which, in turn, led me to the poem I was dying to share with you. So, I wrote it down and sent it to you for your birthday."

„Do you still remember it?"

Tamara closed her eyes.

„ Twas brillig, and the slithy toves

Did gyre and gimble in the wabe;

All mimsy were the borogoves,

And the mome raths outgrabe. "[2]

He burst out laughing.

"This is so absurd it's almost beautiful," he admitted after a while. "I didn't know that."

"Neither did I back then. But it fascinated me. And I wanted it to fascinate you too."

Tamara and Boris had been looking at each other for a good five minutes. Though they were silent, it didn't feel like wasted time. This time, they looked differently, without guilt, fear, uncertainty, or any negative emotions. They gazed at each other with curiosity, discovering more and more similarities with every passing moment.

"What's your favorite color?" Tamara asked after a while.

"Green."

"Mine's blue. And what's your favorite food?"

---

[2] Jabberwocky by Lewis Carroll, Harry N. Abrams, 1989

"Hmm... stuffed cabbage rolls and beef roulades."

"Mine too!" she exclaimed joyfully. "What else do you like?"

"Traveling." He winked at her. "Must be hereditary."

"Where have you been?"

"Recently, Morocco. I wanted to see all those colors with my own eyes and smell real turmeric."

"And what does it smell like?"

"I don't know." He laughed. "I'd recognize the scent anywhere, but I can't describe it. The most surprising thing was a bartender who once added turmeric to my coffee. Just a pinch, but I noticed it immediately. Do you like coffee?"

She nodded.

"But do you *really* like it, or do you just drink it out of habit?"

"I really like it. I don't add milk or sugar. I drink it black, to fully understand its flavor."

He looked at her with admiration.

"Same here."

"Where else have you been?"

"On Venetian bridges. And in Porto, searching for azulejos."

"What's that?"

"Tile mosaics, often blue. Almost every wall of Porto-São Bento station is covered with them. Apparently, there are over twenty thousand azulejos depicting the country's history."

"That's beautiful", Tamara said, visibly moved. "And what else have you seen?"

"The hot springs of Balçova-Izmir, near the Agamemnon Baths in Turkey. And Gaudí's Blue House in Barcelona."

Tamara listened with a faint smile playing on her lips.

"Why did you become an architect?"

"Houses fascinate me. And so do people, who sometimes build things so detached from everyday life that they take your breath away. Did you know there's a shoe-shaped house designed by a sculptor for his wife? Or underground apartments in the Swiss Alps - a hidden bunker-like home. Beautiful, comfortable, fascinating."

"Go on."

"A house made from shipping containers, an egg-shaped house designed to withstand hurricanes with an inflatable frame in the shape of an elongated ellipse. Or a house in California completely covered in mirrors, blending perfectly into its surroundings."

Boris could have talked about his passion for hours, but he suddenly stopped and glanced at his watch.

"We don't have much time left", he said quietly.

"We have more than we've ever had before", Tamara replied.

"And what about after?"

"Just don't forget me. And maybe you'll finally read the letters I sent. Emilia must have kept them all. Maybe she wanted to give them to you for a special occasion?"

"There have been a few of those already, don't you think?"

"Maybe she was waiting until you had a child of your own? I don't know. But I'm sure she didn't do it out of malice."

Boris sighed.

"I love her. Who I am, and how I am, I owe to both of you, though probably more to her."

Tamara couldn't disagree.

"Were you ever angry with her?" he asked.

"Plenty of times. I was angry that she had something that belonged to me, even though I gave it to her myself. I was angry that she got to witness all your firsts -first words, steps, falls, baby teeth, nighttime fears, smiles, and loves."

"I still can't believe we've crossed paths a few times in life." He buried his face in his hands.

"You couldn't have remembered. I was a stranger to you and you didn't register me or keep me in your memories. They were stolen moments, snatched a little forcibly, but ones I desperately needed. Even if it made everything hurt even more afterward."

In the courtyard of the tenement where Boris lived, everything had already turned white. Snow had covered everything carefully, hiding even the dumpster and the old wardrobe someone had dragged out the night before under its pristine layer.

"I love days like this", Tamara said. "I've always loved being thoroughly frozen, imagining myself coming back home afterward, filling the bathtub with water, and brewing a cup of hot tea. Then, slowly, I'd feel warmth spreading through me until I finally reached a blissful comfort."

Boris understood her perfectly. He, too, loved getting drenched in the rain or swimming in a lake until his lips turned blue. Emilia always scolded him, worried he'd catch pneumonia. But he rarely got sick.

"Have you ever eaten snowflakes?" he asked.

"I still do", she replied, sticking out her tongue. "I think they taste like frozen powdered sugar."

"Did you know there's such a thing as watermelon snow?"

"I don't believe you", she said, scrunching her nose in a way that made him smile.

"It's all because of red-colored algae. They say the snow looks like watermelon flesh, and when you step on it, it gives off a faint watermelon scent."

"What kind of algae?"

"It's called *Chlamydomonas nivalis*, and it contains a carotenoid pigment. That's all I know. But I'd love to try that kind of snow."

Tamara pulled a pair of tiny mittens from the pocket of her dress - red yarn with a white pattern.

"I made these for you once, during a crochet class I took. Yes, I did one of those too."

They fell silent again.

"Do you have to go?" Boris asked, his throat tight.

"I do. But I feel calm now. And you should too. They say every person is born with an incredible strength, capable of overcoming all kinds of difficulties, losses, and pain. And even though it sometimes feels impossible, we can regenerate, driven by a deep, primal force of life. All the bad cells in us are eventually expelled and replaced by new ones, free from painful memories."

Boris smiled. Then, he looked at Tamara one last time, gently touched her cheek, and whispered:

"Thank you, Mom."

THE END

About the Author

Natasza Socha is a Polish writer, columnist, and journalist, and the author of over sixty books for adults and children. She has recently begun writing crime novels. She holds a degree in journalism and political science from Adam Mickiewicz University. She divides her time between a tiny village in Germany, where she writes her novels, and Poznan, her hometown.

Her work focuses primarily on women - their strengths, vulnerabilities, and the belief that there is always a tomorrow. Readers appreciate her for her honesty, warmth, and her unique blend of dark humour, emotion, and genuine reflection.